D0391504

she loves you,

she loves you not...

she loves you, she loves you not...

A NOVEL BY

JULIE ANNE PETERS

Megan Tingley Books
Little, Brown and Company
New York Boston

ALSO BY JULIE ANNE PETERS:

Between Mom and Jo
Define "Normal"
grl2grl
It's Our Prom (So Deal With It)
Keeping You a Secret
Luna
Pretend You Love Me

This book is a work of fiction. Names, characters, places, and incidents are the product of the author's imagination or are used fictitiously. Any resemblance to actual events, locales, or persons, living or dead, is coincidental.

Copyright © 2011 by Julie Anne Peters
Discussion Questions copyright © 2011 Hachette Book Group, Inc.

All rights reserved. In accordance with the U.S. Copyright Act of 1976, the scanning, uploading, and electronic sharing of any part of this book without the permission of the publisher is unlawful piracy and theft of the author's intellectual property. If you would like to use material from the book (other than for review purposes), prior written permission must be obtained by contacting the publisher at permissions@hbgusa.com. Thank you for your support of the author's rights.

Little, Brown and Company

Hachette Book Group
237 Park Avenue, New York, NY 10017
Visit our website at www.lb-teens.com

Little, Brown and Company is a division of Hachette Book Group, Inc.
The Little, Brown name and logo are trademarks of Hachette Book Group, Inc.

The publisher is not responsible for websites (or their content) that are not owned by the publisher.

First Paperback Edition: April 2012
First published in hardcover in June 2011 by Little, Brown and Company

Peters, Julie Anne.
She loves you, she loves you not / by Julie Anne Peters.—1st ed.
p. cm.
Summary: When seventeen-year-old Alyssa is disowned by her father for being a lesbian, she is sent off to a small town in Colorado to live with the mother she has never known, where she is forced to come to terms with herself and her family.
ISBN 978-0-316-07874-0 (hc) / 978-0-316-07875-7 (pb)
[1. Lesbians—Fiction. 2. Mothers—Fiction. 3. Family problems—Fiction. 4. Emotional problems—Fiction. 5. Colorado—Fiction.] I. Title.
PZ7.P44158Sh 2011
[Fic]—dc22

2010022853

10 9 8 7 6 5 4 3 2 1

RRD-C

Printed in the United States of America

Book design by Alison Impey

To Sherri,
you rock my world

Prologue

The night Sarah and Ben showed up out of the blue. You should've known or suspected something was wrong. The vibe was weird, but then it had been for a while, and Sarah was... Sarah. Up in your room even, when she kissed you and you lost yourself in her. The moment it all came crashing down.

On the plane ride here, to the vast unknown that is Carly, the stupidest thing kept running through your brain. That toy in Dad's office. You learned at some point it wasn't a toy, that it had a name: Newton's swing. Steel balls in a row suspended on a frame. When you pulled balls back on one end and let them go, the same number of balls swung out from the opposite end. The harder you let go of the balls, the farther out the balls on the other side flew. You even remembered the principle, that for every action there's an equal and opposite reaction. How many hours did you spend in Dad's office playing with those balls? He'd say, "Cut it out, Alyssa. You're driving me nuts."

The physics law works not only on objects but on people. Because of Sarah's action, her force and thrust on your life, you went flying into space and spinning out of control.

Chapter 1

What does a stripper keep in her closet? The left side is packed with low-cut tops, short skirts, and dresses. No real skankwear. The clothes don't reek of smoke or booze. Carly has this silk kimono with an embroidered lotus on the back that's very cool. I take out the robe to hold it up to me in the mirror, and then I hear the front door open. Quickly, I stuff the kimono back in the closet and slither out of Carly's room.

"Alyssa. You're up," she says as I casually saunter down the stairs from the loft. Does she think I sleep all day? She sets her workbag on a chair in the dining room and digs into the front pocket for her cell.

"You got a lot of calls," I tell her.

"Here?" She peers over her shoulder at the cordless in the kitchen.

"I didn't answer them," I say. "I only saw a couple of IDs. Someone named Geena?"

"Did I forget to charge my cell again? I keep doing that. Spacey." She knuckles her head.

"And Mitchell."

Carly sighs. "Did the phone keep you up?"

"No. I wasn't asleep." I wish I could sleep, but every time I close my eyes, I think of Sarah.

Carly slips off her high heels and pads across the dining room to listen to her messages, checking to see how many johns have called. I'm just guessing. She fishes through her purse, finds her cell, and plugs it in. "You're welcome to have people call you here," she says. "I can get you a separate number or switch over your cell service so it's free."

"That's okay." I don't want to tell her no one would call me; no one wants to talk to me ever again. Besides, I won't be here that long.

At the wet bar she pours herself a glass of wine. "Why don't you give me your cell number, and I'll give you mine."

"I don't have a cell," I tell her.

She arches her eyebrows as she sips. Swallowing, she says, "Why not?"

I hesitate. "Dad took it away."

She lowers her wineglass. "Why?"

I don't want to tell her.

She shakes her head. "He's such a prick."

I'd like to agree, but Dad was right to take my phone. I have no control over my impulses.

"Have you eaten?" Carly asks. "I don't even know what you like to eat. What do you like?"

"I'm not hungry."

She cocks her head at me like, *I know you're lying*. With her long fake fingernails, she presses the telephone number pad. I wander over to the French doors, my back to her, watching her reflection in the glass. She removes a hoop earring and sets it on the counter.

"Geena, hi," she says into the phone. "I just got in, so I want to eat and shower before tonight. Go ahead without me. I'll see you at Willy's." She listens and then laughs. "Hey, girl. It's a living."

I take in the view—the bare side of a mountain. If I remember right, Carly called it Caribou Mountain. I feel her eyes on the back of my head, so I twist around and force a weak smile. She pulls the scrunchie from her ponytail and, shaking out her hair, says, "You have my eyes. You should let me give you eyelash extensions."

I stifle a gag.

Her phone rings again, distracting her from me. Her business card says she's a massage therapist and personal trainer. I know it's a cover for how she spends her days. She doesn't even try to hide that she's a stripper by night.

She ignores the caller and turns back around. "You need your brows shaped too." From her bag, she retrieves a leather case. She unzips it, and inside are fake eyelashes and glue and makeup. She pulls a chair out at the dining room table and motions me to sit.

When I don't obey, she juts out a hip and fists it.

I want to say, *Don't tell me what to do. You're not my mother.* Except—she is.

She pats the back of the chair. "Come on. It'll be fun."

"No, thanks." It comes out kind of snotty. As I pass in front of her, I resist the urge to check out her eyes.

The only time we've spent together before now was an occasional Saturday when she was passing through town on her way to New York or Miami or wherever she was working at the time. She'd drop by out of the blue to take me for the day. It always pissed Dad off. He hates Carly.

And now his hate extends to me.

"I'm going to work out for a while before dinner," she says, stretching her arms over her head, interlocking her fingers. "You could join me. We could talk." She smiles.

Does she think I'm fat? I'm not as tall and thin as she is, although I've probably lost fifteen pounds in the last month, with being sick and the trauma around Sarah.

"Would it be okay if I watched TV?" I ask.

"Of course. You can do whatever you want, Alyssa. Consider this your home." She opens her arms to me, like *Come get a hug*. I won't go running to her just because she's here now and I need her. A lump rises in my throat, and I don't want to lose it in front of her.

The plasma TV is in the formal living room, so I veer off that way. Carly says, "Not in there."

The sharpness of her voice stops me cold.

"There's a high def in the family room and one downstairs in my exercise room." The trilling of her cell snags her attention again. As she slides it open, she hustles up the stairs to the loft.

I watch TV for, like, ten minutes and get bored. Up in my room, which is actually a *guest* room, not *my* room, I plug in my nano earbuds to listen to my music. I must fall asleep, because when I open my eyes, it's dark out. Goose bumps prickle my skin.

She keeps the air-conditioning on Siberia. In stocking feet, I make my way to the panel in the downstairs hallway, the electronics control center, and punch off the fan. There's a note on the dining room table, propped up against a bowl of floating daisies.

ALYSSA
OFF TO WORK. SORRY WE HAVEN'T HAD A CHANCE FOR A REAL GIRL-TO-GIRL. IF YOU GET HUNGRY, THERE'S SALAD OR YOU CAN ORDER OUT.
XO CARLY

She left me her American Express card.

I feel weird spending her money, eating her food. Just... being here.

This grip of loneliness begins in my stomach and crawls up my chest and lungs and throat. I pick a daisy out of the bowl and hold it to my nose, closing my eyes, and the bitter odor reminds me of Sarah and home and... everything.

I pluck a petal. "She loves you." I drop it in the bowl and pluck another. "She loves you not...."

A volcano of hurt erupts inside, and I burst into tears.

Virginia Beach

Last September, first day of junior year

You saw Sarah in the hallway. You didn't know her name then; you'd never seen her before. She glanced right, then left. She turned in a circle. You recognized that first-day panic. You told M'Chelle and Ben to go ahead and you'd catch up. "Um, can I help you?" you asked.

"Yes!" she cried. "I'm so lost. I thought I knew where my next class was, but it's not here. It should be right here." She pointed to a wall where a GO WILDCATS banner was taped. "Is this like a tricked-out school or something, where doors appear and disappear?"

"That would actually be interesting," you said.

She laughed. You took her class schedule and immediately determined the problem. "You want 104B, not C. I don't know why they numbered the rooms exactly the same in every wing. It's confusing."

"I'll say."

You handed back her schedule, and she smiled into your eyes.

At the time you thought she looked young, with her braces and ponytail, her too-new jeans and brand-new layered tops right off the back-to-school rack. You remember how terrified you were the first day of freshman year. You said, "I'm going that way if you want me to show you."

"Would you? God, I'd love you forever."

The gauge on your gaydar jumped a few notches. Down, girl, you chided yourself.

She was cute. Too much to hope she might be a lesbian. Too young for you, anyway.

As you walked down the corridor, she said, "I'm Sarah."

"Alyssa." The late buzzer sounded, and you had to hustle to find her class and then get to yours in the adjoining wing. The next time you saw her was in the gym during club week. You and M'Chelle volunteered to man (make that woman) the Gay/Straight Alliance table. You were supposed to talk to people about what the GSA was, the goals and mission, hand out information and permission slips. Was Ben there? He might've had to man (make that girly man) the Gaming Club table.

"Ooh, I love to recruit," M'Chelle said, checking out the freshmen who were trickling in. She rubbed her hands together. "Fresh meat."

"Stop." You elbowed her.

She slapped a rainbow sticker on your forehead, and you immediately removed it.

Almost everyone made a wide berth around your table. Except her. She headed straight for you.

"Hi, Alyssa," she said.

She remembered your name. "Um, hi." You didn't remember hers.

"Hi," she said to M'Chelle, "I'm Sarah."

Sarah. That was it.

"I was hoping there'd be a GSA here. We had one in my middle school."

"Cool," M'Chelle said. "Where'd you go to school?"

"Bethel."

You'd never heard of it. Having a GSA in a middle school was pretty progressive, especially in Virginia.

She took the information sheet M'Chelle handed her. "You don't have to identify as queer—LGBTQ—to join," M'Chelle told her. "That's why it's called Gay/Straight Alliance?" M'Chelle tilted her head to emphasize the inclusiveness.

"Oh, I know." Sarah smiled at M'Chelle and then at you. She had this turquoise shade of blue eyes with flecks of silver. You have a weakness for blue eyes. Alyssa, you admonished yourself. Jailbait.

Still, if she was lesbian.

"It's basically a social group, but this year we're going to do more with diversity issues and tolerance. And we always do Day of Silence." M'Chelle was our newly elected president of GSA, acting all presidential.

Sarah said, "I can't believe we need our parents' permission." She rolled those baby blues at you.

"It's so stupid," M'Chelle said.

To M'Chelle you went, "On three. One, two . . ." In unison, you chanted, "Forge the sig!"

All three of you laughed. M'Chelle said to her, "Are you interested?"

Her eyes held yours, and you felt that hitch in your lower belly.

"Oh, yeah," Sarah said. "Definitely interested." She flattened the info sheet, with permission slip, to her chest and then wandered off, eyeing you over her shoulder.

M'Chelle about died laughing.

"What?" You blushed. "Quit it."

M'Chelle wheezed. "Fire up the barbie. We got us a smokin'-hot rack of baby back ribs."

I rip the daisy to shreds. If I could only go back and erase every moment, every memory of Sarah's existence. If I could only figure out what went wrong.

Carly's makeup kit is sitting next to a freestanding mirror on the table. I press the button on the base of the mirror and it lights up, illuminating my face. I'm someone I don't know anymore. A reject. A throwaway person. Little girl lost. Sure, Sarah. I should never have helped that little girl lost find her way.

Chapter 2

Carly didn't come home last night, or at least I didn't hear her. I don't mean home. *Her* home. Usually I sleep so hard my stepmom, Tanith, has to shake me awake, or my little brother, Paulie, jumps on me. I can't sleep here. Even when I was a baby, Dad said I'd fall into this deep sleep that he thought I'd never wake up from. I bet now he wishes I hadn't.

Carly's bedroom door is cracked, and I tiptoe down the hall to peek in. The bed's made. I want to go snoop around some more, but she could show up anytime. She doesn't seem to keep regular hours.

This is only my third day in exile, and already I'm bored shitless and thinking too much. What am I going to do for however long I'm banished? "Veg in front of the TV," I answer my own question. "Eat and get fat."

Shrivel up and die.

I need to stay busy, keep my mind off things. People.

Maybe I could get a job. I saw an outlet mall when we passed through Dillon and Silverthorne on the way up here from Denver. Carly was babbling away about all the summer activities in the mountains, the boating and biking and hiking trails, how much fun I'd have in Breckenridge, even though it's miles away from Majestic, where she lives. I was trying not to think about home, about Dad and Tanith and Paulie and Sar—

Stop thinking about her.

What is everyone doing at home? I wonder. *What time is it in Virginia Beach?* I check the clock. A little after seven AM. That'd be nine o'clock Eastern. I could call.

Dad might still be at home and answer.

Forget that.

I shower and dress in jeans and a white sleeveless button-down. The only shoes I brought besides flip-flops are leather boots. I remember thinking, *Colorado. Snow. I'll need boots.*

In June? How was I supposed to know it doesn't snow in the mountains in summer?

Carly said I could drive her other SUV, and she handed me the keys to her Mercedes. I was still dazed from the flight and the long drive to Majestic and how fast my life was disintegrating. I just stared at the keys.

A memory slices through the years. Carly bringing me home after we'd spent a day together. Dad and Tanith, the three of us, watching her walk from the porch to the curb, where she'd parked the Corvette convertible.

Dad said, "She looks like a hooker. A high-priced hooker if she can afford that car."

"Paul!" Tanith hitched her head down at me and widened her eyes at Dad.

Dad said to me, "What did you two do all day?"

"We drove to the beach," I told him. "We went shopping."

"Did she tell you what she does for a living?"

I knew what she did. So did Dad. "She's a dancer."

"Oh, right. Like strippers make that kind of money."

I didn't say stripper. I said dancer.

He turned toward the stairs. At his back, I said, "The car's a rental."

I heard Dad mutter, "So's she."

How old was I? Nine, ten? I didn't know what he meant then. I do now. And I know the difference between dancer and stripper.

It scares me to drive anyway, but a Mercedes SUV? She said I could. Still.

Majestic is within walking distance of the house, or at least it seemed close by when we whizzed past. Carly's house is built right into the side of Caribou Mountain—if you can call it a house. It's more like a resort, with an outdoor hot tub and sauna. How does she afford this?

I mean, how much do massage therapists slash personal trainers make?

More than strippers. Not as much as high-priced call girls.

With all my heart I wish for Dad to be wrong. But evidence doesn't lie.

I trudge down the winding access road to the highway. Trucks and semis pass, but I'm too chicken to thumb a ride. Who knows what wackos live in the mountains? About fifteen minutes into the walk, I wish I was brave or stupid enough to hitch. It's so hot out, and I'm soaking wet. I wish I'd packed my sandals. Or Chucks. I didn't bring everything I owned because...

"Because I'm going back," I say out loud. My throat is so dry that my voice cracks. No way I'm staying here. Dad will forgive me and remember how much he loved me before. I know he will. He has to.

"Stop." *Stop torturing yourself.*

Main Street is two blocks of square brick buildings with hokey-looking storefronts. Carly said it was built as a movie set in the 1990s. There's a souvenir curio shop, a liquor store, and a barn with a stenciled sign: USED BOOK EMPORIUM.

There are no HELP WANTED signs posted anywhere. The sidewalks are raised planks with wooden handrails, and I wonder what movie was shot here. Some dopey Western. As I pass the curio shop, I jump back and almost fall off the sidewalk. The window display is a coiled rattlesnake under glass. Snakes scare the bejeezus out of me. I press my heart to calm the pounding.

Across the street is a video rental store that looks fairly new.

As I open the door to the video rental, a blast of air-conditioning hits me in the face. Relief. No one's here. I walk to the counter, and a tall, skinny kid with mega-zits shuffles out from the back. He has green hair. It reminds me of that summer Paulie started swim team at Dad's club and spent so much time in the pool that his hair turned green from the chlorine. Except this kid's color came from a bottle. "Who are you?" he asks.

"Who are you?" I answer.

"Who wants to know?" he says.

I sigh inwardly. "I'm looking for a job," I tell him. "Do you need any help?"

"Does it look like we need help?"

Brat. Okay, the place is deserted. It's possible they'd get a rush, though, right? "Weekends or something? Anything?"

His zits run down his neck to his shoulders. And he's staring at my chest. Perv. I turn to leave and he says, "You sorta look like someone. Do you know Carly?"

I twist back. "Yeah? Why?" How does he know Carly?

"Arlo's hiring."

The smirk on his face answers my question. Small town. "Who's Arlo?"

The kid goes, "Street before the light, take a right. You can't miss it. The Egg Drop-In."

I missed it the first time through. "Okay, thanks," I say.

"If you ever want to browse in the adult section, let me know." He wiggles his eyebrows.

Gross. Now I wonder if Majestic is populated with peanut-sized perverts.

The Egg Drop-In is a restaurant. More like a greasy spoon, but there are customers, at least. All the tables are full. A guy in a wheelchair is ringing up a sale at the cash register. He catches my eye, and I give him a little wave, like hi. He stares at me so long, I think he sees a ghost. Everyone in the room swivels to look.

Now I feel conspicuous, like I'm standing in the middle of the restaurant naked. Time starts again, and people resume what they were doing. Eating, talking, judging me. I approach the front counter, and Wheelchair says to the customer who just paid, "Thanks, Dutch. See you tomorrow." The customer is dressed like a real cowboy. No kidding. Worn, saggy jeans, a cowboy hat, and boots. Is he an actor? His face doesn't look familiar.

Wheelchair stares at me again. I open my mouth to speak, but he rolls through the swinging café doors to the back.

People are so rude here. I survey the shelves and cases. Bagels and muffins, cheese Danish. An espresso machine and a bottle of pulpy orange juice.

"Order up," Wheelchair calls through the opening between the kitchen and the dining room as he skids two plates across the counter. His eyes rise to meet mine, and he fixes on me again.

What?

I have a sudden urge to flee. Just get out of there. As I pivot, this girl nearly bulldozes over me. She juggles a tray stacked high with dirty plates.

"Sorry," I say.

She doesn't budge.

I glance around. *Oh.*

She needs me to...I step one way, and she mirrors my move. We both step the other way. I let out a little laugh. She doesn't.

She shoves the tray between us and cuts through. The name on her badge reads FINN. I watch her dump the tray, load up the hot plates along her arm, then serpentine through the tables and chairs.

Dyke! my gaydar screams. She has that self-confident aura. Plus, she's wearing carpenter shorts and leather hiking shoes. Dark curly leg hair. Hel-loooo.

Wheelchair says, "You're Carly's girl." He's sitting in the

doorway, propping open the swinging doors with both hands. He has on latex gloves, and he reeks of green peppers and bacon grease.

Am I wearing a scarlet letter?

"What do you want?" he growls.

"Um…" Now I'm all rattled.

"Arlo, can we get some grub?" a guy at the end of the counter hollers. Wheelchair shouts, "Finn!" She twists her head. She has this long, black braid that hits her at the waist. So cool. I've never seen hair that long.

Wheelchair—Arlo, I guess he is—waves toward the customer, and Finn scrambles over there.

The doors close and Arlo disappears. He reappears through the order window at the grill, pouring pancakes from a plastic pitcher. I move closer to the cash register to talk to him. "I heard you had a job opening, and I was thinking about applying."

He doesn't look up from the grill. "Come in here," he says.

To the kitchen? Okay. I push through the swinging doors.

He's sitting on a platform so he can reach the grill. He wheels around. "Did she send you here to twist the knife?"

"What? Who?"

He scans me up and down. Then shakes his head no.

Why not? What does he see that he doesn't like? "I really need a job," I tell him. "I'm a hard worker."

"I'll bet you are."

I catch the innuendo, and heat rises up my neck. "I'm not Carly," I say.

He mutters, "I didn't mean that the way it sounded."

Sure, I think.

He glides down the ramp and past me to a refrigerator. He opens it. He reaches up for something he can't get.

I hurry behind him. "What do you need?"

"You! Outta here!" he barks.

I stumble back, and he hollers, "Finn!"

She *whooshes* through the swinging doors.

"The damn eggs!" Arlo yells at her. "Don't put 'em up so high."

I try to catch her eye to telepath *God, what a jerk*, but Finn just retrieves a cardboard tray of eggs from the fridge and rushes past Arlo and me to set them on the counter by the grill. The bell tinkles out front and Finn dashes out, not even glancing my way.

"You better scram," Arlo says.

A guy in overalls appears at the swinging doors. "Could I *please* get a cup of stinkin' coffee in this turd-infested rat hole sometime this century?"

Arlo grins. He wheels forward so fast, he smashes through the doors, almost taking the guy down. "The rats are working as hard as they can, Bullwhacker. Now sit Your Flatulence down and wait your turn."

Overalls chuckles and tramps off.

Arlo scrutinizes me again. "You ever work one of those machines?" He thumbs at the coffeemaker.

"Um, yeah," I lie. Carly has an espresso machine, which I wouldn't even know how to plug in.

He says, "Take the counter."

Now?

Finn flies past me and says, "I got it."

I could've done it.

Arlo asks me, "You have waitressing experience?"

"Tons," I lie again. The only job I've ever had is lifeguarding at Dad's club in the summer. He never let me work during the school year because he wanted me to concentrate on my studies.

I feel Arlo checking me out. What is he looking for? I flex my right bicep.

That earns me a lopsided grin, at least. He rolls backward into the kitchen. Three people at the counter are holding up cups, and before I can even think, Finn's filling them from a pot of brewed coffee. Arlo hollers, "Order up!" as he slides two plates of steaming pancakes onto the counter.

Finn slips behind me. "Excuse me," she says. She has this soft, low voice. As she's picking up the plates, Arlo says to her, "What do you think? Should we hire Carly's girl here?"

Finn whirls and drops the plates. The shattering glass makes everyone jump. Finn is frozen in place, staring at my face, into me so far I feel her eyes ripping through my gut.

She stoops to clean the mess, and I crouch down to help, but she says, "I've got it." Kind of cold. She stands and shakes her head at Arlo.

Arlo exaggerates a smile at me. "The decision is unanimous." He aims the spatula at the exit. "Go home to Mommy Dearest."

Chapter 3

All the way back to the house, I alternate between anger and humiliation. What just happened in there? I almost got the job, but then that Finn blew it for me. Fine. She's not my type anyway.

Not that I care. I've sworn off love forever.

Carly owns a laptop, but I haven't seen her use it. She did say whatever I wanted I could use. I take the computer up to my room, open the lid, and press the ON button. Windows boots. I check my Hotmail and find six messages.

None from Sarah.

I don't know why I think she'd write to me. She'd better not. I begin a letter:

Dear Sarah,
You ruined my life. Remember how much I used to love you? Double it, and that's how much I hate you now.

I don't press SEND. I don't even mean it. It just feels good to get that out.

I lie in bed, and the jumble of emotions turns to tears. What did I do wrong? If I could only figure out what happened, the when and where and how of it. I thought I was the perfect girlfriend, that we were perfect together. "What did I do, Sarah?" What?

October

She came on to you. She started it. "Are you going to homecoming?" she asked.

We were at GSA, getting settled for the meeting, waiting for stragglers.

You told her, "I'm not really into football."

"Not the game. The dance." She bumped your shoulder with hers. She was always touching you, playing with your jewelry, sitting so close that your arms got twisted up. At every GSA meeting, she'd immediately gravitate to wherever you were. If M'Chelle or Ben was there, Sarah would insinuate herself in the middle.

You have to admit you liked the attention, the warmth of human interaction. Your last girlfriend, if you could call her that, lived in Michigan. Your whole relationship played out online. Ben would e-mail or text you: R U HAVING CYBERSEX YET?

YEH, you'd text him back. U SHOULD TRY IT. O WAIT. UR THE EXPERT.

The opportunities to meet lesbians in Virginia Beach were practically nonexistent.

"We usually go to dances as a group," you told Sarah. "So we don't get jumped afterward."

Her eyes ballooned. "Would that happen?"

Ben leaned across your lap to say to her, "Want to see my battle scars?"

Our school wasn't exactly gay-friendly. Or race-friendly, geek-friendly, or eco-friendly.

It was a wonder we even had a GSA. But it's against the law to deny it. Ben was the one who took the initiative for getting it started last year.

M'Chelle elbowed you and whispered in your ear, "Ask Sarah out. She's dying for you to ask her."

Someone tapped you on your shoulder blade. You twisted your head to see Ben miming, Ask her.

You knew she was into you, but she was so young. Did you really want to date a ninth grader? She did seem mature for her age, or you were blinded by lust and loneliness. Those blue eyes. Damn.

You stalled around after the meeting, after everyone had gone. Except Sarah. She always waited to walk out with you. You figured, what would it hurt? One date. "Do you want to go to the dance?" you asked.

She threw her arms around you, almost knocking you over. "Yes, yes, yes, yes, yes!"

You laughed, and she laughed with you. That first shared moment of joy. Admit it, you were hooked.

"It'll be with the group," you told her.

"That's okay. I'll just pretend it's you and me alone." Her smile cast a wicked spell.

It turned out to be the two of you alone because you stole away from the dance and never returned. You ended up making out in the backseat of Ben's VW Bug. God, it all happened so fast. After homecoming, you and Sarah were officially a couple.

In private, anyway.

You couldn't risk a girlfriend in school. If you openly expressed your love for her by holding hands or snuggling, people would harass you. Or you'd get expelled. M'Chelle found that out the hard way. Last semester she got caught in the restroom kissing Carmen, her girlfriend at the time, and the incident was reported to the principal. He tried to expel M'Chelle, but her parents threatened a lawsuit. Your dad's a lawyer, but if you were the one who'd been caught, he'd be on the prosecution's side.

M'Chelle and Ben opened the closet door for everyone else in our school. Now we had an official GSA with twenty members and counting. It was so great to have the GSA, a safe space where you could be affectionate and real.

Talk about affectionate. Sarah would sneak up behind you at the meetings (though you knew she was there) and take your face, tilt it back, and kiss you. Everyone would go, "Ooh. Alyssa and Sarah sitting in a tree..."

She'd plop on your lap and comb your hair with her fingers for an hour. Whatever went on at those meetings is a blur.

Sarah was in gymnastics. You'd go to the gym after school and sit behind the uneven parallel bars against the wall and do homework. Or watch her. Watch her watching you. Showing off for you.

"Do your parents know?" she asked one day as you walked her home—as far as the Starbucks.

"No. Not unless they read the graphic sexts you send."

Sarah laughed. She'd trickle a finger up the bare skin of your arm and go, "You know you love it."

Who wouldn't? You're only human. Everyone wants to be loved and desired.

So many times you wished you could just scream it out: I love girls!

You wanted to tell Dad, Tanith, Paulie. Maybe not Paulie. He was only ten. You hated keeping the secret from Dad, but you were afraid. Not so much about what he'd do to you. What could he do? Throw you out on the street?

Yeah, that was supposed to be a joke.

You asked Sarah—more like confirmed—"I guess your parents don't know. Since you only let me walk you this far."

Sarah's eyes dropped. "I'm sorry. I want to tell them, but they'd kill me. Right before they sent me to one of those Christian asylums to take the cure."

You both laughed about that.

How can so much joy turn to so much pain?

I'm hungry and hurting, so I go downstairs to find something to eat. I hear Carly in her exercise room, laughing with someone. I walk to the foyer and peek my head around the corner.

"Are you Alyssa? Oh my God!" This crazy lady tears up the stairs from the exercise room and crushes me in a hug. I almost gag on her flowery perfume. She holds me back to look at me and says, "You're gorgeous. Carly, she's gorgeous." Through her extra-thick eyeliner and mascara, her smile extends to her wild eyes. "I'm Geena," she says. She doesn't let me speak before smothering me again.

"I heard you were in the Egg Drop talking to Arlo," Carly calls up from the exercise room. She's on the floor stretching, cooling down from her workout. "Why?"

She knows already? It only happened an hour ago.

I call down the short stairwell, "I was looking for a job. Someone told me Arlo was hiring."

"Ooh, Arlo," Geena goes. "Bet he was all over you like gum on hot asphalt." She cracks herself up.

"You don't need to work in Majestic," Carly says. "There are probably lots of summer jobs in Breckenridge or Dillon. If you want a job, I'll put out feelers."

"Me too," Geena says.

I don't want them helping me, especially Carly. I don't want to feel obligated to her in any way. "That's okay. But thanks."

Geena says, "I'd better get going. I haven't even been home yet, and God knows I need my beauty sleep." She lifts my chin and gazes into my eyes. Sighing, she says, "Were we ever this young, Carly? Were we ever this naturally beautiful?"

Carly doesn't answer.

"Later, sugar." Geena blows Carly a kiss and exits through the front door.

Carly seems entranced in her stretching, or yoga, so I lower myself to the top step and watch her. Her eyes are closed, and she steeples her hands together, takes a deep breath, and lets it out in a long stream. A slight smile curls the ends of her lips. She looks serene. I remove my right flip-flop and see I have a giant blister on my big toe. I wish I had a needle to pop it.

Carly pulls her knees to her chest, opens her eyes, and rolls her head my way. "Who cuts your hair?"

Both hands fly up to cover my head. I know it looks terrible. I cut it the night of prom, when Sarah…

"It'll grow out," I say. It already has, a lot, although I'd really just like to shave it all off. That'd freak Dad out.

Carly says, "I don't suppose you'd let me trim it."

I stand to signal this convo is over.

"You're going to have to talk to me sometime, Alyssa. You owe me that."

I whirl on her. "I *owe* you? What about everything you owe *me*?"

"Me?" she goes.

"You abandoned me when I was a baby."

Her face flushes bright red.

I can't believe I said that out loud.

"I didn't abandon you." Her voice is flat.

I mutter, "What do you call it?"

"I left you with your father. But I always intended to come back. And I did."

"Then you disappeared again."

When I was thirteen. No more cards or presents, not even a phone call to check in. "I haven't heard from you in four years, Carly." Not that I care.

Carly goes limp. "I'm sorry," she mumbles into her knees.

Sorry. Is that all she has to say? I head for the main level. Behind me, I hear, "You want to tell me what happened to make your father disown you?"

That stops me short. Who said he disowned me?

"Tanith was less than forthcoming with details when she begged me to take you in."

I turn around. Tanith called Carly? "What do you mean, she begged you?"

Carly pushes to her feet. "I shouldn't have said—I told her I'd have to think about it, is all. When she said your father wanted you gone and no one else in the family could take you in, then of course there was no question."

The tension in the house was unbearable. A week went by after the...the incident. But I didn't know Dad had disowned me. I thought we were going through a cooling-down period, that he'd come around. There'd be tension, sure, but we'd work through it.

My throat catches. No one would take me? All Tanith told me was, "You're going to stay with Carly for a while. I hope that's okay."

No one wanted me?

"Alyssa," Carly says behind me, so close I can sense her hands rising to clutch my arms. I cross the dining area, toward the loft.

Carly follows on my heels. "I didn't plan to leave you. Or abandon you, as you put it. We don't always know what life's going to throw at us, now, do we? Sometimes we just get slammed."

Tell me about it. I start up the stairs. I want to hear her say everything's going to be all right because she's ready to be my mother now the way she never was before, and I need a mother. Desperately. Except I wouldn't believe her. I'm having a few trust issues at the moment.

"Alyssa, please."

The pleading in her voice makes me slow at the top of the stairs.

"I'm here now," she says. "That should count for something."

Yeah. I have nowhere else to go. My grandparents didn't even want me?

Carly says, "You know what? Let's make a fresh start. We'll put the past behind us and begin anew."

Can I do that? It's what I'm trying to do with Sarah. I need to go forward; get past all the mistakes I made, whatever they were.

"You know what I do to forget the past?" Carly says, heading for the wet bar. "I drink my own special concoction. I call it Milk of Amnesia."

I let out a short laugh. That was actually funny.

She smiles up at me. "That's the first time I've even seen a glimmer of happiness in you since you got here." She holds my eyes for a long minute, too long. She has these steel-gray eyes that slice right through you. My eyes.

Holding up a bottle of liquor, Carly says, "I promise it's a cure-all."

Slowly, I come back down the stairs and stand by as she mixes Baileys with red wine and pours two glasses. The color is a disgusting pink. She offers me a glass.

"To us," she toasts.

I clink with her and sip. Dad would kill Carly if he knew she was letting me drink. But Dad has no say in my life anymore. Milk of Amnesia is good. Delicious.

"To survivors," Carly says.

We clink. Drink.

"To overcomers," she says. We clink again.

Is that a word? Who cares? I take a gulp.

"To working girls of the world." Carly raises her glass. "Oh, hey. You know what I just thought of? There's a job at Teva's Nail Salon in Breckenridge. It's only at the front desk, but you could work your way up."

To manicurist? I don't think so. "I don't want to have to drive to work," I tell her.

"Are you one of those eco freaks? Not that there's anything wrong with that," she adds quickly. "You have principles. I like that."

"I just don't feel comfortable driving."

"Don't you have a car at home?"

Another thing I don't want to talk about.

Carly's eyes light up. "There's a job opening at the Emporium."

"The what?"

"The book swap in Majestic. You must've seen it. That big barn?"

Oh, yeah. Across from the video rental.

"I'll call over there tomorrow."

"Don't. Please. I want to do this on my own."

Carly studies me over her drink before a broad smile streaks across her face. "You got that from me, you know."

"What? Stubbornness?"

She touches the tip of my nose. "Independence."

I'm not independent. I'm weak and needy.

"To independence," she toasts.

We clink and drink.

Carly stares at me so intently, I feel my insides withering. "You look so much like me when I was your age. And if anyone asks, that age is currently twenty-five." She smiles.

She's thirty-four. She had me when she was seventeen, my age. I wish I'd known her earlier. So many times I wondered about my real mom, before we met for the first time, what she was like, why she left. But Dad didn't want to talk about her. All he'd say was, "You got her looks. I hope that's all."

I guess I should be grateful for the little time we had. The time we're having now. I have the strongest urge to hug her and thank her for taking me in.

Carly's cell rings, and the moment passes. She retrieves the phone and glances at the caller ID. "I'd better get this," she says. She answers, "Hey, hon. Can you hold on a sec?" She presses the cell against her thigh. "Check out the book swap. If you're anything at all like your father, I *know* you love to read."

Chapter 4

The Emporium sign is faded, and the whole building looks as though it could collapse in on itself at any moment. Majestic is basically a ghost town. Most of the businesses have shut down, and FOR SALE or FOR RENT signs hang in the windows. There's some new construction, though, like Carly's house. Builders' trailers all around.

Dad's always complaining about urban sprawl—when he's not specifically hating on the homos who are moving into Virginia Beach. There's this older neighborhood near our house that's being renovated, and one of the shops has a rainbow flag flying off the balcony. Even though it's on our way to school, Dad makes Paulie and me walk five extra blocks to steer clear of it.

My dad's the biggest homophobe in the world, which is why I knew I could never come out to him. Tanith led me to believe that staying with Carly was temporary, but now I wonder if I'll ever have a home to go back to.

I loathe the thought of having inherited any of my father's traits, but Carly's right. I do love to read.

The front door to the Emporium is propped open with a cowboy boot full of sand. At noon it's scorching outside. A giant fan whirs in the bookstore, where an old geezer is hunched over a rippling newspaper.

The job isn't posted on any window or bulletin board that I can see. I walk up to the checkout desk and stand there, shifting my weight from one blister to another. A woman's on the phone. She finally notices me and sticks up an index finger.

This has to be the dustiest hole in the West. I run my finger along the counter, and it comes away caked. Every surface has this thick yellow pollen from the pine trees. I hear the woman say, "I think I just got a set in, Dutch. Hang on."

She sets the phone aside and rises to her feet. She's, like, six-two. Her eyes widen. "You're Carly's girl."

Scream. "I came to apply for the job?"

She fans her freckled face. "Whoo, I wish this heat would let up. It's the altitude, you know. Makes it feel hotter." She's examining me like I'm Carly.

It's not fair. I've experienced enough hatred and discrimination already in my life to fill a cesspool of bigotry.

"Supposedly you have a job opening?"

Timber Toes breaks off her stare and bends down, disappearing from view. I hear books slide aside on a shelf under the counter. She pops back up and says, "I'm sorry. The position's been filled." She totes a set of tattered paperbacks to the phone.

Sure it has. No one's going to hire me, and the irony is, it's not even because I'm gay.

A rolling cart clattering out from between the stacks snags my attention, and my jaw drops. It's Finn.

I stomp over. "What are you doing here?" She picks up a book from the cart, reads the spine, and saunters down the aisle.

I follow behind. "Why did you tell Arlo not to give me the job? I really needed that job."

"You don't want to work there. I did you a favor."

"Oh, I'm so grateful."

She turns her head slightly to glance at me.

She has olive skin and oval eyes, like she's part Asian. No, not Asian. Native American?

"When did you get this job?" I ask her.

"Yesterday." She peers at the books on the top shelf, her neck stretching taut. Her braid sluices down her back.

"So if you quit the Egg Drop-In," I think aloud, "Arlo needs a waitress in a hurry." I should get over there before someone else applies.

"I didn't quit," she says.

It takes me a minute to process. "You have two jobs?"

"Three." She reaches up and separates two books, then crams the book she's shelving into the slot.

"You can't have three jobs. There aren't that many jobs in this hick town. Plus, you suck at this one." I remove the book and put it in the right spot, between Mc and Ma.

Her eyes meet mine. She has opaque pupils and infinite irises. The darkest eyes I've ever seen.

"Finn, would you mind helping with this donation?" Timber Toes casts a long shadow down the aisle. To me she goes, "What did you say your name was again?"

"Alyssa," I tell her. Not Carly, okay?

"Alyssa. Alyssa," she repeats, wandering off.

Finn hands me a book off the cart and says, "Maybe you could have these done by the time I get back. Alyssa." She doesn't smile, but there's a glint of amusement in her eyes.

I hate her, but she's kind of hot.

No, she's not. She's *not*.

I throw down the book and race out of there.

By the time I get back to Carly's, I'm barely holding back the tears. It's so hot and my feet hurt; my lips are dry and chapped, and I'm chewing grit. I peel off my sweaty tee and jump in the shower. The water is soothing, streaming down my sunburned face. My room has its own shower and whirlpool. I wonder how many guests Carly entertains here. I don't really want to know. I don't want to believe she's a prosti—call girl. Call it what you want.

Over the course of a week, how many times did Tanith have to beg her? What would've happened if Carly had said no?

The cordless phone is ringing when I open the door. It rings constantly. To drown it out, along with my feeling of total rejection, I go downstairs and turn on the TV. One of my soaps is on—*The Young and the Restless*. Tanith watches it too, along with *General Hospital* and *One Life to Live*. She fills me in on anything I missed, or at least she used to.

Dad would get so disgusted at how addicted we were to such drivel, and it was true. The story lines were absurd. Tanith and I would laugh—in private.

I never thought I'd miss Tanith.

I stare at the TV and blank out. Curl into myself. A jagged saw in my stomach rips up my insides.

Damn you, Sarah. Why did you hook up with me in the first place? Did you ever love me? Because I loved you with all my being, Sarah. I risked everything for you. I always thought it was about us, that nothing or no one could tear us apart.

November

Sarah found a place, she said, where the two of you could do it. You'd been putting her off because you knew what a big step it was. You never told Sarah you were a virgin. You let her believe . . . she just assumed . . . you were older, more experienced. You were scared. You didn't know how.

A nor'easter was blowing in off the Atlantic that day, and it was freezing. Sarah's teeth were chattering when she asked, "When are you getting your driver's license?"

"I don't know. Never." You squeezed Sarah's hand in your coat pocket and snugged her closer as she hurried to wherever she was taking you.

"Why?" She had to raise her voice over the roaring wind. "I can't wait to drive."

You'd gone out over the summer with Dad to the school's parking lot to practice driving. Dad laughed at you because you drove like his mother, he said. "You can give it a little more gas," he said. You stepped on the brake by accident and whiplashed both of you. Then you overcompensated by jamming your foot on the gas. Tires squealed, and Dad bellowed, "Slow down! Hit the brake. Turn. Turn, dammit!" He yanked the wheel, and you covered your ears, but the squealing tires mashed with the crunch of the fender against the building.

Dad said, "Geez, are you trying to kill us?"

You almost burst into tears.

He leaned across you and opened the driver's-side door. "I think that's enough for today."

It was enough for forever.

Tanith asked, "How'd it go?" and Dad grumbled, "Don't ask." Later he apologized for losing it, but he'd already made you feel like crap.

"How much farther?" you shouted at Sarah.

"Almost there." The wind whipped up her loose hair. She began to jog, tugging you along by your pocket. You ended up at Gracie Field.

"What are we doing here?"

"You'll see."

She was a plotter. A schemer. You didn't know that then.

Sarah pulled up short at the baseball dugout. Next to it was a structure enclosed in aluminum sheeting. It was locked. Sarah held up a key.

"Where'd you get that?"

"My dad coaches Little League." The key unlocked the door and Sarah pulled it open. The interior was dark and arctic cold. It was the equipment shed. "We can't do it in the dirt," you said. Sarah pointed to a corner, where a couple of blankets had been tossed. She crouched down on the ground and took out of her backpack a handful of heat packs, the kind you put in your gloves or socks. She upended the sack, and an avalanche of heat packs poured out. "The dollar store was having a sale."

You laughed. She had had this all planned out.

She talked too much. "Alyssa, I want you so bad. I've never done this with anyone, so you have to tell me what I'm doing right and wrong."

Like you knew. Instinct kicked in.

"Oh, yeah. That feels good," she said. "How'd you do that? Oh my God. Do you want me to do that to you?"

You clamped a hand over her mouth and said, "Just shut up, Sarah."

Her voice sounds in my head, and I cover my ears. *Shut up shut up shut up.*

There are three e-mails from Paulie in my in-box. None from Dad. Or any of my friends. My relationship with Sarah cost me all my friends.

I open Paulie's first message:

yo morron. its borring w/o u here. its weerd. whydd u go and leav me?

"I didn't leave you," I say aloud. "You were there, Paulie. You know why."

ur laptop, old iPod, cd player and entir dvd set ar now in my posseshun.

"You think," I reply. His spelling's pretty good for being dyslexic. But he's becoming a smart-ass. Who'd he learn that from?

I open his next e-mail.

she cam over. she askt wher u'd gon and i tol her i dint no. she siad i was lying. i tol her to go to h-e-dubble-l.

My heart pounds. She came over?

She siad to tell u

The e-mail ends.
I close it and open the third message.

Paul is not allowed to contact you.

I flinch. Who was that? Dad? Tanith never gets on the computer. She calls herself a confirmed Luddite.

Sarah came over. A little too late to talk, isn't it? Why didn't we talk more? Maybe that was the problem. Maybe if I'd communicated better, or she felt she could talk to me about whatever was bothering her.

How did I make it hard for her to tell me? We were always open, weren't we?

I turn off the computer and resume lying on the sofa, listening to the dark and my breathing in and out. I used to lie in the shed with my ear on Sarah's chest to listen to the steady beating of her heart. I knew—I believed—we were forever. Now I know that forever is relative and that Sarah's definition was different from mine. My loneliness has a sound—the *whooshing* waves in a conch when I hold it to my ear and imagine an eternity of emptiness.

Chapter 5

Carly keeps prepackaged lettuce and a selection of dressings, so I toss together a salad and step out onto the back deck to eat. I slide into a sling chair and rest my ankles on the railing. Caribou Mountain looms over the house like a monolith. It's weird how all the land is cleared, and what few trees there are near the top are spindly and black. A new house is going up on the adjacent lot in Caribou Estates, but it looks like the developer ran out of money or something, because only the framing is done, and no one's worked on it since I've been here.

On the way up from the airport, Carly mentioned this was the driest year in recent history, and I saw a couple of signs warning about high fire danger. Half the trees on Caribou Mountain look dead or burned. Probably spontaneous combustion, as hot as it is.

If I were home, I'd be at the beach or the mall. We'd be at Starbucks pooling our money to see how many caramel macchiatos we could buy. M'Chelle and Ben. Me and Sarah.

There is no more me and Sarah. No more me and anyone.

I wonder where she is, if she suffered any consequences for her actions. I only met her family once—well, twice. She asked me over for Thanksgiving, which was surprising, considering her parents are Christians. It's terrible to associate all Christians with homophobia, but that's how Sarah described them. "They're Christians," she said, and rolled her eyes.

Anyway, the weekend before, Dad and Tanith were on the sofa with their newest Netflix, and when the FBI warning came on I asked, "Would it be okay if I went to a friend's house for Thanksgiving?"

Dad said, "Absolutely not."

Tanith swiveled her head to look up at me. "What friend? Do we know him?"

Dad's head snapped around to Tanith's face, then up to mine.

Not much gets past Tanith. Well, some stuff does.

"No," I said.

"I think it'd be all right." Tanith winked.

"I don't," Dad said to me. "Why don't you bring him here?"

I mumbled, "Just forget it," and left the room.

I heard Tanith say, "Paul, it's fine with me. Alyssa's growing up, you know, and we won't always be together for holidays."

Dad caught me listening at the doorway. He held my eyes, and a thin smile pressed against his lips. Pausing the movie, he said, "When do we get to meet him?"

There is no him! I wanted to shout. There'll never be a *him*.

Why did he always make it so hard? Why does he still?

On Thanksgiving morning, Tanith knocked on my bedroom door. The aroma of turkey and sage and pumpkin swirled through my room, making me hungry. I love Thanksgiving. The food and the spirit of giving and—the whole family thing.

Now it'll never be the same. I don't even know who my family is.

"I talked to your dad last night." Tanith stood in the threshold. "He wants us to have Thanksgiving dinner together, but I got up early to get the turkey in the oven, so we'll be eating around noon or one. Will that give you time?"

I jumped up to hug her. And I almost did. Tanith could be so great.

I'd already told Sarah I couldn't make it. She'd been sulking all week.

Tanith said, "Maybe afterward you could bring your boyfriend home to meet your dad?"

My face flared. "I don't think so."

"Oh, come on. What's the worst that could happen? He knows better than to humiliate you. Although that probably wouldn't stop him." Tanith made a face.

What's the worst? Being disowned. It's beyond what I imagined Dad would ever do.

It was a mistake to go to Sarah's. The first of countless errors in judgment. Why did we have to involve our families? Why?

I'd never felt so uncomfortable or nervous. Sarah has a large family; all these relatives around the table. "What does your old man do?" her father asked me.

"He's a lawyer," I told him.

Sarah's family *oohed*. What did that mean?

Her mom said, "How old are you?" Her accusatory tone of voice made me tense.

"Sixteen," I said.

"You're a sophomore?"

"Junior."

"A junior! You're too old to be Sarah's best friend."

I glanced sideways at Sarah. I had no idea what she'd told her parents about me. "Alyssa's in Spanish Club with me, and gymnastics. She's tutoring me in math," Sarah said.

She was a good liar.

"I hate lawyers," Sarah's dad said. "They're all crooks."

What a jerk. People who assume all lawyers are dishonest are ignorant. At least my dad was honest. He honestly hates me.

Tears sting my eyes, and I force them to *stop*. I'm so sick of hurting.

I need to *do* something. Occupy my mind. I could read, but lately reading doesn't even take me out of myself.

With all this supposed natural beauty around me, I should go exploring.

My backpack is still stuffed with books and clothes and CDs. Tanith didn't give me much time to pack. In the front pocket are a bunch of video games that Paulie must've stuck in there. Carly doesn't have an Xbox or Wii that I've seen. The last thing I want to do is play video games all by myself.

I can't hike in my flip-flops, and it's too hot for my boots, so I slip into Carly's room to check out her shoes. She has racks and racks. On one side are wedge sandals and athletic shoes. On the other are her stripper shoes—sparkly stilettos and strap-on fuck-me heels.

I have the urge to try on a pair, just to see how they feel. I wonder if she takes them off or leaves them on when she does it. The image makes me sick.

I can tell by looking that all her shoes are too big for me, anyway.

The mountainside is loose gravel and steep banks, slick as ice. My flip-flops keep falling off. I need to climb higher, maybe up through the dead trees, where there might be thicker vegetation and more shade.

I trip and grab on to some scrub to keep from tumbling all the way down the mountain. A swarm of gnats buzz in my ear. I swat them away, and six or eight million mosquitoes lift off my arm. My hands flail around my head. Ew, ew, I hate bugs.

Forget this. I could take a drive. If I drive slowly, stay off the interstate...

Even though it's been in the garage since I got here, the Mercedes is caked with yellow pollen and filmed with a layer of dirt. It's obvious Carly hasn't driven it in a while. Every time she opens the garage, though, another whirlpool of pollen blows in. The front seat of the SUV is pushed way back, and it takes me an eternity to find the adjuster and figure out all the knobs and buttons and gauges on the dash. I hear Dad's voice in my head: "Step one: Always learn the car you're about to drive."

He forgot to mention where the instruction manual is.

"Okay, you can do this," I say aloud. I twist the key. A

grinding sound, then the motor dies. Great. The battery must be dead. I try again, and the motor *vrooms* to life, startling me. I sit for a minute, feeling the power. I garner courage. Shifting into reverse, I release the parking brake, give the engine a touch of gas, and back right into the garage door.

"Shit."

I ease forward, shift into park, and turn off the car. I get out and check the damage. Thank God I didn't hit hard enough to dent the bumper or the garage door. I'm the worst driver in the world.

This time I press the garage door opener first and then back out slowly, slowly. Shut the garage. Shift into drive. Inch forward down the access road, riding the brake the whole time.

To the right is Majestic, then a town named Frisco and a highway that leads to the interstate. I turn left.

A semi swerves around the corner, horn blaring, and I jam on the brakes. When the shrieking in my ears stops, I open my eyes. I'm still alive, but stopped dead in the road.

I putter forward again. This road, Highway 102, curves around Caribou Mountain. I drive slowly, getting a feel for the steering, the gas and brakes. I push buttons on the armrest to find the window opener. The hot air outside is stifling, but better than the stale air inside the car. There's a sunroof, so I search the dash to find the control. The button I push blasts hot air in my face, but soon the air gets cooler. Score. I found the AC.

The drive is nerve-racking, but the scenery is pretty. The smell of pine. Fresh air. In Virginia Beach, summer means the smell of salt off the ocean, and humidity that wilts you like wet spaghetti. My clothes are always damp there. Without warning, a dog darts into the middle of the highway, and my foot slams the brake just in time. A person runs into the road to retrieve the dog.

My heart thrums in my ears. I blink, and Finn's standing there, holding the dog. My first impulse is to *go*, don't let her see me. But she's already seen.

I click the turn signal and pull to the side of the road ahead of her. In a few seconds, she saunters up alongside. How do I open the passenger window? Finn's waiting. I press a button, and the passenger window plus the two back windows go down.

"You almost hit us," she says.

"I didn't mean to. Your dog ran right out in front of me."

She eyes the inside of the car. "Is this yours?"

"Yeah, right. Carly let me borrow it."

The dog whines, and Finn shifts him to her other arm.

"Is this your third job?" I ask. "Walking dogs?"

She gives me a funny look. "People get paid for that?"

Apparently not here. The dog is a mutt. Long-haired dachshund-bulldog mix or something. "What's his name?" I ask.

"Boner," she says.

I laugh.

She doesn't crack a smile.

"Seriously?" I say.

A car races up behind us, and the driver honks. Finn waves as the car zooms past.

"Where are you going?" I ask. "You want a ride?"

"No, thanks. This isn't a good place to stop. There's a picnic area up ahead. Why don't you pull in there?" I check out where she's pointing.

She sets the dog down and starts walking along the shoulder again. I signal and merge back onto the road.

The picnic area, overgrown with weeds and long, dry grass, has one table. I shut and lock the car door and then sit on the bench and wait for Finn. She looks both ways before trotting across the highway, carrying Boner. What a name. She's lean and tan. Muscular, but not in a fake I-work-out-at-the-gym sort of way. More naturally buff.

She sets Boner down and says, "Stay." He sniffs the ground and lifts his leg on the end of the picnic table, barely missing my foot. He wanders off through the grass. "Boner, stay," she calls to him. He acts deaf. She shakes her head at me. "Dumb dog."

We look at each other, and something—I don't know what—passes between us. She opens her mouth to speak, but I cut her off. "If you say I look exactly like Carly, I'll smack you."

"Don't move." She raises her hand. "You have a wasp on your neck."

I slap my neck and jump up, flapping my hands around my head.

She lowers her arm and stares at me.

"What? It was a wasp."

Her eyes shift over my shoulder, and she calls, "Boner!" His tail wags up through the weeds. Finn turns her attention to me again.

"Sorry. I hate bugs," I say.

"They're just looking for their next meal. Or a little excitement in their day." One end of her lip curls up.

"Ha-ha."

She steps up on the bench and plops down on the picnic table, resting her elbows on her knees. I climb up next to her. We seem to have forged a truce. She gazes out across the open field, where Boner's digging up something. "I wish I had a dog," I say. Maybe now I can. "We had a dog when I was little, an Irish setter, but it got cancer and had to be put to sleep."

Finn twists her head my way. "I'm sorry."

It's an old memory. Dad cried all the way home from the vet's. After that he said, "No more dogs."

"How old is he?" I ask, jutting my chin toward Boner.

"I don't know." Finn peers back at him. "He's a stray."

A moment of silence passes. It's peaceful. "Shouldn't you be at work?" I say.

"In a few hours. I should be sleeping, but it's such a nice day, I thought we'd get out and hike up to Caribou Lake."

"There's a lake?"

"In the crater."

"There's a crater?"

She sits upright and whistles through her teeth, about splitting my eardrums. Boner's off by some boulders, sniffing around. His tail wags, which means he heard, I guess. Finn says, "Where were you going?"

"I don't know. For a drive."

She reaches into her backpack. "Give me your arm."

"Why?"

She holds up a plastic bottle of bug spray. "Ticks," she says. "And mosquitoes."

Not to mention wasps. I extend my arm, and she grasps my elbow. Her hands are strong and calloused. She sprays me over and under. Even through the toxic fumes, her nearness, her touch, generate heat. I cool it down.

She takes my other hand. She has gorgeous light brown skin. Sculpted arm muscles. She really does look Native American. Kind of a round face. That long, thick, coal-black braid.

"Shut your eyes," she says. She points the bug spray at my face.

I close my eyes and see her in photo negative. A blinding white aura.

She mists my cheeks, under my chin, around my ears. She sprays the exposed skin on my chest and back. For a heart-stopping minute I soak in her sensuality. She oozes it. It's hard to squelch the feeling.

The dog barks shrilly, startling me.

Finn bounces off the bench, dropping her pack, and races through the long grass over to where Boner is. I scramble behind her. She stops, her arm jutting out to the side like a crossbar to halt me.

"Stand still," Finn says. "Very still."

The dog barks, and Finn lunges, catching him by the collar. She hoists him up as he barks and barks. "Shh, Boner. Hush." She clamps his snout. He whines, and she whispers, "Shh," to him.

I say, "What is it?"

Her palm stops millimeters from my mouth. I hear it—a sound, like *chchchchch*.

Finn's arm drops, and she grabs my hand. "Step back very, very slowly." Her grip tightens as she leads me backward. When I falter in my flip-flops, she curls an arm around my waist.

After nine or ten steps, we freeze in place. She exhales a breath and lets me go. "That was close." She returns to the picnic table, dog in tow, me stumbling behind. "They usually don't come up this far, but it's a hot summer. I've seen a bunch of them around the quarry south of town." Finn scoops her backpack off the ground.

"What was it?" I ask again.

She takes out a leash and clips it onto Boner's collar. Then she says to me, "Rattlesnake."

"What!"

"Western rattlesnake. Pretty big one. Not a good idea to be walking around up here in flip-flops."

"You're shitting me."

"You should get some decent shoes."

I'm paralyzed, seized with fear as I imagine snakes everywhere, crawling all over my feet and legs.

"We should get going." She shoulders her pack and tugs at Boner's leash.

"Wait." I rush up behind her. "Can I give you a ride?"

"The trail's just around the bend here." She pivots and walks backward away from me. "I didn't know Carly had a kid your age. She never mentioned you."

"I'm not a kid." And thanks for the slap in the face.

Finn smiles. "How old are you?"

"Eighteen," I lie. "How old are you?"

She doesn't answer. I'm guessing early twenties.

I get in the car and start the ignition, expelling a sharp breath. I drive past her, speeding up so she thinks I'm cool. Yeah, I'm so cool. Watch, I'll run right off the road or get hit by a semi. Out the rearview mirror, I see Finn veer up onto Caribou Mountain and just sort of blend into nature.

Chapter 6

The front door shuts, and I jerk awake. I shift to sit up on the sofa, find the remote, and turn down the sound on the TV. Carly appears on the main-floor landing. "Oh. You're here."

She sounds disappointed.

She lowers herself into the velvet wing chair next to the sofa. All the furniture is new. Matching white leather sofa set and blue velvet wing chairs, which don't exactly fit the whole rustic cabin illusion she's trying to create. How many log cabins have four levels, floor-to-ceiling picture windows, and state-of-the-art electronics?

"What'd you do today?" she asks.

"Nothing. Took a drive. The job at the Emporium was already filled."

Carly makes a pouty face.

"Maybe I could work with you," I say.

"Doing what?" She reaches into her purse for her buzzing cell.

"I don't know." I think, *Handing out numbers to your johns?*

She ignores the call. She's wearing this corsetlike top that pushes up her boobs, and knee-length black leggings. She's poured a pitcher of lavender perfume on herself.

How could Dad have fallen for a person like Carly? And vice versa. I can't see them together at all. Now I wonder if they ever were married. Dad never talked about a wedding, and Carly's kept her maiden name.

Carly rolls her right shoulder a couple of times and says, "I pulled a muscle or something." She winces. "Would you mind getting me the tube of Ben-Gay down in my exercise room?"

As I pass her, she reaches out to clench my wrist. "I'm glad you're here, Alyssa. You could come to work with me, but there wouldn't be anything for you to do."

"I could collect the money off the dresser," I blurt out.

She slices me in half with a look.

Oh my God. Did I say that?

"Most of my clients are on account."

Which means she has regulars. She releases me.

In the bathroom downstairs, she has drawers full of products—skin creams, anti-itch creams, muscle relaxants. The tube of Ben-Gay is half-empty.

"Thanks," she says as I hand it to her.

I sit and watch as she presses a glob onto her fingertips and pulls down the strap of her corset. Traces of glitter sparkle in the sunlight streaming through the high arched window. She glitters her shoulders? Chest too. She doesn't look or dress old enough to have a teenage daughter. I'm not surprised she wouldn't want anyone to know about me. Still, it had hurt when Finn said that.

There's not one picture of me in this whole house. I've checked.

"How did you hurt your shoulder?" I ask. Why don't I just ask if she's a call girl, stop dancing around the truth?

"I think it happened when I was showing a new client how to lift weights properly." She screws up her face. "He's probably at Summit Medical right now in a full body cast."

My nose puckers at the menthol vapor, and I sneeze. I sneeze again. I have a really sensitive nose. Sarah wore this lemon-lime body gel, but it was light and delicate.

Why does my brain always circle back to her?

"Where'd you drive to?" Carly asks as she gets up and goes to the wet bar.

"Around the mountain. Halfway around."

"You shouldn't be wandering in the mountains alone, especially without a phone."

Well, excuse me if I'm restless and bored and I don't have a phone or anyone to call even if I did.

Ice cubes clink into a glass. "You should've called me. I would've rescheduled my appointments for the day, and we could've driven to Vail, maybe. Gone shopping." She returns with two glasses of bubbly liquid, a lime wedge in each. Mine tastes like 7-Up, nonalcoholic. Hers is amber-colored.

"Wow. What are you watching?" she asks, lowering herself to the sofa.

Shit. I get up to retrieve the TV remote from the coffee table and thumb the power off. Did she see the girls kissing on Logo, rolling around in the sand? I'll have to be careful what I watch on cable. Dad would have a heart attack if he knew there was a gay TV station.

"I don't watch a lot of TV," Carly says, curling her legs under her. "What shows do you like?" With her fingernails, she swirls the ice cubes in her glass.

"I don't know. A couple of soaps. *Gossip Girl*." Dad hates all those "trashy" shows. And if there's a gay character, forget it.

Carly turns and looks at me, at the side of my face, until I feel blood rush to my cheeks. "I wish I still had your skin. Come. Sit." She pats the sofa.

"I have stuff to do," I mumble.

Carly says at my back, "Are we ever going to talk about it?"

My heart pummels my chest. I promised myself I'd always be out from now on, but the situation scares me. My friends have all ditched me. My family. I have a little savings left, but not enough to get an apartment or anything.

She adds, "You know I don't have a problem with you being lesbian or bisexual."

I whirl. "I'm not bisexual."

"I have lots of gay friends. Your father is just so narrow-minded and—" The cell in her purse buzzes again, and she holds up an index finger. She checks the ID and answers, "This is Carly." She listens. "Well, how are you, stranger? It's been a while. A massage?" She crosses her eyes at me and rolls her shoulder. "I think I can fit you in." She gets up and walks past me, pressing a palm against my cheek, and then bounds up the stairs, laughing at something the caller said.

This enormous weight lifts off my shoulders, and I think, *Wow. My whole life would've been different if I'd grown up with Carly.*

But she didn't want kids, I guess. Specifically me.

Sarah wanted kids. She talked about it all the time, how much she wanted kids, how scared she was she'd never live a normal life. I kept telling her just because you're lesbian doesn't mean you can't have children.

"Yeah, but it isn't easy," she said. "It isn't... natural."

Ben was there. "What isn't natural?" he interjected. "The sperm meets the egg. They exchange vows. Who cares how it happens?"

Sarah laughed. When was that? Was that when it started?

Carly tramps down the stairs, her hair freshly combed and banded with a scrunchie into a ponytail. She says, "He's a big tipper. Otherwise I'd blow him off."

Did she have to use that expression? "That's okay." I shrug. "You have to work."

Her eyes nail me, like she caught the undertone in my voice. "I won't be long." She heads for the door and then stops. "Oh. Wait. I won't be home. I have to dance tonight at Willy's. I've totally lost track of time. Does that ever happen to you?"

"Yeah," I say. "Don't worry about it. It's not like you'll get grounded."

She laughs as she closes the door behind her.

December

Dad ambushed you when you eased open the front door at one AM. "Do you know what time it is, young lady?"

"I lost track," you said, out of breath after running home from Gracie Field. "Sorry."

"You're grounded." He stormed up the stairs.

"For how long?" You ran after him.

"Until I say."

Bastard.

You stalked to your room and yanked off your coat, threw it onto the floor. Threw all your clothes on top of it, cursing him. *Why was he so hard on you?* Everything you did, you did to please him. You studied hard to get good grades. You did your chores without complaint. You tried to like Tanith. That was the hardest thing, his bringing her into your lives. You'd had him to yourself for seven years before he met and married Tanith. Seven perfect years.

Tanith was never your mother, your real mother. As much as she tried to be.

Dad knocked on your door. "I want to talk to you, Alyssa."

Great. Now you were naked. "Just a minute." You crawled into bed and pulled the covers up to your chin. "Enter," you said.

He stood there with his arms folded. You could feel the menacing vibes emanating from him. "I'm sorry about missing curfew. My watch stopped." Which was a lie, and Dad knew it.

He said, "Are you embarrassed for your boyfriend to meet your family? Are we not good enough for him?"

"*What*? No," you said.

"Then why won't you bring him home? *What's* wrong with him?"

"Nothing."

He approached you. The smell of Sarah was strong on your hands and face, so you bunched up the sheet over your nose.

"There must be something." Dad dropped his arms, sounding more hurt than mad. He sat on the edge of your bed. "You used to bring all your friends home. Is he a drug dealer or something? A gangbanger? What are you hiding?"

"Nothing." You'd never brought "all" your friends home.

Dad stared at you, through you. You started shaking all over. You couldn't breathe. This squeak escaped from your throat.

"I can't understand you," Dad said. "Take the sheet out of your mouth."

You scooted back farther against the wall, pulling the covers with you. Dad's eyes bored into yours, waiting. This torchlike heat scorched every square inch of your skin, like you were burning in hell.

You couldn't do it. The words wouldn't even form on your lips. You could never tell him about Sarah. About yourself.

He waited. He'd wait until you said what he wanted to hear.

You swallowed hard. "Okay, I'll bring him home to meet you."

Dad's eyes warmed. He patted your kneecap and stood. "Invite him for dinner. I promise we'll be on our best behavior—even if he is a weirdo or a nerd. You'd better not be into drugs."

"I'm not."

Dad headed for the door. "You're still grounded," he said over his shoulder as he turned off the light.

You whispered in the dark, "Okay."

Chapter 7

Ben had been my best friend since ninth grade, when we both came out to each other. He was like my brother, only better because I could talk to him about anything. I can't even count all the times he cried on my shoulder after his heart was broken by one boyfriend or another. When Sarah and I got together, he was so happy for us. For me.

I texted Ben to meet me in the media center during my study period and his lunch hour. "Hey," he said, pulling up a chair at my table. "Wassup, girlfriend?"

"I need a favor from you," I told him.

"Anything," he said.

I knew he'd do anything for me. Vice versa.

"Don't say that until you hear what it is."

"Is it lurid? Are we breaking in to Fascinations and stealing vibrators?"

"You wish."

He reached into his backpack and pulled out a Tupperware

bowl and fork. "Want some?" He removed the lid. "It's my mom's linguine with clam sauce. *Delicioso*."

It smelled buttery and rich. "No thanks." My stomach was in knots about what I was planning to do. Ben poised his fork over the bowl.

"Go ahead. Eat," I told him.

He dug in.

"Someone led my dad to believe I have a boyfriend, and now I need one."

Ben snorted. "Someone?"

"It wasn't me." It was Tanith. So what?

Ben twirled linguine on his fork. "Why don't you just be honest with your dad? You're going to have to tell him sometime."

I let out a sigh. "Not in this life."

Ben stuffed the forkful of pasta in his mouth and fake-swooned. "You sure?" He passed the bowl under my nose, and I pushed it away.

"Remember that time I wrote your whole history report when you were all devastated about Devon moving to Ohio?" I said.

A flash of pain crossed Ben's face as he chewed and swallowed.

God. How cruel to remind him.

"Blackmail does not become you." He took a smaller bite, not looking at me.

"I'm sorry," I said, and meant it. Sorry for myself. Sorry for taking advantage of our friendship.

"What does Sarah think about this?" he asked.

"She doesn't know, and please don't tell her."

Ben raised his eyes. "Alyssa—"

"It'll only be for a couple of weeks. A month at the most. Then I'll tell my dad we broke up, and he'll get off my back. I'm grounded, anyway, so I don't know how I'm going to see Sarah outside of school."

Ben finished his linguine in silence. He recapped his bowl, stuffed it back inside his pack, and said, "I hate lying about who I am. You know that. It took me this long to get over the fear of being totally out."

A lump of shame clogged my throat, and I stood to go.

He grabbed my hand. "But for you, I'll do it."

Maybe it was all my fault for putting him in the middle.

My eyelids flutter open to blinding sunlight, and I pull the sheet over my face. It feels stuffy in the house, like Carly forgot to turn on the AC.

My stomach growls, so I drag myself down to the kitchen. No note from Carly. Nothing in the fridge that appeals to me. Carly lives on salad. The microwave clock reads 8:51. How can time move so slowly? At home it seems the summers fly by; I never want them to end.

I take a long, cool shower and get dressed. I choose a book to read but can't get into it. Downstairs, I turn on the TV, and the channel is still on Logo. It's showing repeats of *The L Word*, and it reminds me of Sarah's birthday present. I want to hurl. I want to forget. I close my eyes, and Ben's face comes into focus.

He was convincing. He came for dinner all dressed up. He

hugged me at the door and shook my dad's hand hard. He complimented Tanith on her pot roast. He was a gamer, so he and Paulie talked shop. I could feel Dad's eyes drilling into Ben all evening, and I was sure Dad would see through the facade, but he didn't.

You only see what you want to see. I learned that the hard way.

"How long have you two been going out?" Dad asked Ben.

Ben turned to me. "How long's it been, Alyssa?"

My cheeks burned. "I don't know. A couple of months."

Ben said to Dad, "Nine weeks, three days, six hours, and"—he glanced at his watch—"thirteen minutes."

Dad chuckled.

After dinner, Paulie and Ben set up Guitar Hero, and I went back into the kitchen to help Tanith clean up. She said, "I've got it under control. Go back to your . . . company."

A flash of understanding flickered in her eyes. She knew, or at least suspected.

Before I went up to bed that night, Dad clenched my arm and hand. He stared into my eyes. "He's all right," Dad said. "Nice guy. I don't know what you were worried about."

I lay in bed for hours, wishing I could be what he wanted me to be.

Now I only wish he'd accept me for what I am.

I turn off the TV, slide on my flip-flops, and snag the keys to the Mercedes. The only restaurant in town is the Egg Drop-In.

It's packed. The aroma of coffee and pancakes and fried potatoes makes my mouth water. Arlo spots me through the order window and motions me over. "You still interested in the job?"

"Yeah!"

Arlo says, "Help Finn with the rush."

I see Finn taking an order at a table and, as I make my way over there, some guy whistles at me. Gag. Finn whirls and almost knocks me down. She snags my arm to catch me, and it tingles all the way down to my toes.

"What can I do to help?" I ask her.

"With what?" she says.

"I think I've been hired." I smile.

Her eyes narrow over my shoulder, shooting daggers at Arlo. I think, *Get over it.* I need this job to save my sanity—or find it again. I can't spend one more day alone in that empty house. The bell on the front door jingles, and a group of people dressed in scrubs enter. Finn pulls off the damp towel she has draped over her shoulder and dangles it at me. "Bus the eight top." I take the rag, and she takes off.

"Wait!"

She hurries to the customers at the door and tells them it'll just be a minute.

What's an eight top? There are two empty tables. One is small, meant for two people, and the other is big and round. I'm guessing that's the eight top. I have no idea where to begin. I stack the dirty dishes, along with the silverware, cups, napkins, and syrup, but I know I'll never make it to the kitchen without dropping something. I set down the wobbly stack and disassemble, rearrange with only the plates and cups, but one of the cups tips, and coffee dribbles down my front.

The Scrubs circle the table, and I say, "I'll have it ready for you in a sec."

Finn shows up to help, thank God. She sets a gray plastic tub on one of the chairs and, with lightning speed, clears the table. Pulling the towel off my shoulder, she swabs the plastic tablecloth clean.

She might've told me about the tub for dirty dishes.

One of the women is staring at me; she has been since she arrived. What? I know I have coffee and syrup all over me. I'm clueless about waitressing, okay?

"You're Carly's girl."

My jaw clenches. I don't want to acknowledge it because I don't need to be dissed in front of a whole restaurant full of people. "I heard about you, but I didn't believe it. You must be a huge comfort to Carly."

A comfort? More like an inconvenience.

The nurse, or whatever she is, says to her male friend, "This is Carly's daughter."

The guy's eyes widen. Before he can say anything, Finn shoves the tub at me. "Bus table one, then the counter."

I stumble backward, my flip-flops sticking to the floor where someone spilled syrup. I almost fall on my ass, but Finn catches me. She smirks, like it's so funny. She pulls wrapped silverware out of thin air and sets the big table while I manage to clear the small one by the window in under a year.

At the counter, this guy wads his napkin and sets it atop his leftover fried potatoes. They look awesome. I'm starving. As he's pulling out his wallet, Finn swings by the counter and says under her breath, "We need a new pot of coffee. Can you make coffee?"

I click my tongue, like *If I knew where the coffee was, yeah, maybe.*

There's nowhere to set the tub, and it's heavy. I swing around, and Finn relieves me of the tub and then backs through the swinging doors into the kitchen.

"Thanks a bunch." The customer lays a five-dollar bill on top of the dirty dishes and winks at me.

Finn snatches up the tip. Where'd she come from?

"Oh, hey, why don't you take it?" I say.

She stacks his cup and silverware on the plate and sets them in a new tub.

"You could at least show me what to do," I snap. Everything's moving so fast and I don't know how to make coffee and now I feel tears welling and I try to swallow them.

Finn blinks at me, and it's like she ratchets down. "I'm sorry," she says under her breath. "It's just...I need the money."

I wasn't even thinking about the money, really. She waited on the guy; she earned the tip.

Finn gazes so deep into my eyes, I swear she sees the center of the earth. She says, "I'll make the coffee and show you how later, okay? Just brush all the crumbs on the counter into the bus tub." She pulls the towel off my shoulder and adds, "Swab the counter and chairs. We can sweep up the crap on the floor later, unless some little kid dumps his whole plate, which happens. The napkins are there." She points to another tub under the counter, full of silverware bundled in paper napkins. She's woven a leather thong with a feather on the end through her braid today. So cool.

A *clang* sounds in the kitchen, and Arlo curses loudly enough for everyone to hear. He shouts, "Orders up, goddammit!"

Finn rolls her eyes at me. "How desperate are you? Because working for Arlo..."

"On a scale of one to ten? Eleven."

She stands there a minute, searching my face. I feel it getting warmer and warmer.

Arlo shouts, "I got two waitresses, and they're both deaf as doornails!"

Finn says, "Pretend you don't hear him."

"Hear who?" I say.

She grins. I amused Finn. I quash the urge to feel happy about that.

On the way home, I can't stop smiling because I did it. I got a job. I lasted through the rush, and not once did I think about...

Damn. Dammit.

Get out of my head, both of you. All of you.

I'd never been grounded. I was the good girl, Daddy's little girl. Perfect in every way.

"When I'm grounded, I can have friends over, at least," Ben said. "Your dad doesn't expect Romeo and Juliet to actually be kept apart, does he? Make that Juliet and Juliet."

We were in Ben's VW before school, Sarah and me in the backseat grabbing a few minutes of togetherness before school. It was cold, and Ben had the heater running. Sarah was kissing my neck and nibbling my ear, and the windows were steaming up.

She said, "Ask, okay? I can't stand not being with you."

I did everything Sarah wanted me to do. Not once did I say no. Maybe she saw that as weakness. I asked Tanith about having friends over, and she said, "I'll have to ask your dad."

Because it was always what *he* wanted, what *he* said.

What *Sarah* wanted, *she* got.

Dad said yes. I was shocked. "I'd rather Ben comes here than have you sneaking out behind my back. So, yes, Ben can come over." That was Dad's rationale.

Little did he know how long I'd been deceiving him.

The climb up to Carly's house is heart attack hill. It's not paved, and my feet hurt, and I feel light-headed from dehydration. If I'm going to be walking to work, I need to pack bottled water and get better shoes.

I can tell by the stillness in the house that Carly's not home, or she's sleeping. I creep up the stairs to her room and find it empty, her bed made. A pile of clothes lies on the floor, as if she changed in a hurry.

All I want is a shower. But the whirlpool looks inviting, and I have all the time in the world.

As I'm running a cool bubble bath, I return to the main level and pour myself a Milk of Amnesia. On the rocks. I think, *This is how the bold and the beautiful live.*

I take the drink upstairs, set it on the rim of the tub, strip, and slither in up to my chin. Heaven. The first gulp of my drink slides down my parched throat like silk.

The Baileys reminds me of eggnog. And Christmas.

I remember, they all burst on the scene—Ben and Sarah and M'Chelle. It was Saturday, and Tanith was baking cookies for Paulie's cookie exchange at school. "Oh my God," Ben said. "It smells amazing in here." He walked right past me and into the kitchen. M'Chelle and Sarah lagged behind. Then it was just Sarah. She took my hand and squeezed it.

Dad emerged from his home office, and I pulled away from Sarah fast.

"Hi," she said to him. I freaked, but she smiled and introduced herself. She still had her braces, and her hair was longer, French braided. It made her look even younger than she was.

We all ended up in the kitchen, where I introduced Dad to M'Chelle and Ben. Which was stupid because he knew Ben. Dad snagged a couple of thumbprint cookies from the counter, and Tanith fake-slapped his hand. He winked at me and left.

Paulie and I had been assembling a gingerbread house, and Ben said, "Ooh, let me help with the landscape design."

M'Chelle and I rolled our eyes. So gay. Ben sure knew how to turn it on and off.

Sarah said, "Wasn't there something in your room you wanted to show me?"

Tanith was watching and I hesitated, but Sarah caught my sweater and yanked me back out of the kitchen. "Show me your room," she said in a sexy voice, batting those baby blues at me.

It seemed safe enough. I led her upstairs, where she shut the door and pulled me into her. Kissed me so long and hard, my lips swelled. Then her hands were under my shirt and...

God.

I punch on the jets in the whirlpool and slide down.

...She unhooked my bra...

"Sarah..."

"I miss you so much."

"Me too."

"How much longer do we have to be apart?"

"I don't know."

She said, "I can't stand it. I just want to be out. I hate hiding and lying about what I am. About us. I want to be together." She tried to pull my shirt over my head, but I stopped her.

"We can't. Not here."

She ran her hand between my legs....

I drop my head back and feel the power of the jets. Her power over me.

She got her way. She always got her way, and I gave it to her. I gave myself willingly, Sarah. And you took and took until there was nothing left of me to take.

Christmas

You and Sarah bought each other initial necklaces, hers with an A, yours with an S. You exchanged presents in the shed by clasping the necklaces around each other's necks before making slow, passionate love.

You weren't looking forward to winter break, because Sarah was going to her aunt and uncle's home in Philadelphia.

Now you wonder if she really went. If she was lying to you even then.

But she called you every night. She said how much she missed you. She must've gone.

There was no sign of any change in your relationship. Sarah ended your conversations with a whispered, "I love you so much, *Alyssa*. I wish we could be together."

"*We* are together," you told her. "Distance can't keep us apart."

Distance wasn't your undoing.

But then Sarah didn't call the day she got back from Philadelphia. The day she told you she'd be home. You called her cell. No answer. She had a habit of letting the battery die or forgetting her phone. You called her home. No answer. You didn't leave a message.

Paulie was bugging you. "One more game of Guitar Hero?"

You barked at him, "No! Leave me alone."

He slumped on the floor and pouted. You felt bad about taking it out on him. You'd been grouchy the whole Christmas break. "You play," you told him. "I'll watch."

"But you're spazzier," he said.

You struck a spaz pose, and he outdid you with his twisted limbs. It made you laugh and feel better. Paulie was—is—an awesome brother.

You lay on the sofa, calling Sarah again. No answer. Paulie set up Transformers on his Xbox instead. He talked to himself while he played video games. While he did homework too. Sometimes at night you'd hear him talking to himself in bed. What a weird kid.

Or a lonely kid.

You were crazy with pent-up energy and anxiety. You threw the cell down, jumped up, and attacked your brother, sitting on him and tickling him until he screamed.

You ended up spazzing out to Guitar Hero anyway.

The next day, New Year's Eve, you called Sarah the minute you woke up. Her cell went to voice mail. Same with her home phone. You tried all day long.

Even though it was sleeting and bitter cold, you rode your bike to her house. Cars were parked in the driveway, and the Christmas tree lights were on. You just sat out in the cold because you couldn't work up the nerve to go ring the bell.

You rode back home.

Right before midnight, Sarah finally answered her cell. "I can't talk to you," she said in a hoarse voice. She sounded like she'd been crying.

"Sarah, what?" you asked. "What's the matter?"

"I can't! Okay?" She hung up.

It hit you. She'd done it. She'd come out to her parents.

Chapter 8

I set my alarm for five, not really sure what time I should be at the Egg Drop-In to start work. Arlo'd just grumbled, "Be here tomorrow. And for God's sake, speed the plow." I guess he noticed I was a little slow. Today I was going to wow him.

Traces of cigarette smoke and perfume hang in the air, so I know Carly's been home. I sneak down the hall and see a lump in her bed. I think to leave her a note that says, *How does it feel to get up and find me gone?* Instead, I write, *Got a job in town.*

The bell tinkles over the Egg Drop door when I walk in a little before six. The joint, as they say, is jumping.

"Look out," Finn says. "He's in a mood."

Worse than usual?

Dishes and pans clang in the kitchen, and then something metal hits the wall.

I grimace. She hustles toward the counter, saying over her shoulder, "You'll need to get here by five, at the latest."

Five AM? Finn's eyes are bloodshot, and her hair is kind of messy. As she hands me an order pad, I say, "Rough night?"

She sets a cup on a serving tray, along with a plated croissant, and balances the tray on her palm. Arlo yells out the order window, "Is Sleeping Beauty in yet?"

Finn calls over, "She's been here an hour. Where've you been?"

Thank you, I mime.

Arlo grumbles, "Order up."

I walk over to the window. "Good morning, Sunshine," I say with a smile.

He just looks at me.

"Let me guess," I add. "You're not a morning person?"

"Finn, get her a tee!" he yells.

I scope out the customers. Most of them look like construction crews or cowboys. They're slamming down enormous portions of eggs and potatoes, pancakes and meat.

Instantly my head's covered in cloth. It's a T-shirt like the one Finn's wearing. Mocha brown with a splattered egg imprinted on the back.

"Can we get some effing service here?" one of the guys bellows from a table.

Arlo says in a lowered voice, "It's the jerk squad. Hate those hammer heads." The whole table starts to pound their fists and chant, "Ser-vice. Ser-vice."

Finn passes behind me. "They're all yours." She disappears through the swinging doors.

I don't know the menu or prices, but I've seen enough waitresses taking orders in my life. How hard can it be?

The tee's an extra large, so I pull it over my shirt as I hurry across the dining room. "What can I get you guys?" I ask.

The loudest one goes, "What can I get *you*?" and pinches my butt.

I kick him in the shin. He scrapes back his chair, and I bolt.

In the kitchen, I slap the order pad on the counter by the grill and tell Arlo, "I quit."

He holds up the spatula he's using to flip pancakes. "It's the middle of rush."

"I don't care. That guy just sexually assaulted me."

Finn leans back from the open refrigerator door and meets my eyes.

Arlo says, "What'd he do?"

"Pinched my ass."

I see Finn smirk and duck her head inside the fridge. Arlo hands me the spatula and pivots a wheelie toward the swinging doors, ripping off his latex gloves. Finn carries over a carton of cream and a tub of butter. "They're just messing with you."

"Is that what you call it? I call it sexual harassment."

Finn says, "You've never waitressed before, have you?"

If this is what waitresses put up with, I'm never going to.

She points. "The pancakes are burning."

With the spatula, I quickly flip over a pair of smoking pancakes. Charcoal. At the other end of the grill is a trash can with eggshells and smelly garbage. I dump the pancakes on top, find the pitcher of batter, and pour two more.

Arlo crashes through the swinging doors. "They decided it was in their best interests to leave this fine dining establishment and never return."

Finn cries, "Arlo!"

"What?" He takes the spatula from me.

"They're my biggest tippers."

He flips the gooey pancakes I poured. "Tips ain't worth putting up with that shit."

She slit-eyes me and storms out. It's not my fault. Why would she give me her biggest tippers, anyway? Over the flapping doors, I call to her, "I'm sorry."

Arlo says, "You need a lid." He thumbs to a cup rack by the fridge, where a pair of caps hang on hooks. Meanwhile, he yanks on new rubber gloves.

I hate hats.

"Finn doesn't wear a hat," I say.

"Her hair's pulled back. Wear a lid."

None of the caps look new; in fact, there are sweat stains around the brims. Arlo's sweat, no doubt. My hair looks weird with a hat on.

The night of prom, I sat at my mirror and chopped away at my hair. My form of self-mutilation, I guess. The next day Dad asked, "What did you do to yourself?"

Cut my hair. Duh. He's lucky I wasn't an arm or leg cutter.

Every time he looked at me after that, he clicked his tongue in disgust.

My hair is growing out now, but there are uneven tufts all over, and with a cap on, the sides of my hair stick straight out from my ears. "Do I need gloves too?" I ask Arlo.

He eyes me. "Not unless your hands have been somewhere they shouldn't."

It takes me a minute. Arlo wears gloves to cook because his chair isn't powered, and his hands have to grab the wheels, which are constantly rolling over dirty floors. "Don't just stand there!" Arlo barks. "It's rush!"

Finn sweeps by on my way through the swinging doors. "I've got all the orders taken. Why don't you help plate?"

She clips the tickets onto a revolving metal stand by the grill. Arlo yanks three down at once.

"Where are the plates?" I ask.

The next few minutes are a frenzied blur of Finn showing me where everything is and explaining the menu, how to indicate substitutions, how to plate and stack. She says, "Just follow my lead," and I do. I stand next to her while she takes orders and serves the meals.

The counter is easier to work because there are only coffee and juice and pastries. Still, I drop a cheese Danish on the floor, pick it up, and blow on it. No one sees that, I hope. I burn four bagels before getting the hang of the toaster settings. People scowl. A lady grumbles, "It's about time." One guy makes smooching noises every time I pass by. I burn his bagel to a crisp.

Whenever I clear an order, Finn says, "Nice job."

I don't know if she's being facetious.

Around twelve thirty the crowd thins. I plop on a counter seat and slump over. The cool Formica feels soothing against my cheek. If I closed my eyes, I could fall asleep.

Finn touches my shoulder. "I need to show you how to work the espresso machine and dishwasher."

"I'm hopeless," I mutter.

Finn says, "You did great."

I raise my head off the counter a fraction of an inch. She's fiddling with the coffee machine, her back to me. "I suck, and you know it."

She doesn't turn around. "My first week," she says, "I started an electrical fire and dumped a boiling cup of coffee in a customer's lap that burned her so bad she had to go to the hospital."

"Oh my God." I sit up straight.

"Yeah. I don't know why Arlo didn't fire me. He should have." Finn twists her head around and smiles kindly, sincerely. Arlo wheels out of the kitchen. He points at me and says, "You suck as a waitress."

I shrink in my skin.

Finn goes, "It's her first day."

"Second," I correct her.

He says, "What? Not a morning person?"

I stick out my tongue at Arlo.

Finn adds, "She didn't send anyone to the hospital."

"*Yet*," he mutters. He says to Finn, "I gotta go deposit our millions."

"If you go by Safeway, we need half-and-half," Finn tells him. "And we're running low on dishwasher detergent."

Arlo pops open the cash register, which hits him chest high, and grabs a wad of crinkled bills. As he rolls by, he says to me, "Fill out a W-2." He tells Finn, "Show her the ropes."

Finn does a classic double take. "Where do we keep the ropes, again?"

Arlo waves her off and wheels through the kitchen and out the back door. Tossing a towel over her shoulder, Finn motions me around the counter. "Espresso Machine 101," she says.

She's funny. I command the butterflies in my stomach to stop fluttering. "Why did you give me your biggest tippers today?"

Finn turns slowly to look at me, and the power of her sexuality makes my knees weak. "I wanted to make it worth your while." I have to hang on to the counter to keep myself upright.

A warning flare goes off in my head. *No,* I think. *Please no.*

I promised myself never to get involved with anyone again, ever. All you end up with is heartache. It's not worth it. Even if I think Finn's hot, I'm going to douse every flame that flickers. Every ember.

Carly's gone when I get back to the house around two. She left me a note:

CALL TANITH.

She wrote out the phone number, like I don't know my own number.

All I want to do is veg in the whirlpool. My feet are swollen, and my head's spinning, trying to remember everything Finn taught me today. Trying to get her out of my head. On my way out the door, she said, "Get some decent shoes. You can't work in flip-flops."

That's what I should do. Go buy some Chucks.

The bed moves up to greet me, and I lie down. I must fall asleep, because when my eyes open, I'm disoriented. I still have on the clothes I worked in, and the note is clutched in my hand.

CALL TANITH.

What time is it? Four forty-six here. Two hours later in Virginia Beach. Dad's clearing the dinner table. Or if he's finished, he and Tanith are watching TV or listening to music or reading. Paulie's upstairs playing video games by himself. I'm disowned.

I roll over onto my side. I have a job. A job I got all by myself without Dad's or Carly's or anyone's help.

It feels like more than a job. It feels like liberation. Independence. Like maybe there's life after Sarah.

I startle awake to my alarm. Punching it off with a fist, I stagger out of bed. I slept. I actually slept.

A fuchsia sticky note is posted on the inside of my door, which is wide open.

<u>CALL</u> <u>TANITH.</u>

Message received, Carly. It's six AM in Virginia Beach. Tanith is up making breakfast for Dad. During the school year, she works—worked—as a substitute teacher. She was always there, though, to see me and Paulie off. There when we got home from school.

She answers on the second ring. "Hello?" Her voice sounds clear and cheerful.

My throat closes. I strangle out, "Hi."

"Alyssa, is that you? Hi, honey. How are you?"

For someone who was thrown out of the house? "Great."

"Really?"

No, Tanith. Not really.

She says, "I—we—miss you."

I close my eyes.

"I'm so sorry about this," Tanith says. "He just needs time to—"

"I have to get to work," I cut in. "Did you need something?" My voice regains control. I shouldn't be mad at Tanith. Except, she knew. She could've intervened on my behalf. But no. Whatever Dad says, goes.

"You got a package," Tanith continues. "Well, a box."

"What is it?"

"I don't know. I don't open your mail."

"Who's it from?"

"There's no return address."

A pause stretches the distance between us. "Do you want me to send it to you at Carly's?" she asks.

"I guess. Wait." If it's from Sarah, I don't want it here. "Any idea who it's from?"

"Yes," Tanith says.

My pulse races. "Why don't you just burn it?"

"I can't do that, Alyssa. Do you want me to put it in your room?"

"My room? What room? I don't have a room there anymore, remember?"

Silence. I hear her breathing. "Just open it," I say, adding nicely, "please?"

Tanith says, "I'd be happy to send it to you."

I don't want it! "Just please open it and tell me what's in it."

"Okay. Hold on a minute." I picture her rummaging through the junk drawer for the scissors. "You should call and talk to Paulie," she says. "He really misses you."

"I thought I wasn't allowed to contact him."

"Who said that?" Tanith's voice sharpens. "That's ridiculous. Of course you can talk to your own brother."

Half brother. Whatever. Let's talk about ridiculous, Tanith. You, standing in the hall upstairs behind Dad gazing into the middle distance while he rips into me. While he says, "I won't allow that kind of perversion in my house."

I looked to you, Tanith. Because you knew. You could've told him. You could've stopped him.

"I'm cutting through the tape," Tanith says. "It's in a fog machine box."

My heart aches. Ben and I bought a fog machine for the GSA's Halloween party. Sarah and I dressed as Glinda and Elphaba. She's addicted to *Wicked*. Ben showed up dressed as Glinda too. Which was hilarious at the time.

"I'm opening the top."

I don't need a running commentary.

"There's a layer of peanuts. Unsalted."

Not funny.

"All right. The first item on top is a gray hooded sweatshirt. It looks like your old one."

My stomach twists. Where had I left my hoodie? In the shed?

"There's a pair of sunglasses. They look expensive."

My Ray-Bans. They looked so hot on Sarah that I told her to keep them.

"A red bra."

"You don't have to—"

"Something in tissue. Oh, it's a ring. And a necklace with an *A*..."

My throat closes.

"And earrings."

"Stop," I choke out. "Just...throw it all in the trash."

Tanith expels a breath.

Hang up, Tanith, I think. In fact—

I hang up. Sarah can still hurt me. Fifteen hundred miles between us, and Sarah's still knifing me in the back. Some people know no boundaries when it comes to cruelty.

Chapter 9

January

She couldn't, or wouldn't, answer the phone. The last time you called, her mother answered. "Alyssa, stop calling here," she said. "Sarah is not allowed to see you, call you, or have any contact with you. Do you understand?"

Either Sarah told her about you or she guessed.

The day before you were to go back to school, you came down with mono. Your memory is fuzzy about what happened over the next three or four weeks.

Sarah floated in and out of your dreams. So did Ben. M'Chelle. Did they come to see you? Together? The people and days all collage together. You remember Dad at your bedside, feeling your forehead. Kissing your head, tucking you in. Tanith bringing you soup. You felt Sarah's lips on yours, but that could've been wishful dreaming.

You woke up one time to find her lying next to you in bed, her head nestled in the crook of your neck. Your throat was sore, and you had a raging headache, but you managed to rasp, "Sarah, no. Don't touch me. You'll get sick." You were panicking; Dad might see.

She said, "I already had it." She caressed your face and kissed your eyes.

You wanted Sarah to stay with you, but Dad couldn't find you like this.

The door was ajar, and you could hear voices downstairs. Paulie and Dad and . . .

"Is Ben here?" you asked.

"Uh-huh. Your dad is totally in love with him."

A wave of guilt washed through you. You'd never told Sarah about using Ben as your boyfriend.

"He told me what was going on," Sarah said.

The pain in your head intensified. You wanted to explain, but she pressed a finger to your lips. "I wish I'd thought of it instead of telling my parents the truth about us."

That made you feel like crap.

Sarah traced a finger across your jawline. "My mom accused you of corrupting me." Sarah's eyes twinkled. "If she only knew."

"Sarah . . ."

She kissed you.

You fell asleep, and images kaleidoscoped in your brain. Sarah's eyes, her lips, her fingers in your hair. You sensed people nearby. Dad hovering. Sarah and Ben sitting on the floor in your room. Ben being goofy, cracking her up. M'Chelle dropped in. During a lucid moment, you remembered that M'Chelle had been bringing you your homework. It was piling up, but you couldn't concentrate long enough to focus on finishing assignments.

Sarah and Ben and M'Chelle were laughing. Dad appeared. "You'd all better scat. Let the invalid get some rest."

"Okay," Sarah said. "Thanks for letting us stay so long."

"You're welcome, Sarah. Call tomorrow before you come."

You wondered what Dad thought of Sarah. He'd love her if he knew her. Footsteps on the stairs and then a presence. Dad said, "Do you want anything? Hot cocoa or a toasted cheese sandwich?" Dad had always made you toasted cheese when you were little. Toasted cheese and tomato soup.

But all you wanted was sleep. Did you fall asleep again? Someone brushed your bangs up and planted a kiss on your forehead. On your eyes, your lips. Her lemon-lime shower gel filled your nose. You pulled Sarah down.

A movement at the door snagged your attention. How long had she been standing there? How much did Tanith see?

Enough to know Sarah was more than a friend.

Arlo shoves a tub of dirty dishes at me as I rush through the café doors. He snipes, "You can't wear those to work in." He rolls so close to my toes, he almost runs over them, and I have to jump back.

"I know. I didn't get a chance to go buy any shoes."

"Doesn't your mother have shoes?" He says it like it's a dirty word.

"Yes, my mother does." I throw it back in his face. "If you want me to wear fuck-me pumps."

His eyes meet mine, and his lips twitch. So glad I amuse him.

I wonder what it is between Arlo and Carly. Something.

Arlo rolls over to the fridge and mutters, "Wear a hat."

I pivot to snag a cap off the cup holder, and scoop up an order pad.

A score of hungry eyes eat me alive along the counter. Finn's busy with tables. "Good morning," I call cheerily to everyone. "I'll be with you quick as a bunny." Did I just say that? I get stupid when I'm nervous.

Finn zooms by with a fistful of orders to pin on the rack. She says, "Can you handle the counter by yourself?"

"Sure," I say, not sure at all.

"Can I get a cuppa joe?" This beefy guy wheezes and coughs up bloody phlegm into a napkin. Major ew.

I spill a tall grape juice down my shirt, which makes me look like Sweeney Todd, and then I get two orders of toast sent back because they're cold. I can't figure out how to get hot coffee and hot toast out at the same time. As I slam down two more slices of bread in the toaster, the steam from the espresso machine scorches my hand, and I squeal. A customer comes up behind me and says, "I ordered a cherry Danish, not raspberry. I don't think I should have to pay."

He's holding out an empty plate. I'm about to say, "Okay," when Finn grabs the plate and goes, "Nice try, Gomer. You don't think she's gonna fall for that old trick, do you?" She cocks her head at the guy. He snaps his fingers like, *Got me*, and reaches for his wallet.

Without warning, my arm is jerked backward. "Be careful," Finn says. I was about to pour boiling-hot milk from the espresso machine on my hand. She presses a button to release steam.

"Thanks," I say.

She lets me go but holds my eyes.

I suddenly feel so inadequate and incapable and inexperienced. Finn gives me a brisk hug around the shoulders. "It'll get easier," she says.

"When?"

"Order up!" Arlo calls.

Finn leaves to fetch the plates, but her kindness clings to me.

A woman signals to come over to her table. It's that nurse from the other day. "Alyssa, right?" she says.

"Right." How'd she know my name? I don't have a name tag yet.

"I'm Barbara. I knew your mom when...I mean, I still know her. I don't see her as often." She lifts her plate. "My eggs are kind of runny. Do you think you could ask Arlo to apply a bit more heat?"

"Sure." I take the plate from her.

"Tell him I ordered over easy, but these are a little too easy for me."

I run the plate into the kitchen and say to Arlo, "These eggs," and he almost launches off his chair. "Don't *do* that!" he screams at me. "Don't ever sneak up behind me!"

"God! Don't yell at me!" I shout. I hate being yelled at. Now I'm on the verge of tears, but I refuse to let him see me cry. "These are runny." I set the plate down hard on the counter.

He goes, "They're over easy."

"Yeah, well, she doesn't want to drink them with a straw."

Arlo smiles, and then he laughs. He actually laughs. "You're Carly's girl, all right," he says.

Is Carly a smart-ass too? I want to ask him what he knows about her. Barbara said, "I knew her when." When what?

I wait for the eggs, watching Arlo alternate between

sausage, pancakes, bacon, potatoes, and an omelet on the grill, in addition to the over-easy eggs. He reminds me of those Japanese chefs at Akebono, back home.

Arlo's not that old—maybe forty? I'm curious why he's in a wheelchair, but he'd probably bite my head off if I asked. I'll ask Finn. I'll ask her about Arlo and Carly too.

When I get back from delivering the eggs (Barbara said they were perfect!), Finn is tamping down espresso in a new filter and sliding two shot glasses under the slots. A fine sheen of sweat glistens on her skin, which is so smooth and brown and moist. I reach over her head for more cups and saucers, and our eyes attach across a roiling ocean. I have to pull back or get swept into the vortex.

The toaster sets off the smoke alarm, and Finn hisses, "Shit." She runs to the back for a step stool to yank the battery in the ceiling alarm. Meanwhile, I fork out the crispy critters and slam down two more slices.

The screeching alarm clears out customers fast.

It's almost one, anyway. Closing time.

I go around collecting dirty dishes and tips. I find Finn in the back dumping leftovers into the trash. "God, I'm starving," I say. To prove it, my stomach rumbles. I rinse a fork and dig into a nest of hash browns.

Finn says, "Don't let Arlo see you eating off people's plates. He'll cook for you if you want."

"Really?" He's a fantastic cook. Chef. Whatever. It's clear why this place is always packed.

Her eyes scan down my front. "You take a bullet?" she asks.

The grape juice. I curl a lip at her like, *ha-ha*.

She smiles. We hook eyes again, and it gets intense.

Her gaze lowers to the wad of money on the serving tray. "Those the tips?"

"Yeah." I scoop up the bills to give to her.

"Split it in half," she says.

"No way. You waited all the tables."

She divides the tips anyway and says, "Go buy some shoes," tucking my portion in the front pocket of my shorts. The feel of her fingers gives me goose bumps.

I'm so weak. *Stop it*.

She goes over to scrub the grill. "Could you get the dishes?" she asks.

Cups and plates overflow the sink and grill area. I open the dishwasher, but it's crammed full.

"Are these clean or dirty?" I ask.

She glances over. "Not sure."

I remove a cup, and it's still warm. Clean, I deduce, and begin to empty the dishwasher. A radio is playing classical music. It's always so noisy in here that I hadn't noticed the radio before. I'm not a fan of classical, since that's all Dad and Tanith listen to.

I walk over to change the channel, and Finn's hand clamps over mine. "You have a death wish?" She releases me. "Don't touch that radio. Arlo will kill you."

Now my hand buzzes. I wish she'd stop touching me. Obviously, I'm attracted to her, but I won't allow it. When they say being gay is a choice, they're wrong. The only choice is whether you act on your feelings or not.

Finn resumes scrubbing while I load up the dishwasher with dirty dishes. I see Arlo out back in the parking lot, smoking.

"Why is Arlo in a chair?" I ask Finn.

She deadpans, "He can't walk?"

I mock sneer at her. "Really? What happened to him?"

"I don't know. Ask him."

Sure, and have my death wish fulfilled. "Why don't you just tell me?"

"Because I don't know. I make it a point not to get personal with people."

I wonder, *Does that include me?* "Do you know how he knows Carly?"

She says, "How does anyone know Carly?"

My eyes narrow and hers drop. "I didn't mean that to come out the way it did. I just meant everyone knows Carly." Finn ducks her head and disappears into the restroom, leaving me to ponder the statement. It's a small town. Everyone knows everyone. Or...they know who she is by *what* she is.

I find the detergent and start the dishwasher. When Finn comes out, she's changed into a faded tank. I love the definition of her arm muscles.

"I've got to get to work at the book swap," Finn says. "You okay here alone?"

Arlo's van pulls out of the lot, and I panic.

Finn stuffs her Egg Drop tee into her ratty backpack. "Just set the tables for tomorrow and then lock the doors."

I trail her to the rear exit. "Isn't there a security system or something?"

Finn says, "If anyone broke into this place and stole something, there'd be a riot in town. Anyway, Arlo will be back. He lives here."

"At the restaurant?"

She saunters through the dirt parking lot, straps on her backpack, loops a leg over a mountain bike, and pedals off like a speed racer.

There's a door marked PRIVATE, and I think, *I'll just check it out*—you know, for interest's sake. It's not locked. I flip on the light and see a double bed, made up with old flowered sheets and a folded fleece blanket. A closet. The closet bar's been lowered so Arlo can reach the hangers. Bars and pulleys, like exercise equipment. A small TV. Through another door there's a wheelchair-accessible tub and shower. The front bell tinkles, and I close the door fast.

It's that old cowboy dude. "We're closed," I call out to him.

"I figgered. I was in town and thought I'd come by to shoot the bull with Arlo."

"He's not here right now. He should be back soon."

"You his new girl?" He removes his cowboy hat and flaps it against his thigh, raising a cloud of dust.

I'm nobody's *girl*. He means waitress, I think. He seems nice.

I push through the swinging doors. "Yeah. I mean, yes. Yes, sir." I wait for him to say it—*blah, blah Carly's girl*. When he doesn't, I introduce myself. "I'm Alyssa."

"Dutch." He extends a hand, so I walk up to him and shake it.

His hand is bony, with age spots, like my grandpa's. Paper-thin skin. "If you want to wait..."

"Don't mind if I do." He takes a seat at the window table. "If you got some sludge and fudge, I'll take it off yer hands," he says. A moment passes, and he chuckles. "Coffee and a chocolate doughnut."

"Oh." I must be perfecting the art of the clueless expression. I think, *I'll have to tell Ben that one—sludge and fudge.* Immediately I snuff the thought.

We have one chocolate doughnut left and half a pot of coffee. "Is decaf okay?" I ask him.

"Better'n okay," he says.

I serve Dutch his order. "Thankee, little lady." He smiles and the crow's-feet around his eyes remind me of Grandpa too. I head back to the kitchen, wondering if I'll ever see Grandpa and Grandma again; if being disowned means giving up everyone I love.

"You."

I jump out of my skin. Arlo's sneaked up behind me in the kitchen.

"Fill in on the schedule what days you can work." He hands me the clipboard from the wall. "No more'n four days."

"That's all?"

"Howdy, Dutch," he calls through the swinging doors.

Dutch lifts his coffee mug at Arlo.

Arlo says, "Be right out." He cranks up the fan and goes, "Can you feel that?"

The fan blasts hot air in my face, but it's a relief. "Yeah. Thanks."

Arlo takes a stroll around the kitchen, humming. He's chipper, for once.

"What happened?" I say. "Did you just get laid?"

Arlo widens his eyes at me. Then cracks up. "I like you." He wags a finger at me. He rolls to a stop at the dishwasher and adds, "Go home. I'll finish up."

I want to ask him about the chair, about Carly. But I don't want to push my luck, and right now it feels good to have someone actually like me.

At the house I strip and shower. The grape juice soaked all the way through, staining my bra and the front of my shorts, so I gather a load of wash and take it downstairs.

I open the laundry closet and reach up for the detergent. Then I see this box shoved under the bottom shelf. I don't know why I pull it out or open it.

Yes, I do know: I'm a snoop. I plop on the cold tile floor and remove the first item. A tiny pink knitted cap. The next item: a pair of baby pajamas with little pink flowers. A frilly dress. The whole box is filled with baby clothes.

This warmth flows through me from head to toe. She kept my baby clothes. I must've meant something to her if she kept my baby clothes. Right?

I go through everything in the box. There are sizes from zero to three months, on up to eighteen months.

Eighteen months is almost two years. Dad said she left when I was a baby, but eighteen months means she was there for nearly two years of my life.

I feel uplifted. Elated. She didn't just take off, the way Dad said or led me to believe. How many more lies did he tell about her?

I'm still smiling inside when I go upstairs and fix myself a salad.

I sit on the balcony and imagine her dressing me in all those baby clothes. Pink. Ugh. I hate pink. Was I walking by then? Talking? Did she teach me my first words and witness my first steps?

Why do I have no memory of her? People block out painful events in their past, so maybe that's what I did when she left. But she saved reminders of my babyhood.

I suddenly remember I need to go shopping for shoes. Indoors, I find the business card Carly gave me and call her cell. She doesn't answer, and the call goes to her voice mail. I leave her a message: "Hi. It's me. Um, Alyssa. If you get this, or when you do, I really need to go shopping for work shoes. I thought maybe you could take me. We could go together. Anyway, call me. I guess you know the number." I hang up. Idiot, of course she knows the number.

I wait twenty, thirty minutes. Naturally, today of all days, her cell is off or she's not answering. Maybe she's with a, uh, client. It reminds me of sitting around anxiously waiting for Sarah to call. Will everything always remind me of her?

I can't wait anymore. I'm old enough to go buy my own shoes.

Chapter 10

I have to drive through Majestic to get to the turnoff for Breckenridge or Dillon. The digital clock on the dashboard says it's quarter to three. I hate shopping alone and wonder what time Finn gets off at the Emporium. Since it's on Main Street, and I have to pass by anyway, I pull to the curb and stop.

Nothing's going to happen, I tell myself. She's the closest thing I have to a friend, and God knows I need a friend. Finn's working the front desk. A mom with three little kids is babbling away while Finn bags a bunch of picture books. Finn looks so serious. She rings up each sale on an old adding machine, concentrating on punching in the prices. One of the little kids toddles toward the door, and the mom shouts, "Come back here, Isaac!"

I chase him down, sweeping him into my arms. He reminds me of Paulie when he was little, with his mop of reddish-blond hair and cherubic cheeks.

The mom says, "Oh, thank you," as she takes him from me.

"You're—" Her eyes slit. "Let's go, kids." The woman backs off like I'm a biohazard.

I know loathing when I see it. *Excuse me for contaminating your space.*

She grabs the book bag, spilling half the books, and Finn has to hustle after her to the door. I hear the woman say to Finn, "A guy's been in a couple of times asking about the Concours."

Finn's spine stiffens. "Does he want it?"

"He keeps coming in to look at it." The mom scans me out of the corner of her eye, shifting the baby as she shoulders the book bag.

"But I put a deposit down," Finn says. "A big one."

"Times are tough, Finn. If someone walks in with cash, we'll have to sell it."

"But my deposit..."

The woman ushers her kids out the door.

Finn storms right past me, scoops up the cash box, and heads into the office. Without even saying hello.

Nice. I turn to leave, and Finn reappears with the book cart. She rolls by me, looking pissed. "Hey," I say to get her attention.

She stops. Her anger is palpable.

"What's up?" I ask.

"You heard."

I heard, but I have no idea what it means.

"Why am I working my butt off if they're just going to sell the Concours out from under me?" Her dark eyes go completely black, and she seethes. "You can't trust anyone."

That's the truth. Except I'm a trustworthy person. "First of all, what's a Concours?"

She looks at me like, *You can't be serious.*

"Well, I don't know," I say.

"It's a bike." She takes off with the cart, pushing it to the rear, toward the health section, while I follow.

"Don't you have a bike?"

"The Concours is a motorcycle."

What I know about motorcycles is zip. They're dangerous, according to Dad. How could he know? He's never owned one, never ridden one, as far as I know.

Finn stops at the end of the aisle, grinds her fists into her eye sockets, and curses under her breath. "I want that bike. I *need* that bike."

"How much is it?" I ask.

Finn lowers her arms and blinks at me like she forgot I was there. "Eight hundred. That's all I have left to pay on it. How could they just sell it right out from under me?" Her eyes get moist, and she pushes the cart away.

I almost run to catch up and say, *I'll give you the money.* But I control myself—for once. I don't have eight hundred dollars. After all the expensive presents I bought for Sarah, my savings are nearly depleted.

It obviously means a lot to Finn, and I want her to have her bike. Even more, I want her to believe in trust, in me. Maybe there's some way I could get the money. I'll have to think on it, wiki *how to rob a bank.*

"What time do you get off?" I say. "I was wondering if you'd go shoe shopping with me."

She peers over her shoulder down at my feet and then glances at her watch. Timber Toes passes the aisle, stops, and backtracks. "When you get done with that, Finn, would you mind cleaning up the children's section? Those kids made a mess, as usual." She fixes on me. Pointing a finger, she opens her mouth as if to say something, but then doesn't.

"Sure," Finn says.

Timber Toes adds, "Then you can go. That's all I have for you today." She strides off, making me feel invisible.

Finn shelves a book from the cart, and I pick up the next one. She clamps my wrist. "Don't help!"

I put down the book.

Finn's voice softens. "I get paid by the hour."

In that case...I dump a stack of books off the cart onto the floor. "Oops," I say.

Finn cocks her head at me. "Alyssa."

"Finn."

She shakes her head, but she's grinning. With my help (or hindrance), she manages to add another hour to her time sheet.

When we step outside the Emporium, the brilliant sun is blinding. At home in Virginia Beach, the haze of humidity filters this kind of direct sunlight. "How long is the outlet mall open in Silverthorne?" I ask Finn.

"No idea," she says, yawning.

She looks exhausted and smells kind of ripe. "Do you want me to just take you home?" I ask. "I can go shopping by myself."

We're stopped on the plank sidewalk, and Finn is squinting, shading her eyes with a flat hand. "Does that gas guzzler have AC?" She points to the Mercedes.

"But of course," I say.

"Let's go." She leads the way.

As we get in and buckle up, Finn says, "Go through Frisco and then take a left at Summit Boulevard."

I swing out onto Main. "Do you have a car?" I ask.

"It bit it after three hundred thousand miles. I sold it for parts and bought the mountain bike. I've been saving up for the Concours for months." She grits her teeth.

I don't know what to say.

Summit Boulevard connects all the mountain towns in this area. Traffic is heavy, but nothing like rush hour on I-264 in Virginia Beach. Everyone's speeding, though. A car runs up on me and honks, which makes me freak.

Finn says, "You can go faster than twenty-five, you know."

I hit the gas and almost crash into the car in front of me. I tell Finn, who's bracing against the dash now, "I've only had my license a few months."

She says, "Turn off onto the service road…right…here." She points.

I steer off the highway and slow way down; let out a sigh of relief. There's no one on the service road. Finn rolls her head around on her shoulders and reaches up to stretch. She must sniff her pit because she drops her arms fast. "Man, I could use a swim," she says.

"Is there a pool nearby?"

"Caribou Lake."

"Where is it?" I ask.

"I thought we were going to Silverthorne."

A choice between shopping and swimming? "Where's the lake?"

Finn gazes ahead. "Around this corner, you'll see a turnoff. Right after the sign for Blue Spruce Road."

I see the Blue Spruce exit and then a small blue-and-white sign with an arrow pointing up. "Hang a left," Finn says.

The road is crushed gravel, wide enough for only two lanes. "How far?" I ask her.

"Just keep going."

My eyes stray to her legs, her knobby knees. She has on baggy, khaki shorts and a green camo tee. Well-worn running shoes.

God, it feels good to be with her, to be with anyone. I really need a friend. "Is Finn your first name or last?"

"Yes," she says.

Dark shadows block the sun as we drive into a canyon. The road narrows even more, and I ease on the brake.

"Keep going," Finn says. "It's another two point six miles from here. You'll want to slow *way* down on these hairpin turns in case someone's coming in the opposite direction."

I press on the brake.

"Even slower. How do I open the window?" Finn asks. She punches a button, and her door unlocks. The AC's on, blasting ice-cold. I push the button on the driver's-side door panel for all the windows to roll down.

"We don't need the AC," Finn goes. "It's cooler up here."

"Yeah, it's only ninety-eight."

She sticks her arm out the window and breathes in the air.

"How long have you known Carly?" I ask.

She answers, "I haven't lived here that long."

"How long?"

"Can you see the river yet on your left?"

I peer out my side window, but there's no guardrail, and the drop-off is steep. I feel dizzy just looking. Finn grabs the wheel from me. "Suggestion: Try to stay on the road."

My hands clench the steering wheel tighter. I can *hear* the river, the rushing water. It smells fresh and clean. We pass a sign that says HIGH FIRE DANGER. NO CAMPFIRES. VIOLATORS WILL BE PROSECUTED TO THE FULL EXTENT OF THE LAW.

"Stop," Finn says.

I slam on the brakes, giving us both whiplash.

"Not in the road. Pull into the camping area, and park the car."

I see then that the road ends ahead. I steer onto the dirt and draw up to a horizontal log.

"Oh my God." I blink in case what I see is only a mirage. Through the trees, down a hill, is a magnificent lake seemingly suspended in midair. We both get out, and I lock the doors with the key remote.

"Caribou Lake," Finn announces.

"It's gorgeous," I breathe.

We walk down a well-trod footpath toward the water, and my stupid flip-flops slip on loose dirt. I almost take a header, but Finn catches my arm. She holds on the rest of the way down. She has a strong grip.

Near the shore, Finn slows and says, "We're at the summit of Caribou Mountain." She outlines with her finger. "That's the Continental Divide. Rivers flow to the Gulf of Mexico on the east side and to the Pacific Ocean on the west."

"Wow. Cool. How long *have* you lived here?" I ask again.

"Six, seven months. I worked at Keystone during ski season."

"Doing what?"

"What else? Waitressing. Ski business dried up, and I found Arlo's."

"That was lucky."

She looks at me and makes a face. "You think?"

I laugh. She smiles.

Dazzling blue water fills the mountain crater to the brim. Finn's eyes glaze over, and she inhales a long, deep breath. I watch her chest expand and contract. It's impossible to tear my eyes away. "This way." She motions. We follow the shoreline until it's interrupted by a mound of boulders, a sort of peninsula. Finn climbs the first rock and extends a hand to me.

At the top, the boulders flatten out. Finn sits, and I lower myself next to her. The stone is cool against the bottoms of my legs.

The lake and the mountain air and, oh my God, is that a breeze? This has to be the most beautiful spot on Earth.

"Do you visit Carly every summer?" Finn asks.

I snort.

She turns to me. "What does that mean?"

"It means no." I add, "I'm not here by choice."

She frowns.

I don't really want to talk about it. And I do want to. "My dad disowned me, and this is the only place I had to go."

Finn's eyebrows arch.

I push to my feet. "I thought we were going to swim." I pull my shirt over my head, unzip my shorts, and start down the hill in my bra and briefs. The breeze feels fantastic. I'm sweaty all over and wish I had the guts to go skinny dipping. Finn pulls off her shirt and steps out of her shorts. Damn. Her body's tight.

Water laps over my toes, and I squeal. "It's freezing!"

"It's not that bad once you get in." She splashes into the lake, diving forward and under the water. I tiptoe in, gasping all the way. *Plunge*, I think. *Get your blood moving*.

The lake water is clear and refreshing. And *cold*. It tastes a little metallic, but clean. Not salty like the ocean. I swim out fast, stroking up beside Finn. Compared to swimming in the Atlantic and the Gulf of Mexico, lake swimming is easy. I stop and tread water.

What if I never see the ocean again? What if I never see Grandma or Grandpa in Corpus Christi or my cousins down there?

Last summer Dad took an extra two weeks off, and we drove through Nashville and Memphis. We had to hit all the tourist spots—the Country Music Hall of Fame and, of course, Graceland. But what I remember most is this one night we stopped to camp out. The weather was beautiful. The sky was illuminated with millions of twinkling stars, and the four of us rolled out sleeping bags and tried to outline patterns and shapes in the sky. Tanith had studied astronomy in school, so she knew the constellations. But Paulie saw things like T. rexes and werewolves. I spied palaces, two-headed unicorns, and witches with warts on their noses. Dad and Tanith eventually went to bed while Paulie and I stayed up for hours, making up stories about our stars and playing star wars. He could be a cool kid.

"You okay?" Finn treads next to me. I focus on her face. She looks concerned, vulnerable. I rise up and dunk her with both hands.

She yanks me under by the ankle and blows bubbles at me underwater. I grab for her ankle, but it slips away as she propels up and out of sight. I push off the bottom with my feet and break the surface.

She dunks my head.

I pop back up and splash her.

She splashes me back. We laugh, and then our eyes catch and hold. I have this overwhelming desire to kiss her. I'm thankful when she dog-paddles away. "Race you," she says, flipping over and taking off.

I'm twice the swimmer she is, and I catch up easily. Without warning, she starts choking and flailing her arms. She sinks, and I feel her kicking, clawing at me. Is she faking? If not...

To pull her up, the first thing I grab is her braid.

She coughs and spits out water, yanking her braid away.

"You okay?" I ask.

She flaps back toward the shore, still coughing. I swim up beside her and snake an arm around her waist, ballasting her on my hip, the way I learned in lifeguard training. We reach shallow water where we can stand, and Finn unhooks my hand from her body as she inhales a deep breath.

I slick back my hair. My eyes train on her wet bra, her nipples, and I can't help staring.

She sloshes awkwardly to shore.

We gather all our clothes and, atop the boulder, get dressed wet, which isn't easy. I trip and hobble around, falling over as I'm pulling up my shorts. Finn gets done first and sits, drawing her knees to her chest. I want to wring out her braid because it's dripping. We don't speak for a long minute, and now it feels weird between us.

What happened? I didn't do anything.

Out of the blue, Finn says, "Why did you get disowned?"

I turn to her slowly. "Because I'm gay. Duh."

She seems stunned. Like she didn't know.

This ice floe seems to spread between us, so I lean away. She says, "When did you know?"

"Know what?"

"That you were..." She can't even say it.

"A lesbian?"

She nods slightly.

"I've always known. Haven't you?"

The change in her eyes goes beyond shock. More like absolute terror.

Oh my God. She hasn't acknowledged it yet. How could she not know?

Finn gets up and mumbles, "We should go back."

I think, *You should come out.*

We don't speak again as I put the Mercedes in reverse and nearly plunge off the cliff. Finn reaches over for the wheel, but I correct in time. We start down the mountain. She says, "You should downshift. It'll be easier on the brakes."

"What's downshifting?" I slam on the brakes to hug the

first curve, and Finn tilts to the left, like her weight will shift an SUV. I skid onto a wide gravel area, my heart pounding. Finn moves the gear knob down a couple of notches from drive to D2 or D1. "Downshifting," she says.

I smile weakly. "Thanks."

She asks, "Do you want me to drive?"

Do I ever. I shift into park and get out. We change seats.

Merging onto the road, Finn asks, "So, when did you tell your dad?"

"I didn't."

She glances over.

"He caught me in the act with my girlfriend. Ex-girlfriend."

Finn's eyes expand.

"Yeah. It wasn't pretty."

She downshifts for a hairpin curve.

"My dad's a homophobe," I tell her. "Plus, I'm like his darling little daughter who'll always be five years old and doesn't even know how to spell s-e-x. Let alone l-e-s-b-i-a-n."

I'm back in that moment when Dad caught us. The horror on his face. The revulsion. The moment he decided his little girl was garbage to be thrown away.

We need to change the subject because I don't want to start crying, and I definitely don't want Finn to feel sorry for me. "What are you?" I ask. Besides a closeted lesbian. "Like, part Asian? Native American?"

"Inuit," she says. "Half."

"What's Inuit?"

"It's like Eskimo."

"Really? Cool. Where are you from?"

She doesn't answer immediately, so I try again. "Where are you—"

"Canada."

Canada. Sweet. I almost say, *You know, they have lesbians in Canada. In fact, you can even get married there.*

We reach the service road, and Finn shifts into drive. She checks her watch.

"Are you late?" I ask.

"No. Just need a little shut-eye before I go to work."

"What's your third job?"

She stifles a yawn. "Bartending."

That means she's at least twenty-one. Finn turns into the Emporium lot and parks.

"I could take you home," I tell her. As a friendly gesture. Nothing more.

She has the car door open, and she's bending over with her back to me. "I need my bike," I hear her say. She straightens up and hands me her shoes. "Trade," she says.

"Really?"

"Until you can go shopping."

I remove my flip-flops. She slips them onto her feet and then gets out and opens her mouth to say something. Whatever it is never makes it from her brain to her lips. She raises her hand in a wave.

I watch as she shuffles to her mountain bike, loops a leg over, and pedals off.

Her shoes are grody and worn, full of sand. A half size too small, but I can squeeze my feet in. Her giving them to me like that was such a total act of kindness. It's been a long time since I've felt anyone's kindness; since anyone cared about my needs. My throat constricts, and it takes all the willpower I can muster to choke down a sob.

"Sorry I missed your call today," Carly says. "I was with a client and tried to get you later, but you didn't pick up. Did you get a pair of shoes for work?"

"Uh...yeah." I gaze up the loft steps at her, speechless. She's skanked up, meaning thick, black mascara and a short, stretchy red dress over fishnets.

"Paulie called." Carly hustles down the stairs, although you can't really hustle in stilettos, can you? "He said he'd wait up for you to call him back." She stops on the landing to insert huge, loopy earrings in her lobes. "What did your father think would be accomplished by taking away your phone?"

I don't want to think about Dad. I actually had a pretty good day.

"Alyssa?" Carly bats fake eyelashes at me. I wedge past her and up the stairs. "You didn't *buy* those shoes, did you? They look like Goodwill rejects."

The fumes in the loft are staggering. A sneeze backs up in my nose. Ugh. I hate that plugged-up feeling.

"We can afford new shoes, you know. You don't have to shop at thrift stores."

I say over the railing, "Can I have eight hundred dollars?"

She swivels her head up, and I can see clear down her cleavage. "For shoes?"

When I don't answer right away, she says, "I've paid four

hundred dollars for shoes before, but they were designer. For a special occasion."

I bet, I think.

She cocks her head at me, batting her thick eyelashes. "Are you in trouble, Alyssa? Are you into drugs or something?"

"What? No." Why do parents always assume you're on drugs?

"You know you can talk to me...."

"Never mind." I stomp toward my room.

"Alyssa!" she shouts.

I let out an audible breath and return to the loft railing. I don't want her stripper money, anyway. Or wherever it comes from. I'll find eight hundred dollars someplace.

Carly calls up, "I'll leave you my ATM card. The pin number's my birthday: 1013. But you can't withdraw more than two hundred at a time. I'll just write you a check."

I can't believe it. Dad would never give me eight hundred dollars, no questions asked. Not only would he assume I was on drugs, he'd take me in for testing.

Carly checks her cell and adds, "Call Paulie." She leaves in a cloud of lavender.

I lie down and plug into my nano. I look at my feet, at Finn's shoes, and click my heels together. They're not ruby slippers; they won't take me to Kansas. But they feel magical. I fall asleep with the memory of my hip against her flat belly, my one arm curled around her, and the other stroking hard enough to keep us both afloat.

Chapter 11

She left a note on my door.

CALL PAULIE. TONITE.

She can't spell. She never finished high school, as far as I know. She got pregnant with me. Carly and Dad and I were a family for eighteen months.

I sprawl on the sofa, thinking. Wishing I could go back in time to see how it all went down between Carly and Dad. Wanting to know the truth, to hear it from her. I heard Dad's version: She left. It had nothing to do with you.

I wonder now if he kicked her out, or bullied her out, the way he did to me.

This house is so soundproofed you can't even hear chipmunks chattering or birds singing. No passing cars drive close enough to see their headlights. It's never this dark or quiet at home. There's always a TV on, a video game, kids riding bikes in the neighborhood.

I go back up to bed but can't shut off my brain. What if Carly wanted to stay? Did she plead with Dad to keep our family together? I can't see Carly begging. Did she want to take me with her, though? Was he the one who cut off all contact with her?

Everything I knew, everything I believed, could all be a lie.

I wonder where Carly dances and when she started. Before Dad or after? She said something earlier, before she left the other night. Willy's. "I have to dance tonight at Willy's."

I sprint downstairs and find the phone book, page to... what? Strip joints? Not a category. Men's clubs?

There are no Willy's, but under *Bars* there's a Wet Willy's on Blue Spruce Road. I didn't see a Wet Willy's on Blue Spruce Road today. But then, I wasn't looking. I was under Finn's spell.

How can I go to a strip club? I'm underage.

Carly's left a bottle of wine on the wet bar, corked, but half-full. I pour myself a glass and down it. Then another. My fear or apprehension is slowly replaced with courage or need. I don't want to see what she does. And I do. I have to know the truth about who I am and where I came from.

The access road down the mountain isn't lit, and I miss the turn, swerving into a patch of scrub oak. I hear it scrape the paint on Carly's Mercedes. Shit. I shouldn't do this. I'm not drunk, but I'm not completely sober either.

I have to do it. The AC's cranked up to freezing to keep me awake and alert.

It takes me a year to figure out how to turn on the brights.

My brain jumps back to the car accident, to Sarah, but I force myself not to think about it. Think of Carly. The way she was dressed tonight, like a whore. I hate that word.

Think of Finn. How could she not know the fundamental truth about herself? It's so obvious to me, probably to everyone in town. It's hard coming out to yourself, but if I'd waited until I was twenty-one, I never would've known Sarah. Which would've been a blessing.

No. She loved me once. We *were* in love.

I wonder as I'm driving through Majestic if Finn's ever had sex, if she's a virgin. I'm glad I got *that* out of the way.

Sarah's parents' forbidding her to see me hadn't stopped her from coming over or calling. I loved her for putting me before them. She said when she told her dad she was bi, he said, "What does that mean? You're half girl, half boy?"

We all had a good laugh over that. Especially Ben. I still felt sort of betrayed by Ben for breaking our confidence and telling Sarah he was my "convenient" boyfriend, but I felt more guilty about not telling her myself.

Did everything happen during that time I was sick? Maybe she needed me, and I couldn't be there for her. I know I missed her birthday, January 11, because I was still in bed with mono. I did text her fifteen times, for fifteen years old, with a picture of a burning birthday candle and the message MAKE A WISH, but I wanted to do more. When I could finally stay on my feet for more than an hour, I went to the mall and bought her the white-gold necklace and diamond earrings she'd been drooling over. I didn't care how much of my savings I was using. Sarah was worth it.

Even if I wasn't a hundred percent available, that was no reason to do what she did.

And Ben. It's ridiculous to have to make up a boyfriend. The whole time I pretended, I felt I was betraying my and Sarah's love for each other. I'll never do that again. Still, when did he decide it was okay to ruin my life?

Tanith said to me one day, "Your dad wants me to take you for birth control pills."

I was shocked.

She added, "Do I have to take you for birth control pills?"

I couldn't even look at her. I shook my head no.

She knew the truth. Why didn't she tell him? Tell him so he'd take it out on her and not me.

I'm such a coward. A fraud. I deserved what I got.

There are no streetlights on this stretch of road, and I wonder if I've gone too far. I haven't been paying attention. Two motorcycles roar up behind me, so close that I'm blinded in the rearview mirror. They pass on my left. The one biker is wearing a sleeveless leather vest with no helmet. A girl is clinging to his waist.

My first impulse is to follow them, so I step on the gas. They round the mountain curve and evaporate. Where did they go? Red taillights flash to my right, where I see the Blue Spruce sign. Damn. I missed it.

I have to drive to a gas station near I-70 to turn around, and I see a couple of cars parked on the side of the building with people about my age inside. In the backseat of one car are a guy and a girl, making out. Or it might be two girls. God, I think it is.

The longing seeps back in. After Sarah was out out, she had nothing to hide at school, so she cuddled with me at my locker, and I let her. We held hands in the hall. People said stuff, called us dykes, lezzes. Disgusting names, like cunt lickers and munch fuckers. Sarah put on a brave face, but I knew it bothered her. I tried to tell her she'd become immune to the harassment, that there is a never-ending supply of ignorant bigots in the world. That's the truth.

One day after school these two guys came up behind us—I had Sarah's hands in my coat pocket, and we were nuzzling and kissing—and one guy went, "Lesbos make me sick."

I said to him, "Go to hell."

The other guy yanked on Sarah's hat and pulled it off. She cried out because he ripped some hair with it. I lashed out at the guy but missed. The other guy wedged between us, pushing Sarah to the wall and holding her arms. He said, "Do you even know what you're missing, babe?" and smashed his mouth on hers.

With superhuman strength I didn't know I had, I wrenched him around and kicked him in the balls. The other guy clenched my arm, but I kicked him too. Next thing I knew, Sarah and I were flying out the exit, running for our lives.

Was that the day I decided to get my driver's license? A car would've been a godsend. Those jerks didn't catch up, but they could have.

Sarah broke down. She started crying uncontrollably.

"Baby, it's okay." I held her. "They're just assholes."

She pushed me away. "I can't do this!" she yelled in my face. "It's too hard!" She turned and fled.

I caught up with her at Gracie Field, and she whirled on me. "I hate this! I hate the way people look at me and the way they treat me and what they think of me. I hate lying to my parents and sneaking around."

"I thought you told your parents," I said.

"I didn't tell them everything. They know you kissed me."

"You kissed me first."

"No, I didn't."

She did. But what difference did that make? I wanted it.

"It doesn't matter what people think," I said.

"Yes it does!" she shrilled.

I tried to calm her down. She was crazy. "I hate it! I hate living like this!" She kept screaming, stomping her feet on the dirt like a little kid having a temper tantrum.

I shouldn't have laughed.

Sarah stopped immediately. Her eyes hardened and she said, "I can't do this with you anymore." She stormed off.

"Sarah," I called after her. She wouldn't slow down. "What are you saying?"

She stopped and twisted around. "I can't, Alyssa. I'm sorry."

My stomach was in my throat. Did she mean we were over?

A car turned the corner and honked at us. Sarah's father. She ran over to him. Out of cars and vans, hordes of kids in baseball uniforms streamed onto the field, and Sarah disappeared into the crowd.

That night was the worst night of my life. I called and called and called her cell. Sarah's voice mail picked up every time. I lost count of how many times I redialed. The last time her mother answered.

"Is this Alyssa?"

"Yes," I said. "Is Sarah—"

"Stop calling her. She's not allowed to see you or talk to you. Do you know how old she is? Barely fifteen. You can destroy your own life, but don't take my daughter down with you."

I felt humiliated. Ashamed. Why? I'd never made Sarah do anything she didn't want to do. She'd decided. Fifteen was old enough to decide.

Twenty-one is definitely old enough. Finn should be living out and proud. Last year M'Chelle dated this college girl, and that was cool. She didn't have to play out her whole love life at Homophobic High.

Finn's face materializes in my head. She isn't beautiful in a classic way, like Sarah. Finn has that gorgeous skin and hair and those eyes. I could lose myself in those bottomless eyes.

Forget Sarah. And Finn too. Finn doesn't need her first girlfriend to be some reject on the rebound looking to avenge her ex. And I don't need or want a girlfriend.

I see the sign to Blue Spruce Road and turn left. After a few feet, the pavement ends. Over a blind hill the topography flattens out, and I spy the building ahead. The neon sign: WET WILLY'S. Underneath, flashing naked women and curlicue lights that read: GIRLS, GIRLS, GIRLS.

God, Carly.

A hundred vehicles are parked in a dirt lot. Cars and trucks and motorcycles. Music blasts out the open door.

I should bail. Do I really want to see this?

Yes.

I park in the hinterlands and hike up to the entrance. The bouncer, who's ear-gauged and tattooed head to toe, says, "Can I see your ID?"

"Sure." I finger my billfold in my bag, fumble around, pretend I can't find it. He keeps waiting. Grabbing my billfold, I flip it open and flash my license at him. I go to flip it closed, but he snatches it out of my hand. "Sorry, sweetcakes," he says, handing it back. "Kinder Care is that way." He thumbs toward the road.

"I promise I won't drink," I tell him. "I just want a Coke."

"There's a 7-Eleven in Frisco."

How bad do I want in? Bad. I sling my bag over my shoulder and stick out my boobs. I shimmy up close to the bouncer and say in his ear, "Please?" My fingers trickle down his arm. I sort of vomit in my mouth.

A group of rowdies surge out the door, squeezing us together in the tight opening. Then a van pulls up, and an entire construction crew piles out.

The bouncer calls, "Hold up, boys," and I slip inside.

Behind me, I hear, "Hey, where's that kid?" I skitter behind a booth, between tables, keeping my head down.

The bar is straight ahead. I glance back once and don't see the bouncer, because the place is packed. He'll never find me. I look up and freeze.

Finn's behind the bar. Her eyes rise, and I duck down, scuttling sideways toward the wall, weaving through a clot of hairy bikers and slinking along the perimeter.

I should've made the connection. Finn knows Carly. Finn tends bar. Finn knows more about Carly than she's letting on.

There's a dark corner by the ATM machine, and I huddle there. I can watch Finn without her seeing me.

She's dressed in black. Black jeans, black tee on her lean, narrow frame. She'd be completely androgynous without the braid.

A pair of guys at the bar begin to talk her up. She pours whiskey into a glass of ice with one hand while drawing beer from the tap with the other. One guy makes a joke, and Finn smiles.

Not with her eyes. She just looks tired.

She glances my way. I dodge her gaze, but it doesn't matter, because the lights go out. A blaze of red light strobes in front of me, and a screech, like a flock of seagulls, makes my ears squinch. Guys start hooting and whistling, and I can't see what's happening.

I peer around a beefy dude. There's a stage, and on the right, lit with a red spotlight, is a pole. Dry-ice fog rolls across the floor, and Carly appears onstage. She's changed her clothes—into practically nothing. I have to cover my ears, the whistling is so shrill. I can't see clearly through the mass of smarmy bodies and smoke and haze. A bass beat pounds, and then this oily music comes on.

I sneak a peek at Finn. She's stopped working and stands motionless, eyes glued to the stage.

People begin to sit, opening a view of the stage to me, where Carly squats, her knees apart, behind the pole. She reaches up her long fingers and grabs the pole. Then she slides herself to an erect position and raises her head.

Through the mist and haze, Carly's eyes travel the room,

stop, and fuse to my face. No words are exchanged, because none have to be.

It's not all Carly's show. A blue light illuminates the left side of the stage, where there's another pole, and Geena appears. Guys whoop and catcall. She and Carly must've rehearsed this number, because they slide up and down their poles in unison. So raunchy. At one point they hang off their poles by one hand, lean over, and kiss each other.

That's enough for me. I'm gone before I see how far they'll go.

Chapter 12

I bury my head in my pillow, amp up my music, and cover the earbuds with both hands. I can't shake the image of Carly with her legs spread, clinging to that pole. How could she—how could anyone—sink so low? I had an idea what stripping or pole dancing was, but it's worse than I imagined. My own mother. I have absolutely no respect for her.

A hand touches my arm, and I startle. Her cloying perfume bites my nose, and I roll over in bed. Carly stands there in broad daylight, her arms crossed. "Paulie's left two messages on the machine. You never called him back, did you?"

Shit. I'd spaced out. I wait for her to say more—about last night.

She leaves, and I blow her smell out of my nose.

What time is it? If it's light, I'm late! Then remember I don't work today.

I sit up and see Carly didn't go far—to the doorway. Her hair is down, and she sweeps her too-long bangs across one eyebrow and over her ear. "Are you going to call him?"

She has on tight capris and a plunging V-neck top. She's had a boob job. Those are too high and round to be real.

"Did you hear me? Call your brother."

"I will." *Get out of my room*, I think. I slide out from under the sheets and skitter into the bathroom. When I come out, she's made the bed, and she's perched on the edge of the mattress, waiting for me.

"I only have two clients today, so I should be done around one, one thirty. I thought maybe we could drive to Dillon and go shopping for shoes. My friend Mitchell, who's a state trooper, has a boat, and he said anytime I want to go waterskiing to let him know. It might be fun." She examines her fake nails. "Afterward we can go out for a nice dinner and talk. Just the two of us. We need to talk, don't you think?" Her voice is scary serious.

"I'm... busy," I say, backing into the bathroom and easing the door shut.

She snaps, "Get unbusy."

I hear the bed creak and open the door a crack to peek out. She's still in the room. "From now on, you drink only when I'm here."

I shut the door and lock it. The image of last night won't dissolve, and now another memory surfaces. The way Finn watched Carly, kept her eyes on her.

Like hell Finn doesn't know she's gay. She's cruising for Carly. No wonder she's so evasive whenever Carly's name comes up.

I hear the garage door whir underneath me and head downstairs. Carly's stuck a Post-it to the fridge.

CALL PAULIE BACK. NOW!!!

The cordless phone rests on the table. I really do want to talk to Paulie, except I'm afraid I'll break down. I punch in the number slowly, deliberately, and hear a ring. Tanith answers.

"Hi," I say. "Is Paulie there?"

"Alyssa, hello. How are you?"

I almost snipe, *Peachy keen, Tanith. Strawberry pop with sprinkles on top.* Instead I go, "Okay."

She says, "You sound upset."

Do I, Tanith? "Why would I be upset?"

She doesn't answer me.

"Is Paulie there?" I ask again. "He called and left a few messages, but I was working."

"He's not here. He went with your dad to pick up the RV. So, you have a job?"

A dagger pierces my heart. The RV to drive to Corpus Christi to visit my grandparents. The last two or three summers I whined about going. The drive is long, and it's hot in the summer, and I wanted to be home with my friends.

"What kind of job?" Tanith asks.

"Waitressing."

"That's good," she says. "It's hard work, though, isn't it?"

I don't feel chatty. "I should go."

"Did Paulie tell you he got his purple belt?"

"He did?"

"Oh, shoot. I shouldn't have let the cat out of the bag. He'll want to tell you himself. Act like you don't know, okay?"

I can't even speak.

"He is so excited. I wish you could've been here...." Her voice trails off.

My eyes close. We have this family tradition that every time Paulie advances to the next level in tae kwon do, Tanith bakes or buys a cake. We decorate his room with banners and balloons. Paulie and I spar in the living room until Dad tells us to quit or take it outside. Then we watch one of Paulie's Jackie Chan movies. I'm so sick of Jackie Chan.

"Are you going to be there for a while?" Tanith asks. "I know Paulie wants to talk to you before we go."

I clear my throat. "Yeah. I mean, no." I don't want to be here when Carly gets back. "Tell Paulie major props. Tell him..." I can't go on.

Tanith's voice softens. "I will."

I hang up fast.

March

For your seventeenth birthday Dad got you a car. It was a used Civic, but you laid the love on him. He said, "Look out, buildings."

You wanted to come out to him so badly that day. You knew he loved you. He proved it in so many ways. But when you opened your mouth, the only words that formed were, "Love you, Dad."

He gave you a hug and said, "You're growing up too fast."

Sarah gave you the complete L Word *DVD set. That had to cost. You loved it but didn't know when or where you'd be able to watch it on TV. Not at home, that was for sure.*

Sarah told you her plan was working out beautifully. If only she'd thought of it sooner. The sarcasm dripped.

She had a "convenient" boyfriend now. Guess who?

Dad asked you one day why you didn't bring Ben around anymore, and you said, "We broke up." Dad said, "Then who are you on the phone with at all hours? Who are you spending all your time with?" Meaning every night and weekend, staying out till one minute before curfew.

You said, "Someone else."

Dad leveled you with a look. "Bring him home."

A few days later at dinner, he brought it up again, sort of. "For spring break I was thinking we might go to Maine to visit Mom and Dad." He meant Tanith's mother and father. "We've talked it over and agreed you and Paulie can each ask a friend to come."

How many times had you begged Dad and Tanith to let you bring a friend on these trips?

Sarah. God, could you ask her?

Tanith met your eyes. She telepathed the answer.

You said to Dad, "Um, I was thinking about staying home for spring break. I got really far behind in my schoolwork when I was sick, so I think I should stay here and catch up."

He said, "Stay home alone?"

"I'm seventeen," you informed him.

He didn't reply.

"I'm not planning any wild orgies."

Paulie piped up, "If Alyssa stays, I want to stay too."

Tanith scraped back her chair. "No," she said.

"I have to, Tanith. If I don't catch up, I'm not going to pass four of my classes, which either means I'll have to go to summer school or basically repeat junior year."

"Bring the work with you," she said.

"I can't," you insisted. "Most of it is research for reports. And I have this group project in sociology." Which was a lie. You stood up and took your plate to the sink. "I'm just going to stay home and work. Really concentrate my efforts."

"No," Tanith said.

"Wait a minute," Dad cut in. "I think that's smart. Very responsible." He asked you, "Are you sure?"

"Yeah." You said to Tanith, to reassure her, "I'm just going to work the whole time."

Dad said, "Okay, then. Paulie, you keep an eye on your sister. No hanky-panky." He shot you a warning flare.

"Wait. Paulie's staying too?"

Dad reached out and took Tanith's hand. "We'll make it a second honeymoon."

That wasn't the plan.

You spent half your break doing schoolwork and the other half playing stupid Guitar Hero with Paulie. Sarah went with her family to Florida. She might've told you earlier that she was leaving, so you wouldn't have been forced to babysit your brother for a week.

One morning Paulie came into your room and flopped on the bed. You were half-naked in a tank and jockeys. "Hello? Remember this?" You knuckled his head to imitate door knocking.

"I'm bored. Can we call Ben?"

You resumed reading your history text. "Don't you have any friends?" The image of ten-year-old hoodlums invading the house materialized in your brain. "On second thought..." And you weren't even getting paid to babysit, and you were bummed about Sarah being gone, and you hated yourself for being such a coward. Paulie, with those sad puppy eyes. You slapped the history book closed. "Sure. Why not?"

Paulie grabbed your cell off the desk. "Is he star zero star?"

"What?" You took the phone from him and scrolled through your contacts list for Ben. Star zero star was Sarah. When the phone began to ring on Ben's end, you handed it back to Paulie. "You ask him."

There were weird vibes between you and Ben lately. You weren't sure why. He'd stopped hanging out with you and Sarah. He hadn't been coming to GSA. Paulie said, "Is Ben there?"

You figured you'd take a shower if Ben was coming over, since you'd been slumming all week, and your hair was a grease pan.

As soon as you shut the bathroom door down the hall, Paulie knocked. "Don't come in," you said. You were already naked.

Through the door, he told you, "Ben's not home. He went to Florida for spring break."

Chapter 13

Why can I never see what's right in front of my face? Because trust makes a person want to believe. Trust is more blind than love.

I run upstairs to put on shoes, to get out of the house before Carly returns, and what's right in front of my face? Finn's shoes. Now I hate them, but I don't have anything else to put on my feet. All this time Finn was avoiding the subject of Carly for a reason. The shock on her face when she found out I was gay too. How fake.

My brain is a hornet's nest of anger—mostly at myself. I'm so naive. I drive down the access road, kind of erratically while I'm fiddling with the AC and finding a radio station. Finn's so full of shit. Is everyone a liar? Or do they only lie to me because I'm easily duped?

It's twelve forty-five when I veer into the Egg Drop's parking area in back. I skid to a stop on the cracked, dry dirt. The diner's back door is propped open, and I hear the fan whirring away.

Finn's racking dishes as I enter. I cross over to her at the dishwasher. "Did you enjoy the show?" I say behind her back. "Did you get off on it? Did you think I wouldn't find out about you and Carly?" My rising voice carries over both the radio and the fan. Arlo spins around at the grill, where he's scraping the burned surface.

Finn frowns. "What are you talking about?"

I lower my voice and go, "You know damn well. Are you having an affair with her?" Carly said herself she has gay friends. Does that include girlfriends?

Finn spreads her hands at Arlo like, *I have no idea what this lunatic is ranting about.*

I say, "I was at the strip club last night. I saw you."

Finn blinks. "Saw me what?" she says, but her cheeks flush.

"If you're in a relationship with Carly, just tell me and I'll—" I almost say, *Back off.* Then she'd know.... And I'm *not* interested.

Arlo coughs or something, and I catch him grinning before he returns his attention to the grill. My arm is suddenly clenched in a vise grip, and Finn steers me out the back door. She says, "What were you doing at the club? You're not old enough to be in there, and if you have a fake ID—"

I pull away from her. "Here I thought you were so in the closet that you didn't even know your own self. Bull. Shit."

Her eyes dart around wildly.

I'm furious. At myself for being stupid. At her for deceiving me. I stomp toward the Mercedes.

Finn calls, "Alyssa—"

I whirl. "Just tell me the truth. Are you fucking my mother?"

Finn's jaw drops. My eyes well with tears. Damn.

Finn hurries toward me, and I back up, my arms extended to keep her away. She reaches me because I've stopped; I can't find the keys. "I don't know what you saw," she says, "but you got it wrong. I work at Willy's. I bartend. That's all. Yeah, sometimes after the show, Carly and Geena hang out at the bar, and we talk. We're friends, I guess."

I glare at Finn through my blur of tears.

"Small talk. I barely know Carly. I have a job to do, and I do it."

I sniffle. "Is that the truth?"

She crosses her heart.

I let out a deep, shuddering breath. Why should I believe her? Those soft, brown eyes, melting my core.

I say, "You think she's hot, though, don't you?"

She can't hold my eyes. I knew it! She takes a step back and turns around, saying something under her breath. I must be delirious because I'm sure I heard, "Not as hot as you."

"What was that?" I call out.

She pivots, walking backward. "Do the shoes fit?"

My gaze falls to my feet. "I had to cut off three toes, but yeah."

She smiles. I notice she's wearing hiking boots.

"Thanks. For the shoes."

She vanishes inside.

I stand there a minute, leaning against the Mercedes. Kind of unsteady. Getting my butt burned on the blazing metal and feeling idiotic. But warm inside too.

I know how much work it is to clean up after breakfast, so

I return to the kitchen and grab a bus tub. Finn and Arlo are talking, and the conversation halts. Arlo says to me, "You're not on today."

"I know." I suppress the urge to look at Finn. As I press my rear against the swinging doors to finish whatever needs doing in the dining room, Arlo adds, "This is on your own time."

Yeah, yeah. The tables are cleared, but they need setting, and the floor still needs to be swept and mopped. Finn's and Arlo's voices drift out, and I can't help inching over near the order window to hear what they're saying.

Finn: ". . . a month's advance on my check. Just this once."

Arlo: "No can do."

Finn: "A loan, then. I'll pay it back with interest."

Arlo: "Before or after you skip town?"

Finn snarls. "Forget it."

Awkward silence.

I have to go into the kitchen to fill the mop bucket. Finn grabs the mop from me. "I'll get that," she says.

I snatch it back. "I'll finish." I raise my voice so Arlo can hear. "You go to your other job, your *second* job, or is it the *third* job, so you can make enough money to live and buy yourself some wheels."

Arlo reaches over and cranks up his radio.

Finn throws me a lopsided grin and bumps my shoulder with hers. It electrifies my nerve endings all the way down. As she's filling out her hours, she says loudly enough for Arlo to hear, "Anything you want to know about Carly, ask Arlo. Word on the street is, he's the resident expert."

Arlo swivels his head slowly and cuts Finn a death look,

which she misses because she's already gone. He snaps at me, "Get out of here. I'll do that."

"I don't mind." I roll the mop bucket of soapy water out to the dining room.

Arlo coasts down his ramp and out the swinging doors, crashing into the bucket and sloshing water all over the floor. "You think I can't mop my own floor because I'm a cripple?"

That makes me reel. "I never said that."

"You were thinking it."

"No, I wasn't." I was thinking about using Carly's ATM card to withdraw money from her bank. Could I withdraw four times? Arlo tries to take the mop from me, but I hang on. We have a tug-of-war, and neither of us lets go. I say, "I'm sure you can do anything you want. There's this guy I know at school who's in a chair, and it doesn't slow him down. He's a cool guy." He asked me out my sophomore year and I said no, but not because of his chair. It sort of forced me to come out to him.

"So, you have a thing for this guy?" Arlo asks.

"No," I say.

"Because he's a cripple."

"Because I'm a lesbian." I snatch the mop out of Arlo's hand. My heart jackhammers as I roll the mop bucket across the room to begin in the far corner. I just came out to Arlo, and now he's going to fire me.

He goes back to the kitchen, where he clangs around.

I'm almost done with the floor when he returns. He sits there for a minute watching me. "A cripple could do that in half the time a lesbian does."

Reflexively, I flip him the bird.

He laughs. "Yeah, you're all Carly."

"No. I'm not. And stop comparing me to her," I say.

Arlo doesn't respond. I sneak a sideways glance at him, and he's staring at me. Or through me. Out of nowhere, he says, "You hungry?"

I don't remember the last time I ate. "Yeah. Starving."

"What's your pleasure?" he asks. "Besides the ladies."

Oh, great. Now I'm going to be the brunt of every lez joke he knows. At least he's okay with my being gay. I wish it didn't matter to me what others think, but he is my boss, and I've heard of people losing their jobs when they come out. I need this job. I *like* this job.

"I'm making myself a ham sandwich." Arlo backs into the kitchen. "What do you want?"

"That sounds good," I call out to him.

As I'm dumping the dirty water into the sink to rinse out the bucket, the phone on the wall rings. Arlo rolls over to answer. "Speak of the devil. Hello, Carly." My ears prick up. "Yeah, it's been a while." I turn, and he's looking at me. "Is *who* here? What does she look like?"

I wave my arms, like *no no no*.

Arlo says, "I don't see anyone by that description." He twists away from me. "So, how've you been?" He listens. Chuckles. "Anytime," he says in this voice loaded with sexual innuendo. "Alyssa is an interesting person. What? Oh, sure. She tells me all her secrets. I can't get her to shut up."

I smile. Arlo and Carly talk for a while, like old friends. Mostly, Arlo listens. He says, "Whatever you need. You know that." When he hangs up, he comes over and goes, "She's hacked off at you. You'd better—"

"She can go to hell."

"Whoa." Arlo's chair slides back a foot.

I shove the mop supplies into the closet and stalk past him to the restroom. While I'm in there, I give the sink a wipe down and the toilet a swish. It peels off a layer of my attitude. I find Arlo in the dining room, setting out our lunch.

The sandwich looks awesome. I sit, and Arlo pulls in across from me.

The first bite is heaven. I've never liked mustard, Dijon or otherwise, but with the tomatoes and lettuce and cheese and mayo...I snarf it down. Pointing to my full mouth, I murmur, "Mmm," like *yumtastic*.

Arlo studies my face. Then his gaze lowers, and he says, "You have her eyes."

And that's all. I keep chewing; take a slug of milk from my glass.

"We were lovers. Once."

My eyebrows shoot up. Arlo bites off the end of his dill pickle. "Didn't think cripples could get it up, huh?"

I cast him a withering look. The only person I know with such transparent self-pity is...well, me. I never realized how unattractive self-pity is in a person.

"Oh, I forgot," Arlo says. "You're all sensitive and informed about the plight of the disabled."

I ignore that remark and swallow my mouthful of food. "How long were you and Carly together?"

Arlo chomps his sandwich. "Two years, on and off."

Wow. Sarah and I didn't make it a year. "So, I guess you didn't mind her, um, extracurricular activities?"

Arlo blinks at me. "If you mean the exotic dancing, she wasn't doing that when she first got here. She worked for me as a waitress while she was getting her business going."

I must screw up my face because Arlo says, "What?"

"Her 'business'?"

"The personal training and massage. She had to build a clientele."

"Right," I say.

Arlo narrows his eyes at me. "What's with you?"

I shake my head. "Nothing. Sorry." I'm down to my last bite. "Does she really do those jobs?"

"Yeah, and she's good at them. She has a great reputation."

"As a whore." It slipped out! I didn't mean to say—

Now Arlo's glaring at me.

"Sorry." I wipe my mouth with a napkin. "I just don't respect her."

"Because she's an exotic dancer?"

"Stripper," I correct him. And call girl. My eyes latch onto the half sandwich he still has on his plate. He's balled his napkin and set it on the table, so I know he's done. "If you're not going to eat that..."

He shoves the plate across the table. I practically lunge for the sandwich.

"She makes good money at that club, especially with all the construction crews here lately. Anyway, what's it to you? She's an adult. She can make her own choices."

And suffer the consequences, I think. "Was it when she went back to stripping that you dumped her?" I ask.

A smile curls Arlo's lips. "Thank you," he says.

"For what?" I swallow the last bite. The sandwich is gone, but the memory will live on.

"For thinking I was the one who broke it off."

Wow, I know how much it hurts to get dumped. "I'm sorry. What happened?"

Arlo shrugs. "I was replaced."

My eyes must widen. Major heartache.

He rolls back a little and folds his arms across his chest. "You know, I don't get you. You're awfully judgmental, and toward your own mother, no less."

"She's not my mother. I mean, she is. But she wasn't around for me when I was growing up. Did she ever mention that to you? Did you even know I existed before I showed up here?"

Arlo says, "She talked about you."

"Really? What did she say?"

He opens his mouth and then clamps it shut. He's lying. She never told him she had a daughter. "I'm sorry she hurt you too," I say. "Her specialty is abandoning people."

"Do you have any idea what her life's been like?" Arlo drops his arms. "What she's been through?"

He sounds like he admires her or something. "Childbirth and desertion. Big whoop."

He snatches my plate out from under me and stacks it on his, along with our napkins and glasses, sets them in his lap, and rolls into the kitchen.

Now he's pissed. Why? I get up and follow him. "She doesn't need to degrade herself by being a stripper." And if she actually does do massage and personal training, she must make enough money to live on. "She doesn't need that ginormous house and—"

Arlo whirls on me. "Do you know about Jason?"

My blank look must answer the question.

Arlo sets the dishes on the counter. "Get out of here," he snarls.

Fine. I'll go. At the exit, I say, "Thanks for the sandwich. It was the best thing I've ever eaten in my whole entire life."

That seems to soften him. He glances up over the counter and says, "Ask her about the house. Ask her about Jason and… the rest." His voice catches. "Just ask her."

Chapter 14

Carly doesn't leave me her ATM card, but she does leave two envelopes stuffed with cash. There's a note on one:

> *WOULD YOU MIND DEPOSITING THIS IN MY BANK IN BRECKENRIDGE? IT'S ALPINE BANK, RIGHT OFF MAIN. YOU CAN'T MISS IT.*

The envelope for me is full of twenties and fifties. Eight hundred dollars exactly. I wonder if these are bills that guys stuck in her thong, paid her for lap dances, or worse. Ew. The other envelope has four hundred fifty dollars in it, according to her deposit slip.

A pang of guilt stabs me as I drop the envelopes into my purse. I vow to pay Carly back as soon as possible, even if she doesn't need it.

On the way to Breckenridge, I pass a sprawling school. SUMMIT HIGH SCHOOL, the sign reads. I think, *That's where I'll be going next year.*

It hits me hard. I won't be graduating with my class. All my friends. Ex-friends. In sixth grade my best friend moved away. I remember crying for weeks and weeks. Over time, the memory of her faded, and life went on, but every once in a while a face or a voice reminds me of her. I wonder if anyone at home will remember me, or miss me for very long. There's no one who'd cry over my leaving. No one who did.

I deposit Carly's cash in Breckenridge and take a mini tour. Pretty cool town. You can walk to the ski lifts from the parking lots and lodges. One day I'd love to learn how to ski or snowboard.

As I'm nearing the intersection to turn back toward Majestic, I imagine the scene. Me handing the money to Finn. Her eyes lighting up. Her hugging me. She might even—

It's happening again. I'm losing control. Soon I'll be obsessing and won't be able to stop.

Have I learned nothing? A car honks behind me, and I flinch—the light's turned green. Instead of driving through Frisco, I make a U-turn in a hotel parking lot and head for Blue Spruce Road.

The drive up the mountain isn't as scary as the first time. I roll down my window and breathe in the sweet mountain air. The river is soothing; the sound of rushing water has a calming effect. I reach the parking area at Caribou Lake and pull in.

Retracing the route Finn and I took, I scrabble up the rocky path to the top of the boulders. A soft breeze rustles the aspen leaves, and I sit, extending my legs and leaning back on my elbows.

I love the peace here. Even the screech of a blue jay seems

part of the pastoral symphony. I feel this amazing sense of destiny within the universe, like I'm meant to be here at this time and place in my life.

Arlo's words swirl in my head. I wonder who Jason is. Arlo's replacement? Carly's never mentioned the name Jason—at least, not that I can recall. And what's "the rest"?

An acrid odor pinches my nose, and I sit up. I sniff and the smell is faint, stolen away by a gust of wind. I relax again, close my eyes. The lapping of the water reminds me of Paulie wanting to go to the beach, and Tanith saying, "Let's all go. I'll pack a picnic." Dad had to work or something, so Tanith said, "Why don't you both invite friends."

Paulie said, "Do I have to?"

If Paulie had any close friends, they never hung out with him. I don't think he had a secret stash of friends, the way I did. Immediately, I thought of inviting Sarah and Ben and M'Chelle. No. Not M'Chelle. For Paulie's sake, I didn't ask anyone. It wouldn't be fair to go off with my friends and leave him behind.

That wasn't the real reason.

April

You were walking in the quad before school when M'Chelle caught up. "Are you okay?" she asked, linking her arm in yours. "You seem—I don't know—distant."

You tend to ignore your friends when you have a girlfriend, which is terrible, but M'Chelle was the one who'd been keeping her distance. She didn't have to tell you outright that she didn't like Sarah. You felt her chilly demeanor whenever the three of you were together. "Anything wrong?" M'Chelle asked.

"With me or you?"

M'Chelle unlinked your arms.

That came out sounding dismissive. "I'm fine," you told her. "Just stressed about stuff." Spring break. Florida.

"Are things okay with you and Sarah?" M'Chelle asked.

"Yes," you snapped at her. "Why wouldn't they be?"

"Okay." M'Chelle hesitated a moment, and you wanted to apologize. It wasn't her fault. You wished you could confide in her. She gave your hand a squeeze and said, "You know if you ever need to talk..."

You nodded quickly. A lump rose in your throat, and you swallowed it down. M'Chelle kissed you lightly on the cheek and then took off, flying up the stairs two at a time and leaving you behind.

You did need to talk, but not to M'Chelle. You'd dated M'Chelle the summer between your frosh and soph years—kind of a summer fling. A short one. It never got beyond kissing. The chemistry wasn't there, and you both knew it.

You couldn't bring yourself to ask Sarah or Ben about Florida, because you were afraid it'd come out sounding like an accusation. Or paranoia. Or jealousy. Anyway, your suspicions were ridiculous. A coincidence. Florida is a big place, and a lot of people go there for spring break.

Not to mention Ben is gay.

You saw Sarah waiting for you at your locker, and your spirits lifted immediately. But when you went to kiss her good morning, she turned her face away. "We need to talk," she said.

The first bell rang, and she headed off for class.

You caught her arm. "How about now?"

She cast you that look of irritation, impatience. "Alyssa, I can't. I have a test this period."

Her eyes, those blazing blue eyes, bore right through you. "Later," she whispered.

You sat through American lit and history and psychology, churning up an ulcer. The last time she'd needed to "talk," she told you not to call her anymore, that her mother was monitoring her cell phone history. You told Sarah then, "Just delete my calls," and she said, "Please, Alyssa. This is hard enough."

At passing period you saw Ben in the hall hanging with his friends, and you thought, This is stupid, worrying about something that never happened; that never could happen. You needed to get it out of your system. Coming up behind Ben, you waited for a break in the conversation. When there wasn't one, you touched Ben's arm, and he spun around. "Hey," he said. "'Sup?"

"Can we talk?"

He told his friends he'd catch up with them.

"I heard you went to Florida over spring break."

You detected a slight rise of color in his cheeks. He said, "You heard right." His nose was peeling from sunburn.

"Did you go with Sarah?"

His eyebrows arched. "Was she there?" He snapped his fingers. "Damn. We coulda dissed on Alyss for a week." He stuck out his hip and rested a hand on it. With his bent elbow, he jabbed you. "Places to haunt, people to taunt." Ben strutted off.

He was so totally gay. At least when it was "convenient" for him.

Behind the retaining wall where you always met between first and second periods, Sarah waited. The moment you saw each other, the rest *of the world dissolved. She smiled broadly, and you shrieked, "You got your braces off!"*

She smacked your shoulder and said, "You finally noticed."

You grabbed her and kissed her, and she melted in your arms. After a minute, though, she broke it off. She said, "We still have to talk. We can't be out in public anymore."

"What? Why not?"

"Because I'm afraid it'll get back to my parents."

"You weren't afraid before. What happened?"

"Someone at church told my mom they saw me kissing a girl." Sarah shook her head. "No doubt I'm going to hell."

"Who was it?"

"I don't know. Why does that matter?"

It didn't matter. You understood completely her fear of exposure. You lived it every day. You almost started crying right there because of how much her decision was going to cost you. School was the only place you could ever live your truth.

At the time you wished the truth about you would get back to your parents because then you wouldn't have to tell them—ever.

Unfortunately, there are wishes that do come true.

A breeze sings through the trees, and a pinecone drops near my hand. I pick it up and crack off a brittle scale. Sarah was pulling away. I could feel it; I knew it. I just didn't know how to stop it.

On my way through Majestic, I can't help checking to see whether Finn's mountain bike is at the Emporium. It's not. I wonder if she's listed in the phone book; if I could call and tell her I have the money, or even drive to her place—

Stop.

Shut it down right now. I don't even know her last name. Good thing. Giving her this money is risky. It's acting on impulse, and I need to consider the consequences.

It's a loan, an act of kindness between friends. That's all it has to be. That's all it is.

Carly's in her workout room, running on the treadmill. I guess she has to keep her body toned to shake her booty.

Our eyes meet and I smile. "Thanks," I say. "I'll pay you back."

She slows her pace, and the treadmill's speed decreases. "I thought we were going water-skiing today."

Was that today? "I'm sorry. I forgot." I never agreed to go, did I?

She takes a long draw from her bottle of water, still looking at me. "Paulie called," she says. "Twice."

Shit. "Okay."

She adds, "It's too late. He said they were leaving for their trip."

Paulie. I send him a mental message. *I'm sorry, I'll call you at Grandma's.*

"I talked to Tanith for a while." Carly walks over to the bench outside the sauna and dabs her wet chest with a towel. She's breathing hard, and a sheen of sweat glistens on her skin. "Come sit with me."

"I really need to shower," I tell her. I fan the front of my own stinky tee and turn to leave.

"Tanith told me some things I didn't know," she says at my back. "About the stalking?"

I spin around. "I never stalked her." My sharp voice echoes in my ears.

Carly heads toward me fast, and I step aside to let her pass. "What's her name?" Carly asks.

My heart hammers. I thought we were forgetting the past. "How did you know I was a lesbian?" I ask instead. "Did Tanith tell you that?" I follow Carly to the main level.

She replies, "I've always known."

"How?" I didn't figure it out until I was thirteen.

Carly pours herself a glass of red wine. "You never talked about boys, and the few times I asked if you had a boyfriend, you clammed up fast. Plus, look at you." She takes a drink of wine.

What do I look like? I don't flaunt it. I'm just me. I don't make myself up to look like a dyke, if that's what she means.

She adds, "I'm not as dumb as your father. And I'd *never* be anything but accepting and supportive of you, no matter what. I expect the same from you."

I can't hold her eyes. Carly pours another glass of wine and hands it to me. "What's her name? Your girlfriend."

I take the wine but don't drink it. "Sarah. She's not my girlfriend anymore. She . . . we . . . broke up."

Carly makes a pouty face. "Tell me about the stalking," she says.

"I didn't stalk her," I repeat.

Carly tilts her head to one side.

"I just wanted to talk to her. She wouldn't return my calls." After what happened at my house, the whole fiasco.

"I can tell you need to get this off your chest. Don't bottle it up inside the way I do." Carly motions me to a bar stool.

I'm not sure I want to talk to her.

She scoots the bar stool closer, but I hold my ground. "Fine." She sounds defeated. She gets up and brushes by me to open the cabinet drawer. I almost ask, *Who's Jason?* but before I can get the words out, Carly's beside me, handing me a box. "I got you something," she says.

My chin hits the floor.

"Every girl needs a phone." She winks.

It's an iPhone. Oh my God.

I hand it back to her. "I can't."

She won't take it. "When someone gives you a gift, accept it graciously."

"But I—"

She pads into the kitchen. "Consider it my lame attempt at making up for all the time I lost with you."

That makes me feel guilty. "It's not lame," I say. "It's—" Tempting. Too tempting.

She retrieves salad makings from the fridge while I read about all the iPhone's features on the box. It has a touch screen and a landscape keyboard, video recording and Internet, which means e-mail and text. I can't handle this.

"I have raspberry vinaigrette, blue cheese, or Italian," she calls.

And poppy seed and red wine vinegar. But who's snooping?

"Raspberry's fine," I say.

Carly smiles, a genuine smile. "That's my favorite. Let's sit out on the deck."

I trail her to the French doors, but the second she opens them, heat blasts us like a furnace. Outside, swarms of gnats attack my ears. Carly swats at them. "On second thought…" She holds the door for me as I hurry back inside.

"This heat is so unusual," she says. "It's drier than last year. We haven't had a drop of rain in months, and I'm afraid we're going to have another fire up here. We had a scary one last year."

That must be why all the trees on the mountain are black. I tell her, "I smelled smoke today."

"Really? Probably from one of the forest fires. There are ten or twelve now."

"You're kidding." The local news doesn't play on Logo. "Where?"

"All across the state." Carly sets the salad on the table, along with her empty glass, the bottle of wine, and the vinaigrette. I grab my wineglass and two sets of silverware and napkins from the drawer. We sit across from each other.

"Thank you, Alyssa," she says, spreading her napkin in her lap. "You have nice manners."

Which Dad pounded into me.

Carly drizzles dressing on her salad and then passes me the bottle. She forks a leaf of lettuce and says, "I bet the look on your father's face was priceless when you told him you were a lesbian."

I swallow hard. "I didn't tell him exactly."

"No?"

I hate reliving this. "He found me and Sarah together."

Carly pauses with her fork halfway to her mouth. "Doing what?"

I lower my eyes.

Carly goes, "Oh. My. God." She puts down her fork, throws back her head, and laughs hysterically. Then I laugh because it feels good to laugh. Except then I want to cry.

"He's such a douche bag. I never should have left you with him." She downs her wine.

"Then why did you?"

She shakes her head and resumes eating. "It wasn't the right time for me to have a child. One day you'll understand. I hope." She replenishes her drink from the wine bottle while I munch my salad. She pours her glass full and toasts, "*Santé*."

We clink glasses.

I don't understand and doubt I ever will. "When you decided to come back, why didn't you take me with you then? Why did you come back at all if you were just going to leave again?"

She expels a long breath. "Can't we ever get past this?"

"You brought it up," I say.

She pinches the bridge of her nose. "I have such a headache." She holds her wineglass to her forehead.

Now or never. "Who is Jason?"

As pain so deep and real spreads through Carly's eyes and face, I feel the emotion unleashed on every molecule in the room. "Please, Alyssa. I know I hurt you, but don't get back at me like this." Carly gets up, grabs the wine bottle by the neck, and bounds up the stairs to the loft.

Chapter 15

When I was eight, Dad told me my mother would like to be in contact with me again. He said, "How would you feel about that?" And I said, "Great!"

He seemed sad, like it was a hit on him as a father. It wasn't. He was a perfect dad.

No, no one's perfect. Lesson learned the hard way.

I think Dad would've told Carly to stay away if I wasn't being so horrible to Tanith. This was right after Dad married Tanith and she moved in. Everything she asked me to do, I'd snipe, "You're not my mother. You can't make me." Dad would send me to my room until I apologized. Maybe he thought I'd be nicer to Tanith if I knew the horror of my real mother. Who knows what people's motives are?

I was so nervous about meeting Carly, worried whether she'd like me. Maybe hoping she'd whisk me away to Disneyland or some enchanted kingdom, swoop me up, and carry me off to her palace in the sky.

When I opened the door to her the first time, I actually

gasped. She was stunning. She had on a short, fitted maroon dress with matching shoes and lipstick. She said, "Alyssa? I'm your mom."

She laughed at my speechlessness, or Dad's. He stood there stiffly, clutching my hand. She said, "You can call me Carly," and she shook my limp hand, the one Dad didn't have a death grip on.

All I wanted her to do was hold me and tell me how much she missed me and how we would all be together now. She kissed Dad on the cheek and left a lipstick print. His face turned bright red. She introduced herself to Tanith.

Carly made me feel special. She set me apart from my friends, who had frumpy, ordinary moms like Tanith. I'd talk about my real mom, the dancer, who was off dancing in a Broadway show or making music videos.

Or porno films.

What a stupid, naive kid I was. Now I'm a stupid, naive teenager. I guess people never change.

The next day Finn's eyes are bloodshot, and she looks like death on meth. "Thank God you're here," she says in a monotone. She tosses me a dish towel. "Could you bus for me? My head feels like a bomb went off."

"Big night at Wet Willy's?" I ask.

She presses her thumbs into her temples and drones, "I never drink. I know better."

"Can I get a waitress over here?" Arlo sticks his head out the order window. "I know I have two somewhere, and both of them are overpaid slackers."

Finn bleary-eyes me.

"This should make you feel better." I pull out the bank envelope and hand it to her.

She looks inside, and her jaw unhinges.

Finn says, "Where did you get this?"

I tell her, "I have some college savings. Don't worry about it." I snag the bus tub to head out front, and Finn yanks on the other end to stop me.

"I can't take your money."

"Yes, you can," I say. "I assume it's a loan, right?"

She shakes her head slowly. "Alyssa, no."

"Finn, yes."

She holds my eyes for a long moment, and then lets out a breath. "I'll pay you back. With interest. I promise."

I toss her a casual smile. "I know you will."

She glances at the money again, and the joy that spreads across her face is even better than I imagined. And I put it there. Me.

"Any century now!" Arlo yells. "These orders ain't serving themselves."

I pull the tub away from Finn, thinking, *I do trust her. I don't know why, since I barely know her. But if she says she'll pay the money back, she will.*

The first customer left Finn a one-dollar tip. Cheap bastard. I hope Carly's in no hurry to get repaid. I pocket the tip for Finn, and the front bell tinkles. It's that perv construction dude who violated me on my first day. His crew is lined up behind him. He sees me, and then he glances Arlo's way and nods. I thought Arlo had kicked him out.

The guy walks right up to me. I skirt the table to put hardware between us as he clears his throat. "I apologize for my rude behavior the other day. I didn't mean to pinch your as—er, heinie. Bum."

I want to say, *Yes, you did, jerk*. But I hold my tongue.

He peers over his shoulder at Arlo, who's rolled out the swinging doors and is sitting there with his arms crossed. Arlo hitches his head, like *Go on*. Meantime, I stack a dirty plate and cup in the tub.

Creepo says, "Do you accept my apology?"

Is he talking to me? I keep working.

"Look. Me and the guys want to come back here and eat cuz, I'll tell ya, there's no better or cheaper place in the area. So, what do you say? I promise we'll be respectful and keep our hands to ourselves."

He sounds like a child who's been spanked. He comes at me fast and then drops to his knees, folding his hands and steepling his fingers. "Please?"

Everyone's gawking. Someone yells, "Aw, just tell him you'll marry him." People laugh.

"Okay," I say to him between clenched teeth. I think, *Get up, fool*.

He grunts as he pushes up to stand. "Guys!" He waves his crew over. Extending a hand, he says, "I'm Rufus."

I shake his meaty paw. "Alyssa." I slide my hand out, and it's all smeary.

Each guy introduces himself, like I'll remember their names. One of them—Rick or Dick—points at me and says, "Know who you look like?"

I grab the tub and scramble. When I bring back menus to the table, Rick or Dick says, "Thank you, Alyssa." He smirks.

I say to the guys, "Did Rufus mention how he promised Arlo you'd all double-tip from now on?"

They turn on Rufus, and I leave him to the slaughter.

The stream of customers is steady, and Finn's dragging. I try to pick up the slack, but I'm not as fast as she is. The cowboy, Dutch, comes in and says, "Mornin', little lady." I seat him at a window table, where he removes his hat and sets it on a chair.

"Sludge and fudge?" I ask him.

He smiles. He has these sparkly blue eyes, clear as crystal, like my grandpa's. "Sludge for sure."

I hand him a menu, and he holds up a hand. "Gimme a number twelve, extra green chili, the way I like it. Arlo'll know."

I write the order, printing *Dutch* at the top so Arlo will know.

The rush ends, and the last customers trickle out. "Thanks, Arlo," Dutch calls. "Dee-lishus and new-trishus. Thanks, Alyssa."

"You're welcome." I lock the door behind him. Oh my God. The Scrubs left me a six-dollar tip for a fourteen-dollar tab. Wait'll I tell Finn.

She's at the grill, scraping and looking nauseated.

Arlo rolls up next to me. "Ya done good, Alyssa. You're a natural at this."

"So give me a raise."

"And a comedienne to boot," he says to Finn as he dumps a pile of huevos rancheros into the trash. Finn hustles to the bathroom to hurl.

"How about this instead, to make you official?" Arlo hands me a name tag.

Wow. Cool. I pin it on my shirt, even though I'm done for the day, and the tee is going in the wash later. I stretch out my tee to look. My own name tag.

Finn staggers out, and Arlo says to her, "If Sysco makes a delivery, see if you can finagle an extra case of sugar and creamer." He wheels toward the exit. "Lock up when you're finished. I'm off to get me some." He chuckles on his way out.

Finn's there when I turn around, holding out the bank envelope. "I can't take this."

"Why? Yes, you can." I walk past her. She tries to stuff it in my back pocket, but I smack her hand away and go, "Perv." She tries again, and I snag a spatula and slash the air like it's a sword. Finn smiles, but it's a weary smile that vanishes quickly.

Carly's words replay in my head. I say to Finn, "When someone gives you a gift, accept it graciously."

She hesitates and then says, "Okay. But I promise to pay you back every dollar before I leave."

I look at her. "You're leaving?"

"As soon as possible." A truck *beep-beeps* like it's backing up to the door, and she drags toward the sound. Now I wish I'd never given her the money.

Dad has a list of rules for vacations: no computers or cell phones, don't hog the TV at Grandma and Grandpa's, help out with chores. On my iPhone, which is cooler than shit, I tap in Grandma and Grandpa's number. No one answers, and I don't leave a message. What would I say? "Did you notice I'm no longer a member of the family?" Honestly, I wonder what Dad and Tanith are telling them about me.

I know no one's home in Virginia Beach, but I call anyway. I leave a message for Paulie: "Snot-nose brat boy. I'm finally getting around to calling you back. Timing is everything, as they say. Not that I forgot, or was too busy, or didn't want to talk to you."

That sounds pathetic, plus I'm choking up. "I just wanted you to know I called you back." I disconnect.

I check my e-mail, and my heart leaps. Two messages from M'Chelle. I open the first one:

> im still in shock about everything. ur dads a bastard. im worried about u, Al. call me, ok?

Who told her? It all happened so fast. One day I had a home and a life and friends and a family. Then, *poof*, up in smoke.

The second e-mail is a duplicate of the first, like M'Chelle hit SEND twice. Spaz.

I guess she forgives me. She shouldn't. I'm an ass. I miss M'Chelle. I miss my life. I miss my brother and my grandparents. I dial M'Chelle's number to call her, but I can't bring myself to touch the last digit. If I hear her voice, I'll crumble. And I know what—who—we'll end up talking about. Instead, I e-mail her:

> i'm sorry. about everything. i love u.

End of April

M'Chelle said she needed to talk to you. She came over. You sat on the bed, and she hugged one of your beaded pillows to her chest. "Alyssa, you know I'm your friend, right?" she began.

"Of course."

Her eyes held yours and then dropped. "You should know that Sarah's been hooking up with Ben."

First you froze. Then you laughed.

M'Chelle didn't.

"He's playing the role of her boyfriend so her parents don't get suspicious," you told M'Chelle.

She shook her head. "No, Alyssa. It's more than that."

Your heart beat a hole in your chest. "*Who* told you that?"

"No one," M'Chelle said. "I saw them at Gracie Field after my soccer game. Making out in the bleachers."

Your blood was rupturing every vessel. But still you believed in Sarah. In your friend Ben. You wanted to believe; you needed to believe. So you lashed out at M'Chelle. She was jealous. You'd suspected all along that's why she hated Sarah, and this was confirmation.

"You're wrong," you told her.

M'Chelle picked at a bead on the pillow. "Look, I know what I saw. I just thought you should know."

"You're lying. You've always been jealous of everyone I've ever liked."

"Alyssa —"

"Get out."

M'Chelle slumped her shoulders.

"Get out!"

"Okay!" She threw the pillow on the bed.

After M'Chelle left, hours later, you were still numb and disbelieving.

You'd been driving Sarah home after school, stopping in the Starbucks lot to let her out. She kissed you. Every day she told you she loved you.

You know you promised not to call her, but... She didn't answer. You wanted to try again but then thought, no. You trust her. She'd tell you the truth if there was anything to tell.

The next day she jabbered all the way to Starbucks, something about this discussion she was having in class about gay marriage, and a guy said it was unnatural and against God's law, and other people were gay bashing, and Sarah wanted so badly to stand up and yell, "*What* do you know? How would you feel if everyone was against you?"

"I couldn't do it," she said. "People kept looking at me, expecting me to say something, and I couldn't. I was scared to death. I thought, if I say one word, I'll just start yelling and crying and lose it in front of everyone. Now I feel like I let down the whole GSA. Every gay and bi person in the world."

"*Are* you seeing Ben?" you asked her outright. Because it was killing you inside.

Her expression was unreadable.

"M'Chelle told me she saw you kissing him."

Sarah blinked once and then went, "*What* if I was?"

A million thoughts collided in your brain. She'd been lying to you. She didn't love you exclusively. You were confused, angry. At her, and at Ben too. How could they betray you?

Sarah said, "He wanted to see what it felt like to kiss a girl. So I let him."

That was all? It sounded plausible, you guessed. Ben had never asked to kiss you. Because—gross. Maybe he felt Sarah was safe to experiment with. Maybe you refused to see what was right in front of your eyes.

"Alyssa." Sarah ran her hand down your arm. "I love you."

"I know." You couldn't doubt her. You loved her. You knew M'Chelle had ulterior motives.

Ben. The jerk. You'd strangle him.

Sarah's watch beeped, and she said, "I have to bust." She grabbed her backpack and scooted out of the car. She kissed her fingertips and blew the kiss to you. You caught it. You pressed it to your heart. You watched her round the building, and then you drove out the exit, the way you always do. But something, a nagging feeling, made you retrace your route.

Sarah trotted along the wrought-iron fence surrounding the Starbucks patio, stopping when a car pulled over. Ben's VW. She got in.

Your heart raced, thrummed in your ears. You thought . . . you don't know what you thought.

They didn't kiss or anything. Of course they didn't. Your imagination was in overdrive.

You called Sarah from your car. You couldn't help yourself. Just answer, Sarah. You needed to hear her voice. But another voice sounded in your head—Dad's—warning you never, ever to talk or text on your cell while driving.

Sarah answered.

"Hi, babe," you said.

"Alyssa—"

"Can I talk to Ben?"

There was a prolonged interval. Ben came on. "Hey. 'Sup?"

You felt ridiculous. Unhinged. You couldn't even think of one thing to say to Ben except "fag."

You expected him to counter with "dyke." The way you banter. He didn't say a word. You swallowed and said, "Let me talk to Sarah."

"It's for you," you heard Ben say.

Sarah came on. "What are you doing?"

"Nothing. I don't know. Why is Ben driving you home?"

Sarah let out a long breath. "Because that's what he does. My mom hasn't asked me once about you since I started bringing Ben home. It's working great. You're the one who gave me the idea, Alyssa. Do you have a problem with it now?"

"No." Yes.

Sarah said, "Is there anything else?"

It's the same question you wanted to ask her. Is there anything else?

You hung up and hated yourself. You despised how jealous and bitter and resentful you felt toward Ben, her "convenient" boyfriend, and Sarah, her mother and your father, yourself. You were the one who was jealous. Of Ben! Your friend. The one person in the world who lived openly without fear, who never had to risk exposure and the consequent fallout from his family. Because they accepted him. They loved him. Ben, who got to love freely, who got to spend the time with Sarah you didn't. You thought all this and more, and you felt so sick with jealous rage, you didn't see the stop sign. The other driver in the intersection screeched his brakes and you swerved to miss him, running up on the curb and smashing into a tree. The impact crunched your hood, releasing your air bag and swallowing you, suffocating you until the only screams you heard were the ones inside your head.

Chapter 16

Carly left clothes in the dryer, so I fold and stack them while my laundry is in the washer. I drag out the box of baby clothes and sit there, taking out each piece and smelling it. A faint odor of baby remains. One little sweater has an *A* embroidered on the front. I wonder if Carly did that, if she knows how to embroider. There's so much I don't know about her.

I refold every garment lovingly. I never wanted kids, but I'm starting to rethink that. A crunching sound from the driveway alerts my senses, and I shove the box back into the closet.

The garage door doesn't open, the way I expect for Carly to drive in and park. She must've forgotten something. The doorbell chimes, and I about jump through the ceiling.

Silence, but I can see a shape through the tempered-glass door panel. I tiptoe upstairs to the first landing, then stealthily make my way to the main level and peer out the front picture window. A guy holding a bowling ball is heading back to his motorcycle. Wait. That's not a guy. Or a bowling ball.

I rush down the stairs and fling open the door. "Finn!"

She's already on the bike, making a wide arc in the driveway. I windmill my arms, and the bike grinds to a halt. She putters back to the entrance.

I step outside. "You got it."

She removes her helmet, beaming. "She's a beauty, isn't she?" She props the motorcycle with the kickstand, or whatever it is, and steps back to admire the bike.

Fireball red. Enormous. It's no scooter or ATV. "Sweet," I say. Then I say what I'm really thinking. "Tell me you're not a dyke."

She pretends not to hear, moving to the other side of the bike, putting space and steel between us.

"What kind is it, again?" I ask.

"Kawasaki Concours. Dual overhead cams. It's a 1998, but it's in pristine condition, and I got a dream deal." She fondles the front bumper. "Gets about two hundred to a tank." She rubs off a smudge. "Want to take a spin?"

"Oh my God. Really?"

"Put shoes on."

I'm barefoot. "I'll be right back. Oh"—I pivot—"you want to come in?"

Finn eyes the house.

"She's not here," I say. I don't know where Carly is. Personal masseusing, I assume.

Finn doesn't make a move, but I leave the door open. Behind me I hear footsteps. Finn whistles.

"Yeah, it's a mansion," I say.

She stands in one place for a moment, soaking in the AC or the panoramic view of the interior.

"There's soda and Vitaminwater in the fridge. Help yourself." I lift the basket of clean clothes. "Oh, wait. You like the hard stuff."

"Shut up," she growls.

I sprint up the stairs to the main level with Finn on my heels. This jittery excitement bubbles in my blood, and I try to suppress it. She just came to show me her bike. How cool. Biker dyke. I smile as I dump the basket of Carly's clothes and mine on my bed, slip on Finn's shoes, and run a brush through my hair.

As I thump down the stairs, I see her standing at the French doors peering up the mountainside. She's cradling her helmet under her arm.

"Not much of a view," I say, opening the fridge for a bottled water. I snag two. "If it was me, I'd have built the deck facing south. This way it feels like the mountain's right on top of you."

"They probably wanted privacy." Finn waves off the water. "I don't do plastic," she says.

That makes me feel guilty, like I'm polluting the planet, so I return both bottles to the refrigerator. "What do you mean 'they'?" I ask.

She meets my eyes and then averts hers. She heads for the front door.

Behind her, I say, "You said 'they.' Do you mean Jason and Carly? Did you know him?"

"Ask Carly," Finn says.

"I did. She kind of lost it."

Finn says, "I'm not surprised."

"Why? Where is he?"

She stops suddenly, and I almost plow into her. "It's not my place, and I don't know all the facts. Ask her."

I'm afraid to even bring up the subject.

Outside, I shut and lock the door. The smell hits me again. "Do you smell smoke?" I ask Finn.

She sniffs the air. "No."

"I swear I smell smoke."

"There's a fire near Georgetown, but that's on the other side of the Continental Divide."

My nose never lies.

Finn opens the cargo bag and pulls out a helmet. She hands it to me. We climb onto the bike, and I clamp onto her waist as we putter down the winding access road. She puts a hand over one of mine and yells, "Hold on," as we hit pavement.

All at once we're flying, and I hold her tight, pressing my front to her back. The world skims away.

I've never ridden on a motorcycle before. The noise is deafening. Every bump and thump in the road rattles my teeth. The wind rips at my knees and shoulders and head, so I burrow into Finn's back. She holds up two fingers, which means absolutely nothing to me.

The engine vibrates, and my butt buzzes. She holds up three fingers, and I brace against her, my helmet to her back, my arms so tight around her middle I can feel every rib.

I shout, "We're going to die!"

Finn leans into a curve on the outskirts of Majestic and we nearly tip over. Then she steers us onto a straightaway and accelerates again. Once her hand covers mine in front, and she taps with a finger. Does that mean hold on or loosen up?

At the stoplight for Summit Boulevard, Finn idles. She twists around and says, "You all right?"

All I can do is grin like an idiot.

The light turns green, and Finn hangs a right, accelerating to, like, Mach 1. Ten or fifteen miles down the road, she turns onto a dirt trail and through a copse of pines. She downshifts. Then again. She maneuvers the bike up a steep bank and onto a narrow path, over washboard ruts in the hard-packed dirt. We ride up and up, over a hill. The trees clear, and we draw up to the mouth of a cave, where Finn cuts the engine.

We both remove our helmets at the same time, and I ask, "Where are we?"

"The old silver mine," Finn says. She gets off the bike and holds out a hand to help me.

Warning signs are posted everywhere: DO NOT ENTER. DANGER. NO TRESPASSING.

Finn starts for the entrance.

"We're not going inside, are we?"

She says over her shoulder, "It's cool. You'll like it." She ducks under a crossed pair of planks, where orange painted letters spell out DO NOT ENTER.

"Finn," I call.

"Alyssa." Her voice echoes in the mine.

I cup my hands around my mouth. "I have to pee."

She calls back. "Pick a tree. Hurry up."

God. I hate going in the woods, especially knowing there are snakes and mountain lions and wasps. I finish in a rush and then duck in under the planks, the way she did. Almost immediately the temperature plunges ten degrees. A hand reaches out to grasp mine. "It narrows pretty fast," Finn says. "Watch your head."

I don't let go, and she tugs me forward. The walls and ceiling close in.

She's right; there's room for only one body, like someone chiseled out the entire route by hand. I have to let loose.

"Keep talking so we don't lose contact," she says.

"This is insane."

"Watch your head here."

A spiderweb tickles my face, and I squeal, flailing my hands across and over my head. A movement catches my eye. "What was that?"

The shape of a hand appears, and I grab it. I latch onto Finn's arm.

"They're just bats," she says.

I scream.

Finn claps a hand over my mouth. "You're scaring them. You're scaring *me*."

I claw her hand away. "I'm not going any farther."

She keeps going.

"Finn!"

"Go back, then." Her voice reverberates.

Damn her.

I hurry to catch up, stumbling and scraping my elbow against a protruding rock. The light is dim and growing dimmer, but I catch up to Finn climbing over a heap of rubble, and I quickly scramble up behind her. Then we're up and over.

On the other side is a clearing with a fire pit.

Hazy light seeps in from somewhere above, a kind of frosted, skylight effect. The clearing is tall enough for us to stand, at least, and I rise slowly. It's like a secret hideaway. And it would be totally cool if there weren't bats glomming onto every ledge.

"I hate bats," I say in a small voice. I'm scared of flying, creeping, crawling creatures of any kind.

"They won't hurt you," Finn says. "They're sleeping. At least, they *were* before they were so rudely interrupted by someone's screaming. You probably woke up the vampire bats, and now they're thirsty." She makes a slurping noise.

"Shut up."

She creeps up behind me and goes, "Boo!"

I jump. "Stop it." I reach out to slap her, but she's gone. She's lowered herself to a log at the fire pit, which is the only place to sit. "Scoot a little," I say.

Even though she makes room for me, our hips and thighs touch. I can't help but feel her body heat sizzling my whole left side. She extends her legs toward the pit.

"How did you find this place?" I ask.

"There are lots of hidden treasures if you know where to look."

I get the feeling she's explored every nook and cranny of this entire area.

"How did you get here from Canada?" I ask.

"You ask too many questions," she says.

"Well, excuse me if I want to know about you."

She swivels her head and meets my eyes. "Why would you want to know about me?"

Is she kidding? She seems serious. "I've just never met anyone like you." My whole life has been lived in a closed environment, like an ant colony. I've never been exposed to anyone outside of school or home or my father's circle of acceptable influences. "You're interesting," I say. "You're mysterious."

She laughs.

"Well, you are." Heat rises up my neck, and I hope she can't see the blood infuse my cheeks.

She picks up a stick from the fire pit and draws in the dirt. The electricity between us is almost visible, and if we don't talk or something soon, I'll just start rambling and she'll find out how boring and stupid I am.

"So, are you in a relationship?" I ask. *Oh, nice. Be blunt, Alyssa.*

She looks at me. "I don't do relationships."

What does that mean? "Ever? You've never been in a relationship?"

"They're messy," she goes. "It's better not to get involved."

"That's the truth," I murmur.

"Tell me about her," Finn says.

I hesitate. "Who?" But I know who. It always comes back to Sarah.

She adds, "You don't have to if you don't want to."

Finn's the only person I've felt remotely close to in so long. This cave, or silver mine, seems like such a private, intimate space, and I need to release all my bitterness, let the memories go. Carly's right. I can't keep it bottled up inside. "She cheated on me with my best friend. I thought he was gay—I thought she was. Hell, I thought we all were. Apparently, he and Sarah didn't define *gay* the same way I did."

Finn stops dragging her stick through the dirt and gives me her full attention. I summarize the events leading up to my being disowned. For some reason, I can't relive the bedroom scene yet.

"Pathetic, huh?" I say.

"It wasn't your fault."

"Then why do I feel like I'm the one responsible, that I didn't see it coming, and they played me like the blind, deaf, and dumb idiot I am?" My eyes well with tears.

Finn says, "You shouldn't. You didn't do anything wrong." She snakes an arm around my waist, and my head falls onto her shoulder. She's right. What did I do wrong? I chose the wrong girlfriend. The wrong best friend. Finn's the first one to say it wasn't my fault. But how can she know?

"You've *never* been in a relationship?"

She lets out a deep breath. "It's just easier to avoid all that crap," she says.

I can see every sinewy muscle down her legs. In comparison, my legs are like flabby chicken flesh. "Haven't you ever fallen in love?" Because, yeah, it would've been easier if I hadn't gotten involved with Sarah. But knowing love? Having been loved? I wouldn't trade that for anything.

I face Finn and see something new in her eyes. Need and desire and want.

She jumps to her feet. "We should get back."

"Wait." I snag her wrist.

Suddenly, she's pulling me up and holding me, her arms around my back, and she's kissing me. There's a magnetic force so strong, I can't break free, or don't want to, and her need pulses through me as the earth quakes under my feet, and I'm losing control—

With all the strength and willpower I can summon, I push away from Finn. "Don't."

She opens her mouth to speak, but nothing comes out. Then she stumbles back and scrabbles up and over the rubble.

"Finn," I call. My voice echoes. "Finn, wait."

She caught me off guard, that's all. Which is partially a lie. Do I want her? Yes. Am I ready? No. I don't know.

I clamber over the rock pile and find my way in the dark, scraping my arms against the jagged edges of the mine's wall as I weave toward the exit. In the open, the bright sunlight bleaches my vision.

Finn is yanking on her helmet. She slings a leg over the motorcycle and guns the engine, tossing me my helmet. I catch it, put it on.

Without warning, she shifts into gear, tears off toward the dirt road, and leaves me behind. I yell after her, "Hey!"

She's going to leave me here.

She's almost out of sight before she makes a wide arc in the pine trees, motors over a mound of rocks, and roars up beside me, idling.

She revs the engine. Again. Louder. Again.

She's scaring me.

She revs until my ears hurt, until I get on, and then she tears out of there at top speed, recklessly heading straight down the mountain. I have to close my eyes and smother the shrieking inside my head because I know we're going to crash and die.

Chapter 17

Finn drops me off at Carly's and leaves in such a hurry, she doesn't even say good-bye. What happened? I hope I didn't hurt her feelings or make her think I didn't like kissing her.

I did. I'm just...why didn't she warn me? Work up to it?

I hate hurting people's feelings. The week before prom, Sarah and I got into a huge argument. I wanted to meet her at prom, go together without actually having to explain to my parents. My whole life has been plotting ways to avoid the inevitable.

Sarah wanted it all: the limo, the date, the meddling mother fussing over her daughter's dress and hair, the proud papa taking photos. She wanted to go with Ben so she'd be seen as a "normal" person.

Everything was so fucked up. I yelled at Sarah, "Why do you always have to make everything so difficult? Bitch."

I'd never called anyone a bitch. I made her cry.

I cried myself sick the night of prom. Then I chopped up my hair—don't ask me why. I stayed in my room all weekend, feeling I'd had a relapse of mono. When Dad saw me for the first time, he got pissed about my hair, and I shouted at him, "Stay out of my life!"

He grabbed my arm and whirled me around. "Don't you *ever* talk to me like that!"

He terrified me.

I apologized meekly.

Tanith said, "Oh, Alyssa, why did you cut off all your beautiful hair?"

Because I hate myself, okay?

I still can't do anything right.

I fill the whirlpool and then slide down to let the jets pulse my back and neck and arms. My arms burn where they got scraped in the mine. The stress of the last few weeks and months has lodged in my bones and muscles.

I don't want to hate Sarah. Or Ben. Or Dad. I don't want to believe I have the ability to hate anyone. I don't know how I feel about Carly. I hate her for abandoning me. I hate her for who she is and what she does for money. But I love her too. She's my mother. She took me in when no one else would, and she's trying to make up for the past. She is trying.

This is nice, letting all my anxiety bubble away. I don't know how long I lie there, just numbing out.

An unfamiliar sound jerks me to awareness.

My iPhone. It's ringing. I stand and slosh out of the whirlpool to retrieve the phone from the dresser. "Hello?"

"Alyssa, are you at the house?" Carly's out of breath.

I'm a shriveled apricot. "Yeah. I'm—"

"Thank God. I broke a heel, and I'm supposed to go on in

five minutes. Do you think you could get my silver stilettos from my closet and bring them to the club?"

"Um . . . sure."

"Come to the back door. I'll have someone meet you." She disconnects.

I dry off and get dressed, and then I go to her room and open the closet. She has at least a dozen pairs of stilettos. Two are silver. I grab both and take off.

A gauzy haze dulls the headlights, almost like fog rolling in off the ocean. It's not fog, though. It's smoke. Thick and acrid. My throat burns.

All the muted lights through town are eerie.

Cars cram the parking area around Wet Willy's, so I circle the perimeter, bouncing over old tire ruts. In back I see Finn's motorcycle propped by the exit door. She's standing under the bug light, drinking a longneck beer as I pull up to the building.

When she sees me, her spine stiffens, and I think she'll dart inside. But she doesn't. She lowers the beer to her side.

"Hey," I say. "Can you smell the smoke now?"

"What smoke?" She coughs.

At least she's joking around. I hand her the stilettos and say, "Looking for these?"

Finn hooks her fingers through the straps, eyeing them like they're alien creatures. Geena rushes out. "Oh, hi, Alyssa." She covers her mouth and coughs. "What's all this smoke? Did the wind shift or something?"

Neither Finn nor I answer because we're gazing into each other's eyes.

Grabbing the stilettos from Finn, Geena says to me, "Thanks, sugar." She hustles inside.

Finn steps back, and I clench her arm. "About what happened in the mine..."

She shakes her head.

"You caught me off guard," I say. "I'm sorry."

She peers over my head into the woods.

"That's a lie. I'm not sorry. I liked it."

Her eyes train on me again. They draw me toward her. The lights inside extinguish, and hooting destroys the moment.

"I better get in there," Finn says.

"Yeah, so you can watch the show."

She expels a sigh.

"You know you love it." I push her shoulder playfully and head back to the car.

As I'm unlocking the door, I glance over my shoulder and see that Finn's still there, watching me. Watching me watching her.

Logo is showing a sexy short film, two girls dancing in a bar, getting it on, and I can't watch without thinking of Finn. The solitude in this house makes me want to tear out what's left of my hair. I go around and amp up every radio and CD and TV until the crescendo of sounds splits my eardrums. It doesn't help. I retrace my route and punch everything off.

I go out onto the deck, where the air is so thick with smoke, I can barely breathe. I don't care. I sit on a sling chair, hugging my knees while the gnats begin a feeding frenzy. Forget this.

I remember my iPhone and head upstairs to get it. Bring it back down. I sprawl on the sofa. Wow, I could download a million apps. Out of habit I press 458, our code for *I love you*. Then 498, *I want you*. 458. 498.

May

A knock sounded on the door, and you freaked. You hadn't shut and locked the front door because it was still light outside. Dad and Tanith had gone to a charity event at his law office and left you with Paulie. Paulie wanted to play Guitar Hero, of course, but you barked at him, "I don't want to play your stupid video games!"

Paulie looked like he was going to cry.

The self-hatred and rage had seeped into all your relationships. "I'm sorry," you told him. "I just don't feel like it."

His shoulders drooped. "You never feel like it anymore."

He was right. Something was changing inside you, hardening, and you didn't like what you were becoming. To redeem yourself, you popped popcorn for him and you, and then you curled up on the couch with a book while Paulie played alone.

Paulie said something that took a minute to register. "What?" you asked.

"Can I ask Ben to come over and play with me?"

You snapped, "No!"

Paulie pouted.

Your cell was in your hand, where it was permanently attached. You'd been texting Sarah, 458. ILU. 498. IWU. Over and over, 458, 498, 458, 498 ...

The doorbell rang, and you got up to answer it. Ben stood there.

Paulie rushed over and flung open the screen. "Hey, Ben. Come play Guitar Hero with me." He grabbed Ben's hand and yanked him inside.

Ben said, "Hey, Alyssa. 'Sup?"

"Nothing." Had Paulie called him anyway? Brat.

Ben said, "We came to see you."

Sarah leaped out of the bushes. "Surprise."

The night exploded with stars. Sarah stepped inside and embraced you. A short hug, since Paulie was there. You'd both been so busy with finals and papers and projects, you and Sarah had barely spoken all week. You'd hardly spoken to Sarah or Ben since prom, three weeks earlier.

"Hi, Paulie," she called to him.

He didn't answer. He was too busy restarting the game and jabbering away at Ben or himself. Ben smiled at you. There was something in his eyes, and Sarah's too. She said, "Where are your parents?"

"Out," you told her.

Her eyes softened to a smoky blue. "Can we go to your room?"

You hesitated, but you felt so needy. So lost without her.

"We'll be back," she called to Ben and Paulie.

Ben said, "Take as much time as you need."

You closed the bedroom door behind Sarah and switched off the light. She switched it back on. She went over to your bed and sat, patting the spot next to her.

"I've been texting you," you said. "I know I'm not supposed to, but I've missed you."

Sarah reached out for your hand and pulled you close. "You're so great." She sat you down, turned your face to hers, and smiled. "So amazing."

You held her hand in your lap and said, "I need you, Sarah." You'd never felt the kind of desperate need you had for her. "I love you more than I've ever loved anyone. I don't know what I'd do if I lost you."

Sarah swallowed. "Oh, baby." Her eyes welled with tears.

You kissed her. Looking back, she may have resisted, but it wouldn't have mattered. You didn't want to see. You took her in your arms and kissed her so urgently she had to feel the want and desire rippling through your body. She kissed you back. She wrapped her arms around you, and you both lay back on the bed.

You lay together kissing, falling so far into each other, you'd never find your way out. You wouldn't want to. God, she could turn you on. Sarah came up for air and whispered, "Remember the first time we made love?"

"In the equipment shed."

She smiled. "It was so fucking freezing."

"I know."

You kissed her eyes, her face. Your hands moved up under her shirt, inside her bra.

"Alyssa."

You pressed your mouth to hers, and time slowed. You wanted to consume her, take all of her inside of you. She responded. You rolled over on top of her, kissing her chin and neck.

You never wasted time. You both removed your shorts and underwear and tanks. You spread her arms out on the bed and pinned her wrists. She smiled, that temptress gleam in her eyes, and you bit her neck. You nibbled down her arm, up her side, over her breast. You knew everything she liked.

She was ready. She was going, "Oh God, yes," and you were into it, your lips and hands moving, fondling her breasts while you licked around her belly button, then lower.

A sudden change in temperature made you stop. Sarah gasped.

Paulie slammed the door. Immediately, it opened again, and Dad was there. His eyes skimmed down Sarah's naked body to your frozen face. You wiped off your mouth.

Sarah was hyperventilating and trying to find her clothes, and you got up off your knees and stood there, paralyzed. You realized you were naked in front of your father. You grabbed something, anything to cover up. The beaded pillow. Too small.

He was yelling about your sickness, your perversion, and how you weren't his creation. Not in his house. Not this. You covered your ears, he was so loud. He stepped back into the hall, and Tanith eased the door closed, saying, "You'd better leave, Sarah."

Carly says, "What are you doing up so late?"

The iPhone is still in my hand, and I'm clenching it to my chest, like the beaded pillow, trying to erase that horrible memory. I've lost track of time.

"Thanks for bringing my shoes."

"Sure." She hasn't removed her stripper makeup or changed out of her red dress and fishnets.

She makes me feel dirty. Because I'm a part of her. "Why do you do it?" I ask. "It's so degrading."

She veers toward the wet bar. "I like it, okay?" She pours herself a glass of wine. "It's harmless amusement. It helps me forget."

"Selling your body is harmless amusement?"

She turns to stare at me. Make that *glare*. "If you have something to say, Alyssa, say it."

I thought I just did. "Stripping's bad enough, but...why do you have to prostitute yourself?"

It's as if she turns to stone. "Who told you that?" Her voice is ice-cold. "Did your father say that?"

"He didn't have to. All this stuff. The house. It must've cost a million dollars. No one makes that kind of money as a stripper. Or a massage therapist and personal trainer." My heart is beating so fast, I think it might break a rib.

Carly's expression is completely blank. I can't read her at all. Finally, she says, "I'm not a whore. And for your information, the house cost four million dollars." She picks up the bottle of wine and heads toward the loft.

Chapter 18

Driving in the dark scares me anyway, but the smoke decreases my visibility to a tunnel of soot. All the way to the Egg Drop, I recite, "Four million, four million, four million." For some reason, the astronomical figure keeps my mind on the road and off what happened next with Sarah. The lights of the Egg Drop-In are a welcome relief. "Good morning," I call to Arlo.

He grunts. I don't see Finn.

I'm still raw from the encounter with Carly. She went straight to bed, as far as I know, and I slipped out early, before she got up.

I slide on a cap and head out front to ready the counter and start the coffee. Before I know it, the restaurant begins to fill.

Dutch comes early to grab his window table. "That fire near Kremmling is spreading fast," he says to me, setting his hat on a chair. "If we don't get rain soon, the whole state's going up in flames." He has deep worry lines on his forehead. He unfolds a newspaper and adds, "In my seventy-eight years, it ain't never been this hot and dry for this long. It's a sign, Alyssa. The planet's in trouble. You young'uns better save it, you hear me?"

"I'll do what I can." Like what? Recycle plastic?

As I head off to put in Dutch's order, I see that Arlo has moved his radio onto the order counter so people can listen to the news. The fire reports are interspersed with talk shows and news of suicide bombings overseas.

I catch sight of Finn unpacking boxes of restaurant supplies, and she smiles briefly. A shock wave zings through me.

Orders fly in faster than I can deliver them. I line up six plates along my arms, and Finn comes up behind me. "You're getting good at that," she says.

I concentrate because if I look at her, my knees will collapse. "Thanks. I learned from the best."

"Who's that?" she asks.

I want to jab her with an elbow, but that would require a free elbow.

The rush zooms by, and as the last customer leaves, I feel almost exuberant. That had to be a world waitressing record.

Finn loads the dishwasher, and Arlo rolls right up to her. "If you're done, get out. Who needs you, anyway?" He rolls away.

"Geez," I say to Finn. She starts the rinse cycle and heads for the exit. I hurry to catch up. "What was that about?"

She turns. "You want to take a ride up to the lake? I need to talk to you."

My stomach twists. Talk to me? I'm back there again, frozen in time.

Sarah texted you first: I CANT SEE U ANYMORE.

You called her, but she didn't pick up. You called and called and called. You texted CALL ME!!!

She didn't.

You texted I'M COMING OVER.

She texted you back: NO. DO NOT COME HERE.

You curled up in bed, texting Sarah until her in-box was full. The house felt like carbon monoxide gas was filling every crack and crevice.

The next morning you waited until you saw Dad drive away before venturing downstairs. Tanith was there, in the kitchen, sitting at the table reading the newspaper.

"Why didn't you tell him?" you asked her. She could've minimized the shock, at least. She'd seen what a coward you were, how intimidated you were by him. If she loved you, she could've softened the blow; dropped hints; laid the groundwork for the moment when Dad discovered the truth.

She met your eyes square on and said, "I didn't feel it was my place."

Or maybe she was as scared of him as you were.

Paulie ambushed you on the porch, like he'd been lying in wait. He went, "Geeeeez."

"Shut up," you said. "Forget what you saw."

"I already know you're gay," he said.

"You don't even know what that means."

"It means you love Sarah."

You looked at him, your little peanut brother. Who was older and wiser than you gave him credit for.

Paulie said, "I was coming up to warn you that Mom and Dad were home. I didn't know I'd find you guys—"

You covered his eyes with your hand. "Erase the vision."

Dad had taken away your car keys when he called you "irresponsible." When he said your little accident doubled his insurance, which he refused to pay, and he wasn't sure you were ready to be a car owner. He always made you feel worse than you already did. Every time you fucked up.

"Did Dad say anything else last night?" you asked Paulie. "Or this morning?"

He answered, "No. He just ate breakfast and left."

Don't ever come back, you prayed. You couldn't believe you were wishing that.

Sarah was at school, but she turned and ran when she saw you. You called her on your cell. You texted her. No answer.

You spotted Ben in passing and caught up with him. "Please, Ben," you begged him. "Tell Sarah I have to talk to her."

Ben looked pissed. He plucked your hand off his arm and disposed of it like lint. "Leave her alone," he said.

You wondered why he was mad at you. "I have to talk to her."

"Apparently she can't handle that." Ben veered into the boys' restroom, and you almost followed him. He turned right around and came out. "Sarah was supposed to break up with you. That's why we came over. To tell you the truth."

It was like the ground buckled beneath you. "What truth?" you said.

Ben folded his arms awkwardly and shifted his feet. Looking off, he said, "Sarah and I have been going out for a while. At first I didn't care about her doing both of us, but then it started to get to me." Ben swallowed hard and met your eyes. "I feel like a jerk. I never meant to, you know, steal your girlfriend."

His words slowly penetrated your skull. This was Ben. Your best friend. "B-but-but," you stammered, "you're gay."

He blew out a puff of air. "Not entirely." His arms dropped to his sides. "I'll go as far as bi, but I ain't no straight white boy." He tossed you an offhand grin. Then he must've caught the fire in your eyes, because he said seriously, "Alyssa —"

You socked him in the face.

"Alyssa?" Finn says.

I snap out of it.

"Close up and I'll wait for you out back."

I nod blankly.

She tells me to follow in the Mercedes and then speeds off on her motorcycle like she's trying to lose me. I stay with her, but the smoke is so thick, I have to use my headlights in broad daylight.

We pass Carly's mailbox and the access road. This isn't the way to Caribou Lake, or at least not the way we went before.

Finn's taillights remind me of bouncing buoys in the ocean fog. Her blinker goes on, and I take a right where she turns off Highway 102 onto a side road. Finn stops, and I pull up beside her. I lower the window.

"I need to let Boner out first. The road is narrow and rocky all the way up to the cabin. Put it in four-wheel drive and stay in the lowest gear."

Four-wheel drive. I see a button labeled 4WD and push it.

She's not kidding about the road. It's barely passable, with the huge boulders and rough terrain. Plus the road is practically straight up Caribou Mountain.

A jagged rock splits through the smoke, and I steer sharply to miss it. My left front wheel lifts, dangerously tilting the car until I'm afraid I'll tip over sideways. The ledge drops off, and I crunch to solid ground.

Ahead, I see a fuzzy shape—the cabin? Finn's bike is parked at the door, and I pull in behind it.

I get out, my knees shaking. "You drive that every day?"

She removes her helmet and smears the sweat and ash from her face. I'm not sure she heard me over Boner's barking inside. "Wait here." She opens the door, and Boner barrels out. He races around Finn's legs, wiggling his butt, and then lifts a leg on her bike.

"No!" She scoops him up. "Bad dog." She sets him by a tree, where he finishes his business.

There are three small cabins that I can make out through the smoke. "What is this place?" I ask Finn. It looks like a campground.

"It's a hostel in the winter," Finn says. "Not many people here in the summer. Let me just change my shirt, and I'll be right back."

"Can I use your bathroom?" Because all that jostling liquefied everything inside me.

Finn stalls.

"What? Are you going to make me use Boner's tree?"

She steps inside, leaving the door open for me. "Sorry it's so messy." She picks up clothes and junk on her way through. Boner's chewed a chunk of sofa, and there's stuffing hanging out. "Dumb dog," Finn mutters again. "The bathroom's that way." She points.

The metal sink is an antique, and so's the toilet. It takes me a minute to figure out how to flush—with a chain pull—and the water pressure is low, so I have to pull it twice.

When I come out, Finn's changed from her Egg Drop tee into a muscle shirt with a sports bra. She's opening a can of dog food for Boner, who's jumping and pawing her leg. I check out Finn's digs. A living room area with a plaid sofa (chewed-up corner), a fireplace, a faux furry rug. The kitchen is tiny. There's a pint-size fridge and a gas stove.

"This place is cool," I tell Finn. I mean it. It reminds me of the GSA campout, held each fall. Another thing I'll never get to do again.

Through the open bedroom door, I spy a mattress on the floor. Finn's Egg Drop tee is flung on top. There's no sign of another person, but I ask anyway. "Do you live here alone?"

"No."

I knew it. She was too good to be true.

"I have a dog."

I curl a lip at her. She opens the door, and a gust of hot wind blows smoke and dirt through the room. Boner whines.

"We don't have to go to the lake," I say. "We could hang out here."

Finn eyes me over her shoulder.

"I promise to keep my lips to myself," I say.

Does she crack a smile?

She closes the door.

"Don't you have to work at the Emporium?" I ask.

"I quit," she says.

"Why?"

She leans against the counter, clutching the edge. "I'm leaving," she says. "I gave Arlo my two weeks' notice."

Already? I'm stunned. "What about my money?"

Her eyes sweep the floor. "I'll mail it to you. I promise. I just need to get out of here."

Boner's licked his bowl clean and tipped it over, and now he's shoving it toward us with his snout. We both lean down at the same time to get it, and our hands touch. It ignites every nerve ending in my body. Finn slides the dog bowl out from under my hand and takes it into the kitchen.

"If it's because of me . . ." I say.

"It's not. It's just what I do."

"Run away? Bail on your friends?"

She turns and meets my eyes. "Drift. I'm a drifter."

Unbelievable. I'm mad. Hurt. Everyone I need in my life leaves me. "Where are you going?" I ask. The thought forms in my brain that I'll go with her.

"I don't know. Does it matter?"

It does to me. "I need to know where my money will be coming from."

"I told you I'd pay you back, and I will."

She doesn't have to chastise me like I'm a three-year-old. "I know. I trust you." I say it, but I'm not the best judge of character, and now the only person I feel any connection to here is leaving.

She opens a cupboard and says, "I don't have much to eat."

She holds a box of vanilla wafers. "I don't know how old these are, but mold is a natural digestive aid."

I click my tongue. "Is that true?"

Her eyes gleam. What will I do when she's gone? Die of loneliness. She passes me as she heads for the couch, and I go to sit next to her, but Boner beats me to it. Finn hands me the box of cookies, and I take it. The seal hasn't been broken, so I figure there aren't any mice or spiders in it. Just to be sure, I peer into the box before sticking my hand inside.

The cookies are still crunchy. At home—I mean, in Virginia—they'd be soggy after a day. "Is your family still in Canada?" I ask, passing the box to her.

She takes a handful of vanilla wafers and tosses one into her mouth. She feeds one to Boner, who gobbles it down. "I don't have any family."

"How can you not have family? Where are your parents?"

"I never knew my father," Finn says. "My mother was institutionalized when I was little, and I was chucked off to the foster system. I aged out at eighteen." She passes the cookies back to me.

God. "Then what?"

"Then I left."

Boner whines, so I give him a cookie. "Are you taking Boner with you?" I ask.

"On the bike? I don't think so." She scratches his head. "I'll find him a home." She looks up at me. "Can you take him?"

He lays his head in Finn's lap and gazes up at her with mournful eyes.

"I don't know how Carly would feel about a dog." Especially one that eats furniture. Now may not be the optimal time to ask Carly for any more favors.

Finn pets Boner and feeds him a cookie.

"Won't you miss him?" I ask. I want to add, *Won't you miss me?*

The silence between us lengthens. Wind whistles down the chimney, swirling in the firebox. Finally Finn says, "Did Carly tell you about Jason?"

"After I accused her of being a prostitute, it didn't seem like a good time to ask."

"You did *what?*" Finn's eyes bulge.

I recount the conversation Carly and I had last night.

"Holy..." Finn begins.

"Well, what was I supposed to think? Where is she getting all that money?"

Finn closes the lid on the cookies without answering. She gets up and walks to the kitchen with the box and with Boner on her heels.

"Does she really work as a massage therapist and personal trainer?" I ask.

Finn answers, "Yeah. According to Geena, she has a high-class clientele."

"Enough to pay for a four-million-dollar home?"

Finn twists her head and arches her eyebrows. "Is that what it cost?" She replaces the cookies in the cupboard, and Boner whines. "I don't think her jobs paid for the house."

"Then who did? Oh, let me guess. The mysterious Jason."

Finn fills two canning jars with water and brings them back. She hands me one and goes over to stand by the fireplace.

"Ask her," Finn says.

"I can't!" I cry. "She won't tell me. Why can't you tell me? I know you know more than you're letting on."

Finn sighs before taking a sip of water. "Carly was married to Jason, and they had a little girl, Angelica."

"What?" My heart seizes. "When?"

"Two, three years ago. I don't know exactly. Like I said, I wasn't here. All I've heard are the gossip and rumors, what people say happened."

"What do they say?"

Finn takes a long gulp of water. "Are you sure you want to know this?" She sets her glass on the mantel. "None of it has anything to do with you, and if Carly hasn't told you, maybe she doesn't want you to know."

"It *does* have something to do with me. If I have a sister." It has *everything* to do with me.

Finn lets out a long, slow breath.

"Just tell me the truth," I say. "Someone, please, just tell me the truth for once." My eyes pool with tears.

Finn comes over and sits by me, not close enough to touch, but I feel her heat. "They built that house together. Carly and Jason. He was a doctor. They had a kid together."

"Angelica," I whisper her name. I have a sister.

"She was two," Finn says, "when it happened."

"What happened?"

Finn turns to me. "I'm not the one who should be telling you this, Alyssa. You need to get the whole story from Carly."

I set the water jar on the floor and leap to my feet. As I fling open the front door, I hear Finn call, "Alyssa." The roaring in my ears drowns her out. I want to get home now, as soon as possible, because I have to know. I *need* to know the whole story.

Chapter 19

Carly's bedroom door is closed. I knock but get no response. I ease the door open. "Carly?"

She isn't here. She's been here, though. Clothes from the closets and drawers are heaped on the bed, like she tried on everything and rejected it. Weird that she'd leave a mess like this. She's anal about neatness.

Smoke blows through her open window, the blue-and-white striped canvas curtains flapping like sails. There's a thin layer of yellow ash on her nightstand.

The bed's unmade. King-size mattress, both sides of the sheets crumpled and twisted. She's a restless sleeper. I know that. I hear her rattling around at two or three AM, when she gets home from work. It takes her an hour to unwind or get drunk. The wineglass on her nightstand is empty, and so's the bottle.

She dances to forget. Forget Jason? Angelica? Me?

There's no evidence of a husband and child in this entire house. I've been over every inch—

The baby clothes.

A for *Angelica*. Not *Alyssa*.

I sink to her bed. Three years ago she got married and had a child. Around the same time she forgot I was alive. I was replaced.

I double over, clutching my stomach.

I should go; leave this house. She doesn't want me in her life. She never did, not really. There's nothing of me here. Not a picture, not a memento. There's nothing of Jason either, and Angelica is reduced to a hidden box of baby clothes.

I wonder if she meant to throw out the box and forgot. Or couldn't bring herself to do it. She managed to get rid of everything that reminded her of me.

Can you just obliterate people from your life? I know I'd like to—Sarah, Ben—but it's impossible to erase memories that cut so deep.

The top drawer of Carly's dresser is open, exposing different colored bras. Ugh, what an invasion of privacy to paw through her lingerie. What the hell? It's never stopped me before. Nothing but women's underwear. The second drawer is shirts and shorts. Why am I doing this? I don't even know what I'm looking for. Some memory of me. Anything. As I feel around inside the bottom drawer, my hand hits a hard object, and I grab it.

A digital camera.

I've seen this camera. She used it when she came to visit. She'd stop people on the boardwalk and ask them to take our picture. I sit on the floor and press the camera on. Check the memory—empty. If you have a digital camera, though, you upload the pictures. I jump to my feet and dash down to her laptop.

I look in MY DOCUMENTS, MY PICTURES. Bingo. The folders are labeled by year, the first one three years ago. Nothing before that. Wow, she was thorough in wiping me off the face of the map.

I thumbnail the images, enlarge the first one. A desolate landscape on a mountain. Caribou Mountain? The next picture is a bulldozer.

A series of pictures of the house being built. The construction crew. Boring. The framing going up. A cute guy with a hammer. Is that Jason? I fast-forward through the rest of the folder, but he doesn't appear again.

In the next folder, the living room's been painted and carpeted. Furniture arranged. The leather chair by the fireplace. A guy in the chair. Is that Jason? He's in shadow. The next picture is a close-up. If that's Jason, he's hot. He has short, curly hair and rimless glasses. He looks intent, like he doesn't know his picture is being snapped. He's reading or studying.

The next one shows him again, next to the Mercedes SUV. He has his arms folded and his ankles crossed, like he's posing for a clothing ad.

The next picture is the two of them together on a boat. More like a yacht in some tropical paradise. There aren't any palm trees or giant ferns in the Rocky Mountains. Carly has on a bikini, and her hair is longer and blonder. Both she and Jason are toasting whoever's taking the picture. In the next one, their arms are linked, and they're drinking from champagne flutes.

Jason's built. Tall and buff. Gorgeous guy, if you notice that kind of thing. In another picture he has on jeans and a V-neck sweater. Yeah, he's hot.

Rich, too, apparently.

The next picture is Geena, in a bikini. She's with Carly, sunbathing on the deck. In every picture of Carly, her face seems brighter. More youthful. She looks happy.

In the next folder, there's a series of close-ups of Jason. He has striking blue eyes. Then a full-length picture of Carly. My pulse races. She's pregnant. I punch through a series in which she gets bigger and bigger. She's wearing the kimono. She's out on the deck showing her belly. She, or Jason, wrote in Magic Marker on her belly bulge: BABY, with an arrow.

Then, at the hospital? The baby's been born. Carly has her wrapped in a receiving blanket and is gazing down on her with such joy and tenderness in her eyes. My throat constricts. Did she ever feel that kind of love for me? Dad doesn't have one picture of me as a baby, or the three of us together as a family.

Angelica is a curly-haired blond baby. I have straight dirty-blond hair.

The door opens downstairs, and I slam the cover closed on the laptop.

"I'm sorry," I tell Carly. "I never should've assumed..." God, how to redeem myself. "I know about Jason and Angelica."

Carly removes a bottle of wine from the cooler and reaches up for a glass. "You know what?"

She's speaking to me, at least. "I know you were married. You had another baby." I want to ask, *Is that why you forgot about me?* But I don't. I want to know about my sister. Half sister.

Carly pours her drink. "It seems a lifetime ago."

"Where are they?" I ask. "Will I get to meet them?"

Carly looks at me, and her eyes go glassy. She takes a long, slow drink. "Not now, Alyssa. I'm very, very tired." She picks up her glass and the bottle.

"You could've told me, at least, that I have a sister."

"Not now!"

"*When?*" I shout.

She ascends the stairs, walks into her room, and shuts the door.

The sky through the skylights is a sickly orange color. The same way I feel. I storm into the formal living room just to irk her and curl up in the big leather chair. Everyone leaves. Is that what happened, Carly? Jason dumped you and took Angelica with him? Déjà vu. What goes around comes around, Carly.

I'm suddenly awakened by this sense of danger. Carly's looming over me. Where am I? I fell asleep in the leather chair. "Stay the fuck out of my room," she says. "And this living room is off-limits. Get out and stay out."

I shrivel in place.

"My life is *mine*, Alyssa." She smacks her chest. "Mine." Her eyes film over. She wobbles on her stilettos as she weaves down the stairs and exits through the front door.

She's drunk.

Did I put the camera back? Shit. I should be branded: CAUGHT IN THE ACT.

I want to finish the pictures and see more of the little girl, my half sister, but now I feel guilty. Carly's right. Her life is hers. I have no place in it and never will.

What time is it? The clock on the mantel has stopped. On my way to the kitchen, I automatically switch on the TV. The microwave clock reads 10:28. In my peripheral vision, I see BREAKING NEWS scroll across the TV screen, and a reporter comes on. I sit and amp up the volume. "The Eagles Nest fire has consumed approximately six hundred acres in the White River National Forest, and firefighters are setting firebreaks near Heeney to protect homes and livestock. So far no structures are in the direct line of fire, though the winds, as we know, can shift at any time."

I listen to a report from the meteorologist. A map zooms in with fifteen fires indicated in the mountains. I'm not familiar with this area, or the geography, but I see that Dillon Reservoir is marked, and I know we're not far from there.

"We're keeping an eye on two weather systems. One is currently centered over Oregon, and the other is off the coast of Southern California. In the next twenty-four to forty-eight hours, either or both could bring in some much-needed rain for the western slope and high country. We'll keep you posted on all the fire activity throughout the night and early morning."

It's ominous. The magnitude of destruction. The color of the sky.

The breaking-news ticker rolling across the screen reads EAGLES NEST FIRE 2% CONTAINED. STRONG WINDS EARLIER TODAY HAVE SPREAD THE FIRE TO MORE THAN 15,000 ACRES.

Wind howls through the loft, and Carly's bedroom door flies open. My heart jumps out of my chest.

I go upstairs and stand outside Carly's room. She left her window wide-open, or it blew open, and the curtains are flapping. I know what she said, but I go in to shut and lock the window. I yank the drapes closed and turn. Carly's emptied the entire contents of her dresser onto the floor and bed, like she went on a rampage. For some reason, I feel responsible. I start picking up clothes, folding and replacing them in drawers.

She'll know I was in here. I find her sticky notes and write in my tiniest scrawl:

> YOUR WINDOW BLEW OPEN, SO I CAME IN TO SHUT IT. I CLEANED UP YOUR ROOM. I HOPE YOU DON'T MIND. I DIDN'T GO THROUGH YOUR PERSONAL THINGS AGAIN. I'M SORRY.

I shut her door and stick the note where she'll see it.

Lying in bed, I listen to the howling wind and smell the smoke. I'm afraid to be here alone. I wish I could call someone.

Dad.

Yeah, right.

I get up and find my phone. I call M'Chelle. Her cell rings and rings. Before her voice mail picks up, I disconnect.

Sarah. If I could just call and talk to her—

No.

I go back down to the computer and slideshow through the last set of pictures. Angelica standing all by herself. Angelica smiling with her birthday cake. One candle. Angelica wearing the little sweater with the *A*.

I don't know how many hours elapse while I'm paging through the pictures. Over and over. My eyes ache. I want to close them and sleep forever, but my gaze drifts down to the clock on the monitor: 4:46.

I'm going to be late for work.

No time to shower, and I still have on my work clothes from yesterday. I can hardly see through the dirt, mixed with smoke, that's blowing across the access road. Even with my brights on, I'm driving blind. By the time I park behind the Egg Drop, my nerves are shot.

Flying dirt and debris sting my bare arms and legs as I hurry inside. The radio's blaring. Finn's chopping onions and green peppers. The sight of another human being makes me so happy that I rush over and fling my arms around her.

She stops chopping.

"Don't go," I say softly. Please don't leave me.

Finn's head rests on mine, and I feel her relax in my arms. "Alyssa," she says.

"Finn."

"A tree fell on Arlo's van, and he's stuck at Safeway." She twists gently out of my grasp.

"Is he okay?"

"*He* is. His van's not. We're on our own today. Can you cook?"

"No," I tell her. Tanith does—did—all the cooking at home. "I mean, I could try."

"I don't want you getting burned. That grill gets hot. You wait tables, and I'll man the grill."

I elbow her. "You mean *woman*."

She quirks a smile at me, and my stomach flips.

The reporter on the radio says, "The Keystone fire, fanned by winds, is spreading east toward Silver Plume and Georgetown. That fire is approximately fifteen percent contained. At Eisenhower Tunnel, we've received reports of wind gusts in excess of eighty-five miles per hour. A new fire has sprung up near Kremmling."

Finn goes, "That's close."

A guy hollers from the dining room, "Is anyone working here today?" I recognize the voice. Rufus.

I grab my order pad and head out. The tables are filling fast, and none of the orders have been taken. I yell, "Hey!" Then louder, "*Hey! Everyone!*"

People quiet down.

"Arlo's not here today," I tell them, "so Finn's cooking, and you're all stuck with me as your waitress. I'll get to everyone eventually, but have mercy, okay? If you triple-tip, I'll put you in my will."

People laugh.

Barbara pushes up from her chair and says, "You want me to work the counter? I've waitressed before."

"That'd be awesome!"

I take orders from two four tops and run them in so Finn can get started cooking. I hear the reporter on the radio again. "We have breaking news out of Georgetown. A crew of firefighters was overrun this morning as the Keystone fire exploded out of control. Four people have been airlifted to St. Anthony's."

Someone calls, "Turn it up, Finn."

I stick the orders on the spinner and ask her, "Should we be worried?"

"I'm sure they'll evacuate in time," she answers.

The front bell tinkles, and a blast of dirt blows in with customers. Behind them, I see an aluminum lawn chair tumbling across the street, taking a hop onto the plank sidewalk, and heading straight for our plateglass window. "Look out!" I cry.

Everyone cowers.

The chair hits with a *clunk* and bounces off. People near the windows get up and move.

Every person in the Egg Drop is talking about the fires. A couple of the hospital crew are heading out to volunteer their services. As I race back and forth, I catch snatches of conversation. "The dead lodgepole pines are pure tinder." "Firefighters are spread thin." "More fires south in the Sawatch and the Sangre de Cristos." "Trapped livestock in Heeney." I notice Dutch isn't here today.

The only natural disasters I've ever come close to are hurricanes along the East Coast. Virginia Beach has been spared, for the most part.

Finn says, "Is this grits or gravy?" She squints at my order.

"I don't know." I can't read my own writing.

She says, "I'll just put both on the side."

I load up my arms with multiple plates and deliver all the food hot. It's a miracle.

A lot of people leave early with gobs of food left on their plates, and I don't want to tell Finn, although she probably knows she's not the cook Arlo is. The dining room clears except for a few people at the counter. Barbara hands me a coffee cup stuffed with cash. "Tips," she says.

"You keep them."

She smiles and shoves the cup my way. "You know, the first time I saw your mom was in here. In fact, I think this is where she met Jason."

"Do you know him?" I ask.

Barbara's expression grows serious. "I did. Angelica too. She was a darling."

I set my bus tub on the counter. "Where are they? Carly won't tell me. Where did they go?"

Barbara's eyes change. She palms the back of my skull and kisses the top of my head. Then she shoulders her carryall and hurries out the door.

Why won't anyone tell me anything?

I lock the front door and flip the sign to CLOSED. In the kitchen, Finn's a blur of motion, stacking plates and clanging silverware in the sink and hauling armloads of produce to the fridge. I finish busing all the tables and then collapse—literally—on the floor by the dishwasher. My tongue lolls out the side of my mouth as rigor mortis sets in.

Finn hovers over me. She slides down the side of the

dishwasher to her butt and clunks her head against the stainless steel. "Code blue," she says. "Call 911."

It's quiet except for the wind. At some point Finn turned off the radio. "I have a death wish for whoever got me this job," I say.

Finn nudges me with her foot.

I lift my arms in the air, but the pull of gravity is too fierce, and they fall back to the floor. My head rolls to the side, onto Finn's shoulder. "Something bad happened to Jason and Angelica, didn't it?"

She doesn't answer.

"Are they...dead?" I ask. I shift to sit so I can face her, and she holds my eyes for a long moment before nodding.

"How? When?"

"Alyssa—"

"Tell me!" I bark at her.

"I can't!" she barks back. "I don't know all the details." She scrambles to stand, and I clamp a hand around her ankle.

"Tell me what you *do* know."

She offers a hand to help me up. "It was an accident," she says. "A hit-and-run. I don't know where or when. You'll have to ask someone who was here then."

Oh my God. "Thank you for telling me." At least there's one person in this life I can trust. "Please, Finn," I say. "Do you really have to leave? I want you to stay." I want it so bad I can taste it.

Her soft brown eyes melt into me, and this overarching desire to love and be loved again swells every pore, and I slide my arms around her waist and kiss her.

She doesn't resist. In fact, she draws me closer and kisses me so deeply I lose myself in her, in the moment, oblivious to the raging storm around us. Finn suddenly jerks away, and I open my eyes to see what startled her. Arlo rolls past us, going, "Don't let me interrupt."

Chapter 20

Finn and I stand there, dazed. She ducks her head, grabbing a wet towel to go out and swab the counter. Leaving me with Arlo.

"Who moved my radio?" he asks. "Where the hell is my radio?"

I hurry over and retrieve the radio from the shelf above the grill. Arlo snatches it from me and turns it on. "There's a fire at Caribou Lake," he says. "Some stupid kids were setting off firecrackers. It's already spread into the Estates."

"What?" I say. Oh my God. I go to find my phone in my bag and realize I don't have it with me.

"Is Carly at home?" Arlo asks.

"I don't know. She might be by now."

He rolls to the phone on the wall and punches in numbers. "Carly?" he says. "Do you know about the fire up there?" She is home, probably hungover.

He listens. He says, "You get your ass out of there right this minute or I'll—" She must disconnect, because Arlo slams down the phone.

"You." He points at Finn, who's returning to the kitchen through the swinging doors. "And you too." He aims his finger at me. "You're done for the day. Get out of here, and get Carly down off Caribou Mountain."

As we're logging our hours, Arlo adds, "And don't ever let me see anything like that again. My heart's too weak."

The thick cloud of smoke billowing off Caribou Mountain is visible at the edge of town. A huge airplane roars low overhead, and I hunch over, like it's going to hit me. I turn on the radio but can't find a local news station. The sight of Carly's mailbox is a relief. Finn follows me on her bike all the way up, and we park in the driveway. Everything looks fine.

I get out and Finn idles. She pulls off her helmet. Carly flings open the front door and surges out. She says, "Where have you been? I've been calling your cell all morning." She looks and sounds pissed.

"I don't have it with me."

Her eyes pan to Finn. "So, you bought your motorcycle. I wonder where you got the money."

Finn looks at me and then back at Carly. The way Finn jams on her helmet and revs the engine lets me know she's figured out I lied to her.

"Wait." I lurch for the handle grip. "Don't go."

She stalls for a long minute before raising the visor. "They'll do a reverse 911 if you need to evacuate."

"What's that?" I ask.

Carly returns inside.

"You'll get a call telling you to get out."

My grip on the bike tightens. "Take me home with you."

She lowers the visor and backs off, speeds away.

Damn.

When I get inside, Carly's on the phone in the dining room. "Uh-huh," she says. "Thanks, Mitchell. Love you too." She hangs up. "They have the Caribou fire under control. Unless the wind whips up again, we should be safe. What's going on with you and Finn?"

My face flares. "None of your business," I say. Did Arlo snitch on us? "I know about the hit-and-run," I tell her.

"Then drop the subject," Carly says. "And stay away from Finn."

My first reaction is, *Don't tell me what to do.*

Carly adds, "I know her type."

"What do you mean by that?"

Without answering the question, Carly says, "Pack up everything you brought, in case we have to evacuate." She bounds up the stairs, her cell attached to her ear.

Dad's wise words ring in my ears: "If people would stop and consider the consequences...How stupid can you be?" We were watching the news, and there was a report about a judge who'd gotten his hand caught in the cookie jar. That's how Dad put it. The judge was identified by a high-priced call girl as one of her regular clients. I guess Dad knew the judge. He said to me, "Don't ever be that stupid, Alyssa. I can stand anything but stupidity."

When I wrecked the Civic, Dad said to me, "How could you be so stupid?"

I wanted to tell him you don't always know the consequences beforehand. Or you do, but you don't think about it at the time. I wanted to tell him you can't live your life scared of every action you take. Sometimes, Dad, what's in the cookie jar is worth the risk.

I shove everything in my backpack and then lie on the bed, listening to my music. I wonder how long Carly and Jason lived together before the accident. As long as Carly and Dad? Her life with Jason was different, that was for sure. Dad and I lived with Grandma and Grandpa while Dad was in college. Carly must've lived there, too, for a while. Then Dad went to law school and got a job in Virginia Beach, and we moved to the house we have now. I shouldn't say *we*. I need to stop thinking of it as my house.

It'll never be mine. Nothing's mine. Even this house is Carly's and Jason's and Angelica's.

She has no right to tell me who I can and can't see. She's never been my mother, and she isn't now.

I find my iPhone under my pillow and listen to Carly's voice mails. "Where are you? Call me." She called three more times. That's hardly "all morning."

I add Carly's name and number to my contacts. I add home. Not my home anymore, but Paulie's if I ever want to talk to him. Which I do, and will.

I love Paulie. He's my brother. We will stay in touch.

If Angelica were still alive...

A hit-and-run. Carly must've been devastated. I know I

would've been. All she has left, besides a box of baby things, is this house, which is probably a constant reminder, which is probably why she doesn't spend much time here.

I've been pressing numbers on my phone unconsciously. It rings on the other end, and Sarah answers. "Hello?"

My heart stops. "Hello?" she says insistently. I immediately disconnect. It's . . . it's just so automatic.

I can't have a phone. I can't handle a phone.

End of May

You called and called. You texted her. You IM'd, even though she asked you not to IM, because her mom always monitored her online activities. She either removed you from her buddy list or blocked you.

You asked Tanith if you could borrow her car. "It's an emergency," you said. You're not even sure why she let you, since your driving record wasn't exactly stellar. You drove by Sarah's house for an hour, maybe two. It was growing dark, and you drove past her house again and again, calling on your cell and texting. You knew the dangers of driving and texting, the consequences. But it didn't matter. The only thing that mattered was getting in touch with Sarah.

You parked at the curb to text her again, when Ben's VW rounded the cul-de-sac. Ben and Sarah got out. They walked to the door holding hands, and then Ben kissed her. Sarah kissed him back. No, *you thought.* This can't be real.

The front door opened, and Sarah's mom appeared. She said something to Ben, and the three of them laughed. Sarah kissed Ben right in front of her mother, and then she disappeared inside. Ben zoomed away.

You called Sarah. No answer. You called again. You threw the phone on the seat of the car and stormed up to her front door. You rang the doorbell; you fisted the door. Her mother answered. "What are you doing here?"

"I need to see Sarah."

"She's not home," her mother said.

Liar. You saw Sarah inside. She slipped around the corner in the hall.

"Sarah!" You trampled her mother to get in. You had hold of Sarah's arm, and she was struggling, but you just wanted to talk to her. She screamed and tried to fight you off, and then her mother was on you and someone else too. Her brother? They dragged you out of the house.

The door slammed. You rang the bell.

"Go away," Sarah's mom shouted.

You rang and rang and rang.

You stood there ringing the bell and calling Sarah's name until the cops came.

The rest is a blur. Except the part where Tanith had to bring you home because your father wouldn't even come and get you at the police station.

I have no control over myself; not then, not now. Even though I knew it was over, I just needed to hear the words from her own lips. Is that so much to ask?

My phone rings, jolting me to the present. I fumble around with it in my hand. What if it's Sarah, checking to see who called her? Or Sarah's mom?

The ID reads CARLY. "Hello?" I answer.

"I'm sorry," she says. Her words slur. "I din mean to yell a' you."

Where is she? When did she leave? There's music and laughter in the background.

"That's okay. I'm sorry I went through your stuff. I'm sorry I called you a—"

She starts crying, and I feel like crap. Geena comes on. "Arlo, is that you?"

"No. It's Alyssa."

"Alyssa. Sugar. Listen, Carly's a wreck, so I'm going to take her home with me tonight. Are you okay up there alone?"

"Yeah." Not really. I hate it here alone.

"I don't know what set her off," Geena says. "But when she gets like this, it's best to let her work through it. I'm sure she'll feel better tomorrow. She'll call you then." Geena hangs up.

I know what set her off. Me.

Good job, Alyssa.

I go to the kitchen and stand at the French doors, gazing at my reflection. I look like a ghost. I am a ghost to Carly. She must see me as her past coming back to haunt her.

I wonder if Carly and Dad too see me as the consequence of their stupidity.

I trudge upstairs and flop on the bed. Shadows of fire-breathing dragons dance on the walls and ceiling, and I sense the fire all around me, engulfing me, burning me alive. I wonder, if I die, will anybody care?

Chapter 21

I'll care. I refuse to let self-pity rule my life. I switch on all the lights—from my room to the kitchen, dining room, living room, laundry room, and exercise room—to make it feel less eerie, more inhabited. I turn on the TV. No breaking news. I wish I knew Finn's number. Does she even have a phone? What time is it? Midnight? One? She's probably working at the club.

I'm not going there. I won't chase her. I *won't* stalk her.

Carly's computer beckons, and I switch it on. The websites for the Denver news stations are all about the fires, but I don't see Caribou mentioned. The Internet is distracting, at least. As I'm surfing online, checking MySpace and Facebook, I don't feel so alone in the world.

A sound overhead draws my attention. A flurry outside the window. I glance up at the skylight and see drops of water. Is that...rain? I run up to the kitchen and open the French doors. It's raining!

I step out onto the deck and breathe in the smell. Wet dirt

and smothered ash. Mother Nature to the rescue. Leaving the French doors ajar, I dash down to the entrance and fling open the front door. The rain beats on the gravel drive, kicking up dust and dirt. I step out and raise my face to the sky. Cold, glorious rain.

It feels like I've been in a coma for months, and when my alarm *bleeps*, all my senses are reawakened. At four AM it's still dark outside, and the rain is pounding outside my window, and I've never heard a sweeter sound.

I take a shower and get dressed. Carly's door is closed, and I have the strongest urge to go wake her up, take her hand, and fly downstairs to dance in the rain together. Then I remember she stayed with Geena.

Stupid idea, anyway.

As I back out of the garage, rain pummels the Mercedes so hard, I think it's going to dent the metal. It takes me a minute to locate the windshield wipers. Even on the fastest wiper speed, my view is distorted. The headlights barely illuminate the access road. It's a solid wall of water. I downshift to the lowest gear and inch my way along, glad to meet up with the highway.

I drive slowly, carefully. When I get out of the car at the Egg Drop, my foot splashes into a puddle. Shit. I can't believe I'm still wearing Finn's shoes. Soaked now. Why haven't I gone to buy shoes for myself? Because I wanted to keep a piece of her close? That sounds like Psych 101. I'll go today. I should've worn my boots, anyway, with all this mud.

Arlo's van is here, the hood crushed like a soda can. I don't see Finn's motorcycle. She'll have a rough ride down Caribou Mountain on those slick rocks, if she even tries. There's nothing between us. Nothing. She's leaving, and she doesn't want a relationship.

Arlo's chopping onions, swiping tears off his cheeks.

"Good morning," I say.

"What's good about it?" He rolls past me with a container of chopped onions on his lap.

"It's raining," I reply.

He says, "You think?" He sets the onions on the counter and returns for the peppers. "Where's the traitor?"

Is that how he thinks of Finn?

She can quit if she wants. It's her life.

Finn blows in, bundled in an orange slicker. As she unties the hood and yanks it back, our eyes meet. "Wet," she says.

"Extremely." I can't suppress a smile.

Arlo rolls by, retrieves a carton of eggs from the fridge, and says to Finn, "Why don't you just go now? I'll cut you a check, and you're on your way."

"I'll go when my time's up," Finn tells him.

He looks from her to me, and I know what he's thinking. I also don't care. I'm out now, and so is she.

Finn says, "I'll get the coffee started."

"I'll help." I follow her.

Two boxes of doughnuts are stacked on the counter, and I start unloading them. "If it's still raining when we get off, I'll give you a lift home. Do you have a phone? Let's exchange numbers in case you need to call me."

Arlo yells, "Is this the pancake batter you mixed yesterday?

Who made this soupy shit? And why are there still order tickets on the spindle?"

Finn gives him the finger, which he can't see.

"He loves you," I tell her. "He just doesn't know how to express it with a Hallmark card."

She snorts.

Without thinking, I encircle her braid and run my hand down it.

I see the goose bumps rise on her skin.

Arlo cranks up his radio to earsplitting volume. "We interrupt this broadcast for a bulletin from the National Weather Service."

We both turn to listen.

"A flood watch has been issued for Eagle, Pitkin, Summit, and Park counties, including the towns of Heeney, Silverthorne, Dillon, Frisco, and Breckenridge and homes and businesses along the Blue River."

I ask Finn, "Does that include us?"

She says, "It's only a watch."

A weathercaster comes on. "We're keeping an eye on two converging weather patterns that could bring heavy precipitation for the western slope over the next twenty-four to forty-eight hours. The good news is the Eagles Nest fire was eighty percent contained, and the firebreaks have held. Those living east of the Divide will benefit from the rain, but flash floods are possible with this much rainfall in so short a time."

Arlo shouts out the order window, "Open the joint up, Alyssa."

Me? Wow, I've never been the one to open. I mean, BFD. You unlock the door and flip the sign from CLOSED to OPEN. Can I handle that much responsibility?

People are lined up outside in the pouring rain. The first one in is Rufus. He says, "Arlo here today?"

"Yeah."

He hollers to everyone behind him, "Arlo's back!"

There are cheers and applause. I hope Finn doesn't catch it. She's standing at the cash register, breaking open rolls of coins. If her feelings are hurt, she doesn't show it.

It's amazing how neither fire nor rain can dampen Arlo's popularity. In fact, the rush extends an hour longer because customers stay to chat about the weather or keep dry. I don't get to flip over the CLOSED sign until after two.

I'm wiped. Finn and I clean up and get ready for tomorrow without exchanging a word. There's so much electricity in the air between us, though, one spark and the whole place would explode. That's what it feels like to me, anyway.

Arlo doesn't leave before us, the way he usually does. He rearranges his pots and sharpens his knives. I roll my eyes at Finn, but she's avoiding looking at me. She opens the fridge to put away the carton of creamer and calls to Arlo, "We're going to need butter before tomorrow. Do you want me to stop at Safeway?"

"No!" He points a knife at Finn. "You go away."

She reaches for her rain slicker, and I snag the hood before she can pull it up. "You can't ride your bike in this," I tell her. "Let me take you home." I call to Arlo, "I'll stop at Safeway for supplies, if you want."

Finn opens the back door. Outside, it's a curtain of water, and the parking lot is a river of mud.

Right behind us, Arlo goes, "Where's Noah when you need an ark?"

His voice in my ear distracts me, and Finn pulls away, taking off in the rain.

"Finn!" I holler. I hear the bike engine roar to life. "She can't drive in this. It's dangerous."

Arlo says, "Finn does whatever the hell she wants."

I whirl on him. "Why are you so mean to her? You're the one who's driving her away. What's wrong with you?"

Arlo deadpans, "You want a list?"

I expel exasperation. He's so deliberately irritating. I can understand why Finn would quit at the first opportunity.

"Do you need a ride?" Arlo asks.

All I can think is, *I hope Finn makes it home.* Why didn't I get her number? I'm obsessing again, but I can't help it.

"Alyssa?"

"What? Oh. No. I have Carly's SUV."

Arlo goes over to the bread drawer and pulls out a loaf of sourdough. He says, "That's not Carly's."

"What do you mean?" I fill in my hours on my time sheet and see I'm not scheduled for tomorrow. Finn is. I write in my name. Maybe Arlo won't notice. Sure, and mold is a digestive aid.

"The Mercedes. It's not Carly's."

"Whose is it?"

Arlo saws off two thick slices of bread. "I'm making myself a grilled cheese. You want one?"

I'm famished, of course. "Sure."

"Grab the butter and cheese. Get mozzarella, cheddar, Swiss, and Asiago." He saws another slice. "It was Jason's."

I look at Arlo. Carly's letting me drive Jason's car?

"Bring it over here." Arlo motions me to the grill. He moves to the side and says, "You're going to do it."

I dump my armload of cheeses. "But I don't know how to cook."

"It's never too late to learn. Spread butter on each slice of bread. Usually I just dunk 'em in melted butter, but we'll keep it low-fat." He holds a hand over the grill. "Do lesbians care about their figures?"

I just look at him.

"I'm just askin'. Is that a priority with your kind? The whole beauty-queen routine?"

How do I know what lesbians' priorities are? I don't even pretend to represent. "I shower occasionally," I tell him. "Twice a week I run a comb through my hair."

He chuckles. "I can tell."

Something bothers me about what he said earlier, before the homosexist remark. "I thought Jason and Angelica…I thought it was a hit-and-run."

"Stack the cheeses yellow, white, yellow. For presentation and flair."

A toasted cheese has flair?

"I guess Carly got the Mercedes fixed?" I say.

"They weren't in the SUV," Arlo says. "Turn the grill down so you don't burn the bread before the cheese melts."

I follow his instructions. "They were in another car?"

"Now the top slice of bread. And…flip."

The first sandwich falls to pieces.

"That's okay. Get the cheese back on the bread. Flip faster, like this." He demonstrates with a flick of the wrist.

I try.

"Beautiful!" he cries.

I feel like I just won *Top Chef*.

"Jason was taking the baby to day care, and he got a call from Carly, raking him over the coals about taking her car because his had a flat. They'd been fighting; she knew he was cheating on her."

My eyes widen at Arlo.

"Anyway, he'd taken the little girl out of the car seat and was locking the door when she ran out into the street. Jason ran after her, but a car came tearing around the corner going way over the speed limit, according to witnesses, and hit Jason. He'd just gotten to the girl and picked her up. Jason died instantly. The little girl lived for a day."

"Oh my God," I gasp. "Angelica."

"Huh?"

"Her name. It was Angelica."

"Right. They called her Angie." He holds a plate, and I use the spatula to slide the wrecked sandwich onto it. Another plate for the good one. "You gotta slice it diagonal." He hands me a serrated knife. I saw through the bread, and he goes, "Beautiful. Now you can cook."

Yeah, sure.

Arlo takes a bite out of the messed-up sandwich, which I would've eaten. His eyes roll back in his head like, *rapture*, and it makes me smile.

The grilled cheese is good. Better than good. So much better than the grilled cheese Dad used to make for me. I pull up a step stool and sit, so I'm eye level with Arlo. "Was Carly... I mean, I know she must've been devastated afterward."

Arlo chews and swallows. He chomps off another bite. "She had a breakdown. Stayed with Geena for a while. Geena says she'd wake up screaming, 'My girl! My baby girl!' "

I hear Carly in my head, screaming, reliving the accident. I know I would.

"Then," Arlo says, "she woke up one day, and she was over it."

Like snap, you're over this major trauma in your life? I don't think so. She just buried it.

"She moved back to the house and picked up where she left off." Arlo sets down his sandwich. "Milk." He rolls to the fridge, calling over his shoulder, "Everyone admired the way she was able to carry on."

The end of that phrase is left unspoken: *like nothing ever happened*.

My girl! My baby girl! Angelica was Carly's girl. I wonder if Carly ever woke in the night screaming for me? For the loss of me? Or was she like snap, over it?

Carly's been home. She left me a note:

> ALYSSA
>
> BE CAREFUL OUT THERE. I'LL CALL YOU WHEN I GET A CHANCE.
>
> C

I sit at the table with my phone and wait. And wait. I call her, and her voice mail picks up. I don't leave a message.

I hate this, sitting around waiting for a call. How much of my life has been wasted sitting around waiting for Sarah to call?

The sky's so dark that it looks like the middle of the night, and the rain hasn't let up a bit. I check my e-mail; there's only spam.

I watch TV for a while. Every time I feel myself drifting off, the wind kicks up and hammers rain against the picture window. There's a continuous scroll along the bottom of the screen with flash flood warnings for Eagle, Summit, and Grand counties.

The phone in my hand rings, and I almost drop it. "Hello?"

"Alyssa, are you home?" Carly says.

"Yeah. Where are you?"

I hear a guy's voice in the background and Carly going, "Oh, thanks, honey." She says to me, "I probably won't make it back tonight. This rain is washing out roads, and already there's a mudslide near Breckenridge. Now they're saying it's going to get worse overnight."

A bolt of lightning strikes so close that the hair on my skin stands up, and the charge zings my feet and legs. "Carly?"

We're cut off.

I try to call her back, but all I get is a busy signal. I disconnect so she can call me.

She never does.

There's another lightning flash, and a thunder boom shakes

the house. I scrunch into a ball on the sofa. Thunderstorms scare me to death. Paulie'd always come running to my room, and we'd hide under the bedspread together.

Rain pummels the roof.

A streak of lightning splits the sky, and the TV flickers and then goes black. All the lights go out. Now what? When we lose electricity at home—which happens all the time because the wiring is old and we get lots of thunderstorms in Virginia—Dad goes to the garage to check the breakers. I've watched him flip them back on.

I creep down the stairs to Carly's garage. I wish I knew where she keeps her flashlight. It's pitch-black, and the floor's wet, and I don't have any shoes on. If lightning strikes, I'll fry.

My phone's in my hand, still, so I touch it on to use the lighted panel. I'm a freaking genius.

There's the box. Sure enough, a bunch of the breakers are tripped. I flick them on one at a time and see lights illuminate behind me. The TV blares upstairs.

As I'm returning to the main level, a bolt of lightning illuminates Carly's exercise room. Oh no. There's water streaming in from under the window or the foundation. She has a closet with towels for the sauna, so I grab a stack and pack around the wet places. The sky lights up, and I see streams of water sluicing down the mountain.

What if the whole house floods? Or floats away? That won't happen, will it? At least the main level isn't on the ground floor. I wrap in a blanket on the sofa, surfing channels, trying and retrying Carly's number. The line's dead, and I feel cut off from the world.

The phone in the kitchen rings, and I leap up to answer.

"Alyssa?"

"Finn? Oh my God. Can you come over? I'm scared and Carly's house is flooding and I don't know what to do!"

Finn says, "Where's Carly?"

"I don't know. She left. She's not coming home tonight."

"How bad's the flooding?"

"It's seeping in around the foundation. I put towels all over to soak up the water."

"Okay," Finn says. "That's good. You'll be fine."

"No, I won't."

Lightning streaks through the sky, and I hear Boner howl in the background. "I can't leave," Finn says. "Boner's freaked out."

"Then I'll come there."

"No! Don't even try to drive on these roads."

I feel so desperate for company. "Will you talk to me, at least?" The lights flicker, and I tell her, "The electricity keeps going in and out."

"Keep calm. I'm here."

I remote off the TV. "Stay on the phone, okay?"

A clap of thunder combines with Boner's barking. "Boner, come here. That's a good boy. I've never known such a wimpy dog."

"Have you had a dog before?" I curl up on the sofa and shiver.

"My last foster family did. It wasn't my dog. Nothing was mine."

I know how she feels. I want to know the when and how

and where of her. "Tell me about your foster family. Were they in Canada?"

"Tell me about your family," she replies. "Back in Virginia."

How does she know where I'm from? I bet everyone in town knows all the dirty details of my life. "I'd rather not talk about them," I say. "What are you doing right now? Do you have a fire going?" I wish I could build a fire, but the fireplace is in the formal living room, and I have no idea how to use it.

"Boner and I are in bed. He's under the covers. Boner." She laughs softly. "He's licking me. Boner, stop. What are you doing?" she asks.

"Talking to you. I was thinking of taking a whirlpool bath, but I might get electrocuted."

"Yeah. Don't do that."

"You should come over and try out the hot tub. Before you leave," I say.

"Maybe I will."

Maybe if she did, she wouldn't leave. We start talking about work, and Arlo, then music and movies and I don't know what else. At one point, Finn says, "I hope the minutes don't run out on my phone. I've never talked to anyone this long."

"Wow, I feel honored." She's never had a real friend. Friends can talk on the phone for hours. We jabber until my eyelids are heavy, and I don't know if I'm dreaming or if I really hear Finn whisper, "G'night, Alyssa. Wish you were here. Sweet dreams."

Chapter 22

The ringing phone in the kitchen jolts me awake. I roll over—right off the sofa. The caller ID says it's Arlo.

"Hey, boss man," I answer.

"Don't go out today," he says. "Just stay put. The state patrol closed Highway 9 and Summit, and there are high-water warnings everywhere. Is Carly there?"

"Um, I don't know." I didn't hear her come in.

"It doesn't matter. She can take care of herself." He sounds grouchy. Behind him, I hear, "Do you think we'll be getting a pastry delivery?"

"Is Finn there?" I ask.

Arlo says, not to me, "Hell, I don't know. If people come out to eat today, they're daft in the head." He goes, "Alyssa? Everything bolted down there?"

Everything but me. I hang up and race upstairs to get dressed for work.

* * *

Thank God I brought my boots. They're leather, and the rain will probably ruin them, but they're all I've got. They're not that comfortable, anyway. They're too narrow, and they pinch my toes, but Paulie (via Tanith) gave them to me for my birthday.

I only have a hoodie, so I check the downstairs closet for a raincoat or a parka. Carly has a full-length fur coat. Is it mink? Ick. I'm not about to wear a dead animal.

I crank everything on in the car—the wipers, defroster, headlights—and start down the access road. It's slick and slimy, and my foot naturally jams on the brake, and then I feel the back end fishtailing. I steer in the opposite direction, but there's no traction at all. The car is sliding, swerving, and I can't control it, and all I see are gray shadows blurring past me, branches scraping the windows, and I skid, slide, and scream, "Stop! Stop!" Oh my God, please stop.

The brakes catch suddenly, and I'm jerked backward and then forward. If I hadn't latched my seat belt, I'd have been propelled right out the windshield.

At last I reach Highway 102. Fuzzy headlights are the only visible patterns as semis roar by, splashing waves of water over my hood. I'm not religious or anything, but I make the sign of the cross and pray for my life.

The high-water warnings are no joke. I hit low spots on the highway and feel like I'm driving through a riptide. My heart is pounding as I putter along, getting blinded by every eighteen-wheeler that passes.

The Egg Drop-In sign is such a welcome sight that I want to cry. Water ripples down the street, and the incline to the parking lot is pure muck. Finn's bike is parked next to the building, covered with a tarp. How did she manage to get here?

When I blow through the back door, both Finn and Arlo stop what they're doing to stare at me.

"Are you on crack? What did I tell you?" Arlo snipes.

"Am I late?" I ask Finn. "I wouldn't want to get docked for being a minute late."

She doesn't smile. "Are you okay?"

"Barely."

Arlo growls, "Do you ever listen to anyone?"

I blink. "What?"

He clenches his jaw.

"How'd you get down the mountain?" I ask Finn.

"Very slowly," she says. She holds my eyes, and the way she looks at me makes me forget I could've died out there. Her eyes are bleary, and mine must be too. Neither of us got more than two hours of sleep.

"I called around, and your mother's with Mitchell." Arlo spins his chair away. "Her latest conquest."

Finn shakes her head at me. Sneaking up behind Arlo, I take the handles of his chair and sing in his ear. "You love Carly."

He flaps a hand at me.

"You want to marry her."

He pivots. "I don't love her, and I pity any guy who does. She's a selfish, thoughtless bitch who only ever thinks of herself and what's in it for her. Or haven't you figured that out yet?"

I flinch.

Arlo snarls, "Get out of my way."

I step aside to let him pass. He slams out the swinging doors into the dining room.

Finn mimes wrenching out a heart from her chest and breaking it in two.

Really. He's hurting bad.

It's so awful out, I can't imagine we'll stay open long. I'm wrong. Throughout the morning we get dozens of people in the restaurant. "Fools," Arlo mutters under his breath every time the bell tinkles. The rain beats on the roof, and Finn and I have to keep emptying buckets and tubs from the leaks in the ceiling. The forecaster on the radio reports flash floods and closed roads, accidents everywhere. "A rollover accident near Heeney has left one person dead," I hear.

Arlo says, "Dutch lives in Heeney."

"Oh my God. Do you know his number?" He hasn't been in the last couple of days, and I've been worried about him. "When was the last time you talked to him?"

Arlo rubs his chin. "Don't remember." He goes over to the phone.

I tell Finn, "I'm afraid to drive home. Will you drive the Mercedes?"

"I have my bike."

"Can't you leave it?"

"My Concours? And by the way, why did you lie about the money being yours?"

"What does it matter? You're paying it back, right?"

Arlo hangs up. "He's not answering. I'll go over there if the road's open. Bring your motorcycle in overnight," he orders Finn, like he overheard our conversation—on purpose.

"Really?" Finn says.

"No, not really. I'm a heartless bastard who's driving you away, according to your guardian angel. Bring it in, goddammit. Unless you're scared I'm going to go joyriding, which I just might."

Finn zips into her rain gear and slogs out for the bike. When Arlo turns away, I give him a hug around the neck. "Thank you. Do you need help getting into your van?"

He spins. "Do I look like I need help?"

"Shut up," I say.

His eyes shoot poison arrows at me.

"It's treacherous out there, and I don't want you to get stuck because you're so stubborn that you'd sit outside and drown before asking anyone to come and help you."

Arlo's eyes mellow but don't let loose of mine. He says, "You're not Carly's girl."

"No. I'm me."

He reaches out and takes my hand, pulls me closer to him. In this confidential tone, he says, "Jason wasn't the only one cheating."

As I'm trying to process that, Arlo adds, "Since you worked today, you'll need to cut your hours later."

Damn. Nothing gets by him.

Finn crashes in and wedges her motorcycle between the back wall and the storage cabinets, and I feel Arlo watching me watch her. He pulls me down closer to his mouth and whispers, "Word of advice: Don't get attached to a moving object."

It takes three tries for Finn to back out of the deep ruts I carved on my way in. Highway 102 has heavy traffic, like the big rigs are using it instead of the interstate.

I'm thinking about everything Arlo told me, trying to piece together the whole puzzle. Of course. "Carly was having an affair with Arlo while she was married to Jason."

Finn goes, "You finally figured that out?"

I slap her arm. "Why didn't you tell me?"

She says, "I don't spread gossip or rumors."

Unless she's coerced. What else does she know?

She concentrates on the road, her hands clenched tightly around the steering wheel. Her jaw is set, and she seems worried.

"What?" I ask.

"The rain," she says. "I've never seen it like this. It isn't natural. I have a feeling something bad's going to happen."

The edge in her voice sends shivers up my spine.

At the end of Carly's driveway, we pull in by the mailbox and stop.

I gasp. A river courses down the access road, obliterating it completely. "How do we get to the house?" I ask Finn.

"I don't know. Is Carly up there? She'll never get down."

Finn's concern for Carly stabs me with a pang of jealousy. Ridiculous. I fish out my cell from my bag. Twelve missed calls.

Carly.

Carly.

All of them from Carly.

She answers on the first ring. "Where the *hell* have you been? I've been calling you all morning."

Hello to you too. "I was at work."

"I know you took your phone because it's not here."

What'd she do, ransack my room?

"I didn't hear it ring," I say.

"I got you that phone so we could stay in touch. Where are you now, Alyssa? Answer me."

God, let me get a word in. "I'm at the bottom of the hill. The road's flooded."

"Don't you think I know that? Why do you think I was calling? All the roads are washing out. There's a twelve-car pile-up on I-70, and traffic is being diverted. You shouldn't be out driving at all."

"I'm not, actually." I glance over at Finn. "Finn's here. We're wondering how to get to the house."

"You're not on her motorcycle, are you?"

"Of course not. We're in the Mercedes."

Carly expels an irritated breath. "You can't drive up."

"I *know* that."

"You can't walk; it's too muddy. And if you try to drive, you'll get stuck. Let me think." There's a prolonged silence.

"She's thinking." I roll my eyes at Finn.

Finn replies, "With your four-wheel drive, we might be able to make it to my place. It's more rocks than mud."

Carly comes back on. "They shut down I-70 in both directions. Let me call Mitchell and see where they're sending the stranded motorists. Stay there. I'll call you right back." She hangs up.

I tell Finn, "She's finding out where the stranded motorists are being sent."

My phone rings. "The Red Cross is setting up a temporary shelter at the rec center in Dillon," Carly says. "Do you know where that is? Ask Finn if she knows where the new rec center is."

I ask Finn. She doesn't.

Carly says, "Use the GPS."

Like I know how. "What are you going to do?"

"Wait it out," Carly says. "This rain can't last forever. Call me as soon as you get to the rec center. I mean it, Alyssa."

Her concern seems sincere. "I will."

"What'd she say?" Finn asks as I disconnect.

"She says we should go to your place until the rain stops."

We get torrential downpours in Virginia Beach, especially if a tropical storm off the Atlantic moves through, but they don't last this long. Finn drives slowly, swerving toward the shoulder every time a semi rumbles past, yet we still get cascaded with water. The *fwap, fwap, fwap* of the wipers is calming, or maybe it's the fact that Finn's here beside me. "What other places have you lived?" I ask her.

"I lose count. Why?"

"I'm just trying to make conversation, okay? Do you ever let anybody in?"

She hesitates. "Nobody wants in."

"Until now," I say.

We're quiet for a minute.

"This bad feeling you have. Do you get them often? Do you have, like, a sixth sense?"

She frowns at me.

"Well, you might. You never know."

"I do see dead people. Dead drunk."

I slap her arm. "Quit it."

We drive on in more comfortable silence. "This oil rigger gave me a lift once," she says out of the blue, "and it was raining like this. The guy was going too fast, hydroplaning, and we slid off the road into a ditch. The rig rolled and caught fire."

"Oh my God. Seriously?"

"If the tanker hadn't been empty, we would've been toast."

I shake my head. "My worst fear is burning alive. After being eaten alive by bugs and bats."

That makes Finn smile a little.

"Do you believe in destiny?" I ask her.

Finn blinks over at me. "Not really."

Sarah was a big believer in destiny. She said if she hadn't gotten lost that first day of school, she never would've found me, the love of her life. That's what she used to call me. If Ben wasn't my friend, they never would've met. If Dad hadn't disowned me, I'd never have ended up in Majestic. If Finn had been fried alive…

"What do you believe in?" I ask her. Say trust. Say truth.

"Reality," Finn answers. "Creating your destiny. Owning it."

Can you create destiny? "Is that why you up and leave? Drift?"

She doesn't respond. She clicks on the turn signal and shifts into four-wheel drive. We start up the steep incline to her cabin, and Finn downshifts and then floors the gas pedal to grind through the mud and try to catch anything solid beneath the tires. We bounce violently over boulders and scrape metal on rock as the car bottoms out. Finn doesn't slow down. I grip the seat like I'm on the bow of a rocking boat, and we make steady progress until, at last, I spot the cabins. "Yay!"

She parks as close to the front door as possible. We open our car doors in unison, and rain from the cabin roof splats my head and runs down my neck. Finn sloshes around the front of the Mercedes.

As soon as she opens the door, Boner jumps on her, and she crouches down to lift him up. "I'm sorry, I'm sorry, buddy," she murmurs to him, nuzzling him close. "You're okay."

The cabin is freezing. Finn says, "I'll go get wood from the shed. Be right back." She hands me Boner.

I see that her unzipped duffel in the bedroom is half full. She can't leave. I have to keep her here. I set Boner down on the bed and overturn her duffel, spilling the contents onto the floor.

Finn enters with an armload of split logs. "I'll build a fire if you'll feed Boner." She heads out again.

I find a can of Pedigree in the cupboard and a manual can opener, which requires a mechanical engineer to operate. Finn returns with a second load of wood. She's soaked. While I'm working the opener, I'm thinking I'd like to dry Finn off. I'd love to unplait her braid to see how long her hair is. On her knees at the hearth, she blows on a wad of lit newspaper to get the kindling started. It crackles and pops. Boner whines, and I set his food on the floor.

Finn's got the fire roaring, and she sits on the furry rug, hugging her knees. I lower myself next to her, and a shudder of cold races through me.

Finn pulls a blanket off the couch and drapes it across both our shoulders.

The fire is mesmerizing. Finn's face is illuminated, and her dark eyes glimmer like stars. "You're so brave," I tell her. "To just leave home and make it on your own. I could never do that."

She looks at me. "Sure you could. You did. We all do whatever we have to do to survive."

I can't look away from her. The gaze between us becomes intense, and then Finn breaks it off. "You're braver than me." She picks at a frayed corner of the blanket. Boner waddles up between us, and Finn straightens her legs, pulling him into her lap.

"How?"

"You know who you are. What you want."

"And you don't?"

She stares into the fire. She scratches Boner's ears. It's warm now, and I let the blanket fall off my shoulders. Reaching across, I run my open hand down the length of her braid and she closes her eyes.

My phone rings in my bag, but I ignore it. "What are you running from?"

Finn opens her eyes and turns to me. "Who says I'm running from anything?"

"Know what I think? I think you're running from your truth." I think, *Or trying to find it.*

She buries her face in Boner's fur. With both hands, I reach over and undo her braid. Her hair is kinky where it was wound together, and I rake my fingers through it. So soft. Finn sets Boner aside, takes my hands in hers and kisses my palms. She pulls me in close to kiss me. Sweet and tender. It's impossible to fight the longing, even if I wanted to. I wrap my arms around her. We kiss, and I feel the rush from my head to the tips of my toes. Finn breaks off the kiss to remove her wet shoes. I pull off my boots, and we resume where we left off. The heat of her internal fire radiates through me, and all my pleasure zones ignite. We lie back on the rug and kiss and touch, and my promise never to love again melts away. There's only us and the fire and the heat.

Boner barks, jerking me awake. Finn's gone. My last memory is the two of us under the blanket, naked, intertwined on the floor. I sit up, pulling the blanket up with me. "Finn?"

She appears in the bedroom doorway. She's dressed and carrying her repacked duffel. "I have to go now. Will you take me to Arlo's to get my bike? Will you find Boner a home?"

"No," I say automatically.

"Please," she pleads.

I can't believe this. "You used me. You played me."

"No. Alyssa . . ."

I drop the blanket and crawl on my hands and knees to gather all my clothes, and Finn is there, but I push her away. "I hate you!" I shimmy into my shorts and shirt. I can only find one boot. Fuck it. I snatch Boner off the couch and head for the door.

"Alyssa—"

"Shut up!"

A keening wail of pain lodges in my throat as rain pounds the windshield. It didn't mean a thing to her. I don't mean a thing. The Mercedes tips to the left, and I rev the motor so hard it screeches. Then the tires catch, and the car vaults over an embankment, landing hard and bouncing my hands off the wheel. I clutch it harder.

Beside me, Boner whines. "It's okay," I tell him. "She didn't want you either."

I see a light in my mirror, like a flashlight beam, and I floor the gas pedal. I feel the car lifting, sliding, slipping, and I'm thrown from side to side within the confines of my seat belt.

I can't—*won't*—let her catch me. The Mercedes jerks forward and smashes into a solid object, and all I see is window and ceiling, rain, black, rocks, blur. I'm revolving, and the car is somersaulting down the embankment. It rolls and hits hard, my shoulder crunching against the window.

The spinning stops suddenly. The only sound is the beating rain and my rasping breath. I open my eyes.

"Boner?"

He's in my lap, and I'm clutching him hard. He's panting.

I'm alive. We're both alive. The windshield is fractured into a mosaic of glass, the passenger door crushed in. The top is jagged metal, inches away from my head. A light through my window blinds me, and Finn yells, shouts my name, and jiggles the door handle.

Go away, the voice echoes in my head. *Just go.*

Pounding. A blurry figure with a metal tool is whacking at the door, which busts loose and flies open. Hands reach in for me. I try to lean away but can't, because my seat belt has me strapped in.

"Are you all right? Oh God." Finn's feeling me all over for cuts or missing limbs, broken bones, and all I feel is numb. "Alyssa." Her face is close to mine. "Can you see me?" She holds my face between her hands. "Can you hear me?"

She unbuckles my seat belt, and this pain rips down my neck and arm. Do I scream? I feel myself falling, Finn's arms winding around me, pulling me out of the car. The ground whirls, recedes, and I fall off the edge of the world.

Chapter 23

I have to hurl. When I sit up, someone sticks a plastic container under my face to catch the vomit. It's Barbara.

I'm in the ER. Bells ping and buzzers go off. "How are you feeling?" Barbara asks.

My stomach heaves again.

She smooths my hair, and I lie back down. Hot tears burn my eyes. "Finn said you were in an accident. Do you want to tell me about it?"

I shake my head no, and my brain implodes. She says, "You have a dislocated shoulder, but no broken bones, thank goodness. The doctor should be in soon. I know how much it hurts right now. Try to relax."

She can't possibly know.

"Don't move. Deep breaths." She injects something in my IV, and immediately my muscles go limp. The pain ebbs. I'm about to close my eyes, when I hear a familiar voice. "Barbara?"

Barbara pulls back the curtain. "We're here, Carly."

Carly crosses the threshold and stops.

"It's only a dislocation. She'll be fine."

Carly looks as green as I feel. I wish she'd come closer and hold my hand or hug me and tell me everything's going to be fine. It's a dream; tell me that.

She doesn't cross the threshold, just stands there like all the medical equipment makes her nauseated. The doctor shows up to reset my shoulder, and Carly leaves. I want to call to her, *Don't go*.

The doctor asks, "Were you wearing your seat belt?"

"I always do."

"It saved your life," he says.

Dad will be happy to know his incessant nagging paid off.

While the doctor's talking, he does something to my arm, and I feel a pop, then a pain so intense I must pass out. When I regain consciousness, my arm's in a sling.

Barbara's there. She says, "Can you sit up, Alyssa?" With her help, I swing my legs over the side and raise my torso. Dizzy. She steadies me. "Your arm's going to hurt for a while. Your chest too, from the seat belt. Let me know if it gets worse or if you start feeling pain here or here." She pokes me in the stomach and ribs. "Call me right away if there are any changes."

Carly's hanging back. Barbara rubs my good shoulder and says, "As soon as you feel you can walk, you're sprung. Take your time."

She brushes by Carly, who murmurs a thank-you.

"Boner," I say.

"What?" Carly frowns.

"The dog."

"He's okay," Carly says flatly. "Geena has him."

Thank God.

Carly doesn't talk to me as we drive away from Summit Medical in a car I don't recognize. Where's her SUV? I don't want to tell her about the accident. I will. I mean, I know I have to. Right now all I want to do is crash and sleep. Never wake up.

Carly pulls into a parking lot that's definitely not home. "Where are we?" I ask.

"The rec center," she says. "Where you were *supposed* to go."

God, how I wish I'd listened.

Two Red Cross vans are parked in front, and there are lines of people at the entrance. "What's happening?" I ask, still feeling dazed.

"They're bringing all the motorists here," Carly answers.

"How long have you been here? How did you get out?"

"Mitchell sent a helicopter for me. I need to help inside." She holds the car door for me as I slide out and stand shakily. It's still raining, though not as much. A trickle.

Carly opens an umbrella and hurries me into the building. Someone calls, "Carly, do you know if there are more blankets and pillows?"

She says, "I'll check." There are rows of cots and crowds of people. Carly says to me, "Take that cot over there. Get some rest, and we'll talk later." She doesn't give me time to respond before she rushes away.

Come back, I plead silently. *Stay with me.*

I sit on the cot. Then I lie down and try to get comfortable. Not easy with my arm in a sling. It doesn't hurt as much as it did. A constant dull ache. I have someone's Crocs on, and I wonder where my boots are. I remove the Crocs and try to sleep, but it's noisy, so I dig my phone out of my bag. There are five voice mails, all from yesterday. The first one: "Alyssa, where are you? Why don't you answer your phone?"

The next one: "Alyssa, why aren't you at the rec center, where I told you to go? No one's seen you. Where the hell are you? Pick up, dammit. Call me!"

With the phone to my ear, I close my eyes, and disembodied images of Finn and me together swirl in my brain, and this voice asks if I'm cursed. If I'm doomed to fall in love with the wrong person over and over again.

Plows and tractors rumble on the road outside the rec center all morning. A couple of cops in uniform show up to announce that one lane of I-70 eastbound has been cleared, and a cheer erupts.

Townies help people pack their gear and head out to their cars. Carly's across the room folding cots. She looks beat and harried, but still strikingly beautiful. A familiar voice makes my head swivel. Arlo. I get up and migrate over to the coffee station. "Heard about your accident," he says, serving me a cinnamon roll and coffee.

What did he hear and from whom?

"Damage report." He motions with his chin to my arm in the sling.

"Dislocated shoulder."

He waves it off. "Minor inconvenience. I could use some help here."

You never realize how much you miss a limb until it's incapacitated. I take over serving rolls with one hand. "How'd you end up in a chair?" I ask Arlo.

"Skiing accident. I was sixteen. Bunch of us got stoned and decided it was too crowded on the slope and why didn't we just ski out of bounds? I wasn't that great a skier anyway, and I wrapped around a tree at full speed. Snapped my spinal cord."

"God."

"Yeah, we were hotshots all right." Arlo serves up two coffees, and I hand out cinnamon rolls on paper plates. He adds, "Too bad we don't get a do over in life. Just one chance to change the future."

"Or two or three," I mumble.

Arlo shrugs. "C'est la vie, kid. You take what you get."

I hand out a cinnamon roll to a cowboy dude, who smiles and says, "Thankee, ma'am." I turn to Arlo. "Dutch."

"He's safe," Arlo says. "His place got flooded out, so he's staying with his sister in Steamboat Springs."

I exhale relief.

"Alyssa, there you are!" Geena's leading Boner on a makeshift leash. "Thank God you're all right." She practically mauls me. When I wince because she squeezed my sore arm, she pets the sling and says, "Here, let me do that, sugar." She yanks the spatula out of my hand.

"I can—"

She hip checks me away from the coffee station. "You want me to take Boner?" I ask.

"Is that his name?" Geena looks at Arlo, and they both laugh.

Boner hangs close to Geena, like he'd prefer not to be in my presence. I don't blame him.

Carly appears out of nowhere. "Where's the Mercedes?" she asks me.

"Um..." I swallow hard. "I wrecked it."

"Where?"

"It was raining so hard, and the rocks were wet—"

"Where is it?"

"I was trying to get home."

"From *where?*"

"Finn's." A lump in my throat makes my eyes well. "She's gone." The tears spill over the rims.

Carly blows out a breath. "Oh, Alyssa."

I hiccup a sob.

She puts her arms around me in a loose embrace, careful not to squeeze my sling, and then leads me over to a cot, where we sit. "I'm so stupid," I say.

"No, you're not. You just trust the wrong people."

Okay, that hurt. It's true, though.

"Finn's one of those seasonal employees who show up to work during ski season and then take off." Carly adds, "With my money."

No, I want to say. *She's different*. But she's gone, and she took more than Carly's money. A part of my heart feels ripped away.

"I suspect Finn never stays in one place long enough to put down roots. Sort of like someone else we know?" She arches her eyebrows.

I think she's talking about herself.

This ruckus kicks up around us, and people race out the front door. Geena dashes over. "Carly, I just heard there's been a gigantic mudslide on Caribou Mountain." She grabs Carly's hand and yanks her up.

"I want to come too." I stand.

Geena links her arm in my good one and tugs me along. I see Boner's switched alliances to Arlo, or vice versa. In the parking lot, Geena remotes open the locks on the silver Lexus we drove in from the hospital, and we all get in, me in the backseat. Geena catches my eye in the rearview mirror. "Buckle your seat belt, sugar."

I would have anyway. Lesson pounded home.

We have to pass Majestic, and my jaw drops. The whole town is flooded. The Egg Drop-In is submerged up to the plate-glass window. "Oh my God," I breathe. I wonder if Arlo's seen this. His home. His business.

Highway 102 is passable but barricaded right outside of town. Geena drives up to the ROAD CLOSED sign, and a state trooper halts her. She leans out her window. "Hey, handsome."

He lowers himself so his head is framed in the window opening. He and Carly exchange knowing glances. Is this Mitchell?

He looks at me. "You must be Alyssa. We were ready to send out a search-and-rescue unit for you."

"Sorry," I say in a small voice.

Geena says, "We need to go see if there's damage to Carly's house."

"I can't let you through." His eyes never leave Carly's face. "It's bad, Carly," he says.

She gazes out the front window.

Geena says, "Can you take us as far as possible so we can at least see? Pleeeease?" She puts a hand on his forearm.

He's still looking at Carly. "Okay. Follow me. But slowly." He walks over, gets in his cruiser, and motions Geena to drive around the barricade after him.

The magnitude of the mudslide is unbelievable. The whole side of the mountain caved in. At the edge of the mud and debris, the three of us get out and inhale audibly. As far as the eye can see, there are uprooted trees and bushes, fallen boulders, construction rubble. I raise my eyes to where everyone else is looking—at the gaping hole in the mountain. Where Carly's house used to be.

Geena starts to hyperventilate. "Oh my Lord, my Lord." She covers her chest and then her eyes. She throws her arms around Carly.

Mitchell says, "The dam breached at Caribou Lake, and after the fire last year and the dry conditions this year . . . then all this rain at once . . ."

Carly peers up over the avalanche of refuse and scrap wood. She lets out a long, slow breath.

I don't know what to do or say. What do you say? I know the cost of that house to Carly. All her possessions. The personal loss. The one time she may have tried to put down roots.

Carly interrupts my thoughts with laughter. She laughs until tears run down her cheeks. Mitchell takes her arm.

"No, it's fine." Carly shakes him off. "I'm all right."

Geena widens her eyes at me like, *Carly's hysterical.* I have to agree. Geena reaches for my good hand. "You're staying with me. Both of you. Until you rebuild, Carly, and everything's exactly the way it was."

Carly returns to the Lexus and gets in. Mitchell leans down and says something to her, and she touches his face tenderly.

Geena and I gaze up the mountain for one last look. She kind of leans into me, like she might collapse. When we climb into the car, Carly twists her head over the seat back. "Do you remember where you left the Mercedes?"

Bile rises in my throat. "I think so. It's close to Finn's cabin."

Carly says to Geena, "Since 102 is closed, we'll have to drive all the way around the mountain. Do you mind?"

Geena says, "Of course not."

The Mercedes is a crunched heap of black metal perched on its side, with the roof bashed in.

"Oh my Lord." Geena slaps her hand to her chest. "How did you get out of there alive?"

It's a miracle, I think.

Carly seems unaffected. Or she's seething inside.

"I'm sorry," I say.

She digs out her cell and makes a call to someone. Her insurance agent?

I can see the cabin from here. No sign of Finn, not that I expected her to be there, waiting for my return. She's long gone.

We have to drive up the hill to the cabin to turn the Lexus around. *Don't cry, don't cry*, I think. *Don't look back.*

The cell in my bag rings. I can't find it fast enough with my one good hand to answer. The number isn't in my contacts. I have a voice mail waiting, received last night.

I key into my messages, and Tanith's voice sounds in my ear. "Alyssa, we heard about all the mudslides, and we're worried sick about you and Carly. We'll be back home in a few hours, so please call us and let us know you're safe." She pauses. "Do you want to say something to Alyssa?"

Do I hear Dad breathing? A year elapses, it seems. He doesn't speak, but he doesn't hang up either. Say it, Dad. Say, *I miss you, honey. I love you. Please come home.*

The call cuts off.

Chapter 24

Geena lives in a cottage, I guess you'd call it, with a white picket fence and a vegetable garden. It's about three blocks down the street from Arlo's. I can see where the water rose around the foundation, but it's already receded, and it doesn't look like she sustained any damage inside. She has a guest bedroom with two single beds, frilly bed linens, and lace curtains.

The realization hits me: Carly and I have nothing. The clothes on our backs.

Geena says, "Everything I have is yours. You know that, sugar." She kisses Carly's cheek. Carly mumbles something about phone calls to make, and I beg off Geena's recitation of food options with a headache. I go into the bedroom to lie down.

What do people do who lose everything in a natural disaster? Start over, I suppose. At least Carly has friends, a place to stay until she rebuilds.

Watching her yesterday helping people, the way she put aside her own personal tragedy—even though she didn't know yet about the house. *You're wrong, Arlo*, I want to tell him. Carly's not selfish. She reaches out to others. To me. And she's strong. Stronger than I'll ever be.

Out the bedroom window, I see Boner digging a big muddy hole in Geena's backyard. I almost yell, *Bad dog*, then Finn's voice echoes in my ears, and I try to block it out. How could she, after she knew my past? She got what she wanted and then left. Talk about selfish.

Voices drift down the hall to the bedroom, and I listen at the door. The cop, Mitchell, is here. I get up and venture down the hallway, and he's sitting at the kitchen table eating cherry pie and drinking coffee with Carly and Geena.

He glances over at me. He has these aquamarine eyes and auburn hair.

Geena says, "Oh, hi, sweetie. You feeling better?" She scoots back in her chair. "Sit here."

"I'm fine."

Mitchell speaks up. "They're clearing 102 now, so I expect by tomorrow we can begin the recovery operation on your home. We'll salvage as much as we can, Carly."

"Don't bother," Carly says with a yawn. "There's nothing I want."

Nothing? Not the baby clothes? The pictures?

How about my stuff? Not that I had all that much.

Geena walks over and feels my forehead under my bangs. "No fever. You look awfully pale, though. Come. Sit." She steers me to her chair, and I practically fall into it.

Mitchell smiles at me. He has kind eyes. And the way he looks at Carly, you know he's in love with her. "Well, ladies.

Always a pleasure." He stands and snags his trooper hat off the back of the sofa cushion. He thanks Geena for the pie, and Carly walks him out.

Geena says in a lowered voice, "He's a hottie, isn't he?"

I wouldn't call him hot. Not like Jason.

She adds, "You want dinner now? You must be starving. We eat dessert first around here. I have apple or cherry pie, and ice cream, and every kind of Lean Cuisine they make."

"No," I tell her. "Thanks. I just want to sleep." I drag myself up from the chair, and my eyes catch the movement out the kitchen window. Through Geena's potted herbs, I see Carly and Mitchell at his cruiser. He pulls her into his arms and kisses her.

Geena says, "What size are you?" She clamps her hands around my waist. "I bet you can wear all my skinny clothes."

The kiss goes on and on.

"You have your mom's bone structure. Lucky you."

Lucky me.

Carly returns, sweeps through the living room, and retrieves her coffee cup from the kitchen table. She refreshes it at the coffeepot and says to me, "We need to talk."

Geena goes, "That's my cue." She grabs her purse and heads for the back door. "I need to pick up my bc pills, if the pharmacy's open. I'll get you girls toothbrushes and shower gel and shampoo. What else?"

Carly's staring at me.

"Oh, and dog food." Geena heads out. "Boner," I hear her say. "What a name."

Carly pats the chair back, and I sit down. "I'm sorry about wrecking your Mercedes," I tell her. "I'll pay for the damage."

She slides into a chair across from me. "I have insurance." She takes a drink of coffee. Setting down the cup, she says, "I talked to your father."

My pulse races. When? Why? Is Carly the one who gave Tanith my new cell number? My eyes fall away from Carly's unwavering gaze. "He hates me for what I am."

She lifts her cup and says, "I'm sure he doesn't hate you. He doesn't understand that you're your own person, that you make your own choices and decisions. You need to let him know."

"I tried. He won't accept me. He refuses to believe I'm a lesbian."

"Oh, I think he believes it." A wry smile crosses her lips, and she sips her coffee.

"I'm sorry for...for judging you," I say. "I had no right." The same way others have no right to judge me. They're not God. Dad has no right. I need him to accept me, support me, honor my decisions. "Tell me about Jason and Angelica."

She sets down her cup and presses her fingers into her eyes. "Alyssa..."

"I know it's painful to talk about them, but I kind of feel they were my family too." I add gently, "Please?"

She sighs. "What do you want to know?"

"How did you and Jason meet? I heard it was at the Egg Drop."

"Christ. Nothing gets past anyone in this cow town. Yes, I was working as a waitress, temporarily. Waitressing is good experience to have, by the way. You'll always be employable.

Jason was in his first year of residency, and we just clicked. You know?"

Chemistry. You have it or you don't. "How could you afford to build that house?" I know doctors are rich, but aren't first-year residents just starting out? On TV they are.

"He was loaded. His family was—is—wealthy. He had a trust fund that'd take care of us for the rest of our lives."

Wow. "Does he have a lesbian sister around my age?"

Carly lets out a short laugh. "An only child. Sorry."

"Damn. So how long did you date before you got married?"

"Not very. I found out I was pregnant, and we hurried it up." She lifts her cup to her lips again. "I keep making that mistake."

My face must color because Carly adds, "I don't mean Angelica was a mistake. Or you either. You were just unplanned."

As in *unwanted*?

"Let's get back to what I wanted to talk to you about. I'm not rebuilding the house. I should've sold it to begin with. It only reminds me of the past, and it's not good for me to live in the past. Mitchell isn't going to like it, but I've decided to take the insurance money and do what I've always wanted to do." She gets up, carrying her cup to the sink. She doesn't go on.

"Which is?"

She pivots. "Sail around the world. See places I've always wanted to see. There's a yearlong cruise that I've been looking into. It stops in two hundred forty-two ports in sixty-two countries."

Leaving me where? I try to sound enthusiastic when I say, "How cool."

"You'd go with me, of course."

"What?" I jump up and throw my arms around Carly. "Oh my God." We'll start fresh, new. We'll leave the past behind and sail away into the future. I can finally move on. "Thank you, Carly." Thank you, thank you, thank you.

I can't go. It's impossible. I still have a year of high school to finish, and I don't want to travel around the world. Maybe someday, but not yet. I just want one place to call home. I like it here in Majestic; love it, in fact. For the first time, I feel I am making my own choices and decisions.

When I tell Carly the next morning, she says, "Are you sure?"

"I am."

She pooches her lips. "I hate to go by myself."

"Take Mitchell."

She screws up her face. I guess I know what that means.

"Take Geena. You two have fun together."

Carly fixes on my face. "Are you absolutely sure, Alyssa? You won't think I'm abandoning you again?"

I click my tongue. "Go. You deserve it."

"I do." She smiles. "I work hard for a living. I should go now, while I still have my youth."

While I can still party is what she really means.

"There is one thing," I say. "It's something you said about

talking to Dad. Letting him know how I feel. I think I need to do that in person. I know you've already given me eight hundred dollars—"

"I'll buy you a plane ticket. Just tell me when."

I need a day or two to work up the nerve. To warn Tanith. "Maybe Friday? And I promise to pay you back every penny of that eight hundred dollars. Eventually."

Carly comes over and presses my head to her chest. "I know you will. And if you don't, hell, it's only money. I could make that much tricking in one night."

I look up at her and she laughs. We both do.

There must be some hidden meaning in people always giving me shoes. Like that saying "Walk a mile in my shoes"? My mystery Crocs feel weightless as I make my way down the plank sidewalk to the Egg Drop-In to check out the destruction. "Alyssa?" a voice sounds behind me.

It's Timber Toes, from the book swap. I have to shield my eyes from the sun, she's so tall.

"I heard about the house and your car accident. I'm so sorry. Are you and Carly all right?"

"Yeah. We're fine. Thank you for asking." I hold my arm in the sling closer to my chest.

She says, "It's going to take Arlo a while to get back on his feet. I mean"—she winces—"get his place in order. If you'd like to work at the Emporium until he has his restaurant up and running, I could use the help. Fortunately, we were spared a lot of water damage because we're on the west end of town."

She's nice. I misjudged her. It's a bad habit that I need to work on. "I love to read," I tell her.

Her eyes light up. "Me too. My partner, Vickie, and I have a feminist book club that meets once a month. Maybe you'd like to join."

Her partner? "Uh, yeah. That'd be cool." My gaydar is totally on the fritz.

"Well, say hi to your mom." Timber Toes smiles kindly. "Poor thing. She's endured a lot."

"She has."

"She's a real survivor."

She crosses the street and waves.

I vow to find out her name. In fact, I'm going to learn everyone's names—and their business. Business that's none of my business. I make my way to the Egg Drop parking lot, and it's still a swamp. Arlo ambushes me at the back door. "Where have you been? You were scheduled to work today."

He has to be kidding. The water's gone down, but there's mud everywhere, a thick layer on the floor, dirty water lines all around the perimeter of the walls. Arlo tosses me a wet sponge, which I catch with my good hand. "Heard about the house. How's Carly taking it?"

"Guess," I say.

"She's leaving the mess for someone else to clean up?"

"She's just leaving. Moving objects, you know."

Arlo nods. "What about you?"

"I'm staying. You can't get rid of me that easily."

Does he look happy? Relieved? Probably because he'll still have slave labor.

"Where do you want me to start?" I ask.

"The john," Arlo says. "People are going to be needing it."

My favorite job.

He calls at my back, "And use bleach so we don't get mold."

Mold. It's a digestive aid.

God, I hope the memory of Finn fades faster than Sarah's. I see Finn's bike is gone, if it was ever here. It all feels like a nightmare I'm never going to wake up from.

Arlo calls louder to me, "If you need a place to stay, I'll set up a cot here at Chez Cripple. That'll get tongues wagging."

I hadn't thought that far ahead. "Thanks."

The front bell tinkles, and a herd of footsteps thunder into the dining room. I stick my head out of the restroom to see who it is. Everyone. Like, everyone who's ever eaten here. Rufus drags in the biggest Shop-Vac I've ever seen. "Sheesh," he goes. "You think it's worth cleaning up this dump, Arlo, or you just want to demo the place and start from scratch?"

Arlo says, "Aw, it ain't a total loss. And, thanks. I really appreciate your help."

Someone says, "Hey, we're family. And we're effing hungry."

I smile and go back to scouring, feeling part of it all, this town, this family. It's a totally awesome feeling.

Chapter 25

"Booger brain," I hear a kid yell in the airport concourse. Paulie. Even from a distance, I can see he's grown taller. Beside him, Tanith waves. Paulie runs up to hug me, and then he notices the sling.

"It's okay." I hug him hard with my one arm. He smells like sand and surf and boy sweat.

Tanith says, "We're so glad you're safe and sound."

Am I sound?

She answers my unspoken question. "He had to work today."

Sure he did.

We head down the concourse, and I take Paulie's hand. I don't care if it disgusts him to be seen holding hands with his sister. "I missed you, bat breath."

"You too." His face is freckled and tan, and his hair is bleached by the sun. Paulie babbles about their vacation, how cold the Gulf water was this year, how great the waves were for body surfing. He and Dad had gone out on a catamaran.

Paulie says, "Now that you're home, we can go to the beach every day."

I look at Tanith, but she's avoiding my eyes. She didn't tell him. She starts rambling about shopping to replace all the clothes I lost, and buying me winter gear, but her words sieve through my brain. What will I say when I see Dad? Am I capable of confronting him?

We drive by the mall where M'Chelle and Ben and I hung out. Where I bought Sarah's ring. We pass Gracie Field, where teams are playing baseball. The dugout and shed. Starbucks.

Surprisingly, I don't feel sad. I don't feel anything.

I can't wait to get out of here.

My room is tidied, disinfected. The smell of Pine-Sol lingers in the air as I empty the contents of my small backpack onto the bed. The iPhone. A few essentials Carly picked up for me. The closet door isn't shut, and I see it—the box from Sarah.

I drag it over, intending to haul it to the trash can out back, but the top flap is open, and there's a note on top.

Tanith never mentioned the note. She had to have read it; it's not even folded.

I sit cross-legged on the floor.

DEAR ALYSSA,

I'M SORRY. I JUST DON'T KNOW WHAT I WANT YET. I DON'T KNOW WHO I AM OR WHAT I AM. I KNOW YOU CAN NEVER FORGIVE ME.

SARAH

P.S. I DID LOVE YOU.

I stare at her admission. It barely fazes me. Maybe the meltdown will come later, but I don't think so. Why do I choose these girls who don't know who they are or what they want?

Paulie flings open the door and barrels in. "I brought these back for you." He flops on the mattress and dumps out a pail of seashells.

On the bed, we immediately begin to sort through the shells.

"How'd you know I'd be back?" I ask him.

"Guitar Hero."

What a peanut head.

"Which one's your favorite?" he asks.

No contest. I pick up the perfect sand dollar. The zigzag etchings resemble Native American art, and my thoughts drift back to Finn.

Where is she now? I wonder. Finn's on her own journey, and I know how frightening it can be when you're first coming out to yourself. You don't want to be different. You don't know how people will react. You want to believe it doesn't matter what others think, but it does. I want to believe I'm a forgiving person. I think that's within my power to decide. I'm not angry with Finn. Anger eats you up inside and eventually turns to hate. Then self-hatred. I can't live that way, and I never want to.

The sand dollar is delicate. I rub my thumb across the pattern and wonder how far it traveled. How long it was adrift before it found its way to me.

Paulie says, "These new people moved in down the street, and they have a kid my age who's into video games."

"Yeah? Cool." Paulie needs a friend.

He adds, "She's a girl," and sticks out his tongue halfway.

I give him a noogie on the head. "Don't be sexist."

"I'm not. She already beat me twice at Madden."

I laugh. Headlights split the dark outside my window, and I peer over the sill to see Dad pulling into the driveway. My stomach clenches. The garage door rolls up, and he disappears inside.

I cringe at Paulie.

He rests a paw on my shoulder and says, "No worries, sis. I've got your back."

Who's got my front? I almost say.

Dad doesn't come upstairs. An hour passes, and Paulie goes to bed. I sit in the dark waiting to hear footsteps, creaking floorboards. At last, a tread squeaks.

I swing off the edge of the mattress and pad to the door.

Dad's head is down as he reaches the top step. He either sees or senses me. His eyes rise.

I tender a smile.

His gaze sweeps down my body and fuses to the sling. "Are you okay?"

"Yeah. Nothing broken." *Except us*, I want to add.

He turns around and walks back down the stairs. I hear his office door close.

No, not this time. He won't shut me out. I go down the stairs and knock on his door. He says, "Who is it?"

"Me," I answer.

He doesn't say come in. After a long second, he goes, "I'm busy."

Bastard. He's going to hear me out whether he wants to or not. I open the door and enter, closing it behind me.

He's sitting at his desk in the dark, his back to me, and I switch on the overhead light. He swivels in his chair, blinking, then swivels back around.

"First I want to say I love you. You're my father, and I'll always be your daughter."

"No," he goes. "I don't know who you are, but you don't belong to me."

Don't cry, I think. *Get through this.* "You need to know how difficult you've made it for me to be honest with you. I know you hate gays, so I couldn't tell you I was one. But I've known since I was thirteen."

"You can't know. You're a child."

"I'm seventeen. I knew then, and I know now."

He twists his head around, and his eyes are slits. I feel his hatred seep through my skin. My hands are shaking so hard that I have to cling to the door handle behind me, and I'm trying to control the trembling in my voice. "Do you know what it feels like to have to lie and hide the truth about yourself every single day? All I ever wanted was to come out to you and have you love and support me."

He mumbles something under his breath, and I say, "What?"

He says louder, "I don't. I never will."

"I can't change who I am, Dad."

He doesn't respond to that. And now, I think, this conversation is over.

I go to exit and see the Newton's swing on his sideboard. I pull out two balls and release them as hard as possible, and the opposite two balls go flying. The clacking of the balls still reverberates as I close the door behind me.

In the foyer I nearly collapse because my knees feel so weak. But a tiny spark of pride glints inside me. I did it. I came out to my father. He may never understand or accept me for who I am, but you know what? That's his choice. I only hope I can accept him for who he is.

Tanith's sitting out on the porch when I tiptoe downstairs in the morning. It's early, and I don't care to wake the sleeping monster. I curl into a wicker chair opposite her and say, "Do you want me to tell Paulie?"

She shakes her head. "It's my responsibility."

"I don't mind. Maybe if he heard it from me..."

Tears overflow the rims of Tanith's eyes, and I see she's got a wadded-up Kleenex in her hand.

"It's not your fault," I tell her.

"I don't know how he could turn his back on you like this. It's just so cruel." She dabs her eyes.

I go over to her and sit on the armrest, looping my arm around her shoulders. "I love you, you know." She needs to hear that because it's true. I've never told her how much I appreciate her. She's always been there. Not a day went by when I didn't know Tanith would be there to take care of me. "You've been more of a mother to me than my own mother. I'm sorry I've been such a pain in the ass."

"Oh, Alyssa..."

Tanith leans into me, and I rub her arm. I feel bad for her, caught in the middle. She blows her nose and composes herself. "I talked to Carly today and made all the arrangements." Tanith tells me I'll be living at Geena's, house-sitting, until Carly and Geena return from their cruise. "Since you're not eighteen, I told Carly you'd need a guardian."

"I can take care of myself," I say.

"You still need a legal guardian. She said she had someone in mind."

Oh, great. I'll be under the watchful eye of Mitchell, the cop.

"Are you packed? We should head out to the airport soon," Tanith says, standing.

I embrace her. We stand for a long minute, hugging and rocking each other. I think we both wish we could make up for the past, but what's done is done. We have to move forward.

She says, "I'm going up to tell Paulie now."

"I'm going with you."

She opens her mouth as if to protest but doesn't. If he starts crying, I will too, and so will Tanith, and we'll flood the house with tears.

We don't have to tell Paulie. He's standing at my bedroom door, staring at the suitcases packed with all my stuff. He turns slowly, his eyes moving up to meet mine. He gets that same look on his face that Dad cut me with and says, "I hate you." He tries to storm past me, but I clench his wrist and he goes limp. Hanging his head, he bursts into tears.

I look to Tanith, and she squats down beside him. "Paulie, you'll see Alyssa all the time. She'll come home for holidays. Right?" She glances up at me.

"Absolutely," I say.

"And I already have a trip to Colorado planned. I've been dying to learn how to ski. You want to ski, right?"

Paulie doesn't reply.

"I'll call you every week." I tousle his hair. "We'll e-mail."

"It won't be the same," he says with a sob.

"No." It won't. But it's what I have to do.

The hardest thing I've ever had to do, claim my independence. Redefine my family. I envelop both of them in my arms and choke out, "I love you guys so much."

I bend down to tie my new Nikes, ones I bought myself, and Carly says, "I hate leaving you here in Majestic all alone."

"I'm not alone." As if on cue, Boner groans from under the coffee table. "Everyone in town is my new best friend."

Carly says, "That's the truth. You're like the town mascot."

I think, *More like the adopted daughter*.

Carly's sitting on Geena's flowery sofa, paging through the pamphlet for her cruise.

"Well, I better get going. If I'm one minute late, Arlo has a hissy fit."

"Oh, did I tell you? He's agreed to be your guardian."

"What?" I wasn't going to mention the guardian thing, in case Carly had forgotten. Arlo. Hmm. That is going to be interesting.

"Alyssa?" Carly glances up and meets my eyes. "I just want you to be happy. That's all I ever wanted for you. I figured leaving you with your dad was the best I could do for you at the time. Who knew he'd turn out to be such an asshole?"

Yeah, who knew? "I want you to be happy too." Everyone

should just be happy. "I'll see you later," I say, but Carly's already refocused on her cruise.

After being closed for repairs the last week, the Egg Drop-In is back to normal. In fact, with a clean coat of paint and new linoleum, the place is all spruced up.

I grab my cap off the rack and hear Arlo say, "Unload the supplies before you put out the pastries."

"Good morning to you too." I skirt the counter and almost collide with her. I can't speak, can't breathe.

Finn says, "Hi."

I look from her to the swinging café doors and then back to her. "What are you doing here?" I ask.

Arlo yells, "Did you hear me, Finn?"

She shouts, "They heard you in Frisco." To me, she says, "Working."

"Since when?"

"Since I came back. Since I heard you—"

"Alyssa. I need you to help me prep," Arlo barks. "Get those damn supplies unloaded, Finn."

"In a minute." I raise my voice at Arlo. He must feel the static in the room because he says, "Well, whenever you girls can spare an hour or two. You know we've got all day."

Finn holds my eyes, and all the feelings come rushing back. The love and longing and pain of her leaving. I turn to go and she says, "Do you have my dog?"

I turn back. "Is that why you're here?"

She walks toward me and I take a step back, but she grips my arm and pulls me into her, into a kiss. My legs give out, and she holds me up, pressing me so close I feel every beat of her heart and mine in sync. We're both breathing hard, and I swell with her sensuality. She places her hands gently on both sides of my face and says softly, "You got me involved."

A smile curls my lips. "Who, me?"

She kisses me again. And again. Or continuously.

"No no no no no." Arlo rolls up behind us. "Not here. Not now. For God's sake, this is a public establishment."

In our kiss, Finn and I both start laughing.

Arlo says, "I can't have this, Alyssa. Stop it right now."

I cock my head at Arlo. "Or what? You'll ground me?" I tell Finn, "Arlo's my legal guardian."

She lets out a laugh.

I smile. "I know, huh?"

He crashes through the swinging doors, and my eyes fix on Finn again. I ask her the question: "How long are you staying this time?"

She doesn't take her eyes off me. "I've gotten real attached to this place. *Real* attached."

The heat between us flames again.

"Could we *please* get ready to open?" Arlo hollers.

It's almost impossible to break away, but duty calls. I spy Rufus out front, peering in through the window, and something else.

I walk toward the door, holding up two fingers at Rufus to let him know we're almost ready. The shape in the street materializes. Finn's Concours.

On the front, between the handlebars, she's posted a sign: FOR SALE. MAKE ME AN OFFER I CAN'T REFUSE.

she loves you, she loves you not...

Questions for Discussion

1. What pressures (external or internal) are placed on Sarah and Alyssa through their relationship?

2. Discuss the use of money and gifts to express affection. Why does Alyssa feel the need to give gifts to Sarah and Finn to express her feelings? Is she "buying" their affection? How does Carly begin to express her affection for Alyssa through gifts?

3. How does the town or community play a role in this story? Discuss the differences between Alyssa's environments in Virginia and Colorado. Is one community more or less accepting than the other?

4. Is Carly a good mother? Why or why not? What about Tanith? Why or why not?

5. Can you sympathize with Sarah's and Ben's confusion about their sexuality? Why or why not?

6. What is Finn's role in Alyssa's healing process? How does Finn's character change over the course of the story?

7. Do you think Alyssa's father will ever understand and accept her? Is any of his anger justified? Why or why not?

8. Discuss the role of friendship. Which characters are loyal and dependable friends: M'Chelle? Ben? Geena? Arlo?

9. How do different characters run away or hide parts of themselves: Carly? Finn? Sarah? Do you understand their actions? Why or why not?

10. What do you think the future holds for Alyssa? Finn? What about Ben and Sarah?

IT'S OUR YEAR. IT'S OUR NIGHT.
IT'S OUR PROM.

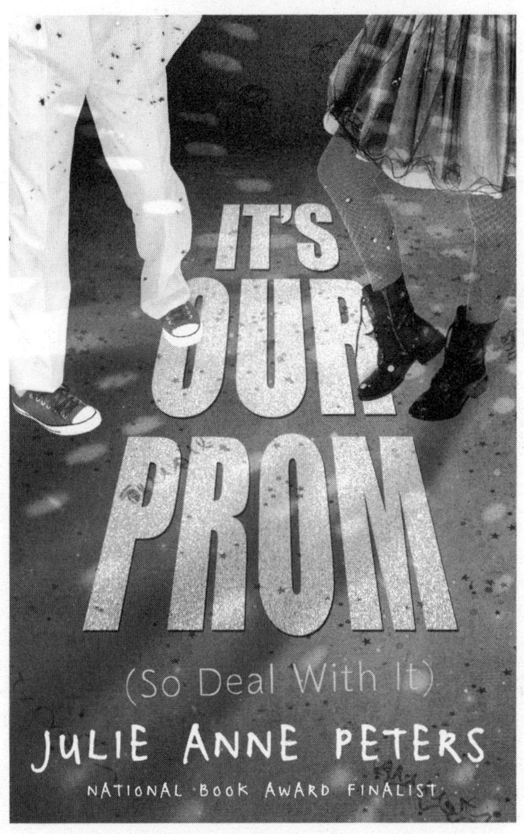

A compelling new story about friendship, love, and the trials of planning an alternative prom— turn the page for a sneak peek!

AZURE

There must be an epidemic of flu or cold virus going around, because when I walk into my last class I see Mr. What's-His-Sub, the same guy I had in third period. He says, "Your teacher didn't leave any lesson plans, so you can use this time as a study hour." Good idea. I pull out my cell and scroll through my pics from Friday night.

We made our usual entrance to the theater, walking down the side aisle all the way to the front. As we crossed the curtain, Luke and I waved to people in the audience, while Radhika shielded her eyes as if she didn't know us. People turned to see who we were waving to, which was hilarious because we didn't know anyone. Then the three of us climbed the steps to the back row and scooted in with our tub of popcorn and supersized Icee to share. Luke plopped down next to Radhika, so I stepped over them to sit on the other side of her. I still remember the first whiff of her jasmine-scented shampoo, and how my breath caught.

Luke started pitching popcorn in the air and catching it in his mouth. "Radhika," he said, tossing a kernel to her. She stuck out her tongue, but missed. Luke grabbed a fistful of popcorn and threw it high in the air, all of us opening our mouths like hungry chicks, and laughing when most of the popcorn landed on our laps or the floor. I picked out a kernel from Radhika's hair and ate it. She turned and smiled.

That's the first picture I snapped on my cell. I study it and imagine her lips on mine. Shiver.

The next pics are a series with the three of us, heads together, making silly faces, or sipping from the Icee. Me, Radhika, and Luke.

How long had it been since the three of us had gone out together to a movie? Too long. I missed "us."

I'm so engrossed in scrolling through the pictures over and over that when the bell buzzes, I'm startled back to the present.

"Get a lot of homework done, did you?" the sub says to me on my way out.

I turn slowly. "Yeah," I go. "I read *War and Peace* on my iPhone."

"I've been waiting for you." Mr. Gerardi, the principal, ambushes me as I shut my locker door. "Follow me." He turns and lumbers down the hall of doom toward his office.

I grimace. Last week Luke and I had the bright idea to superglue UNISEX over the faculty restroom sign. It seemed only right; the Diversity Club has been campaigning for a unisex bathroom for the last three years. Now we have one.

We get to his office and Mr. Gerardi says, "Sit down, please," as he circles his desk. He folds his hands on top and smiles one of those smiles that looks like it hurts every muscle in his face. "I have a proposition, Azure," he says.

Uh-oh. When my dad says that, it means do or die.

"Is this going to take long?" I ask. "Because my ride's waiting."

"It might," he answers. "Do you have another way home?"

"Let me make a call." My heart thrums in my chest as I text Luke:

In deep shit. Go ahead w/out me. Blame you later.

After I drop my cell in my bag, Mr. Gerardi says, "Do you remember how last year you circulated the petition to eliminate prom?"

"It wasn't just me."

"But you started it."

Did I? Luke was the one who got all the signatures. I'm about as popular as herpes.

"If I recall correctly, your complaint was that prom wasn't inclusive."

"Because it's not," I say.

His smile is stuck in place and it's creeping me out. "Apparently, one of the board members got hold of the petition and agrees with you. Prom should be an event for every student in school. Although I don't see how it's not inclusive—"

"It's elitist." I edge forward in my chair. "It's so expensive only the richie rich can afford it, then the populars are the only people who go, so they can be seen. You have to take a date or you're labeled a loser."

Mr. Gerardi's smile fades from his face. He doesn't respond, so I go on.

"The tickets are seventy-five dollars, then you have to buy a dress and shoes you'll probably only wear once, or rent a tux. There's the cost of the limo, and probably dinner before or after." Not that I'd know. I've never been to prom. "I bet it comes to three hundred dollars. I'd have to work for fifty years to make that much money. Even then, I wouldn't go because right now I don't have a girlfriend."

I choke. TMI.

Mr. Gerardi must space my last comment because he asks, "If it was cheaper, would you go?"

"Not the way it is. I mean, the geeks, freaks, and uniques, like me, don't feel welcome at prom. It's a dance, but it could be so much more."

"Like what?"

"Like…I don't know. I haven't thought about it. Because nothing will ever change."

He plasters on that fakey smile again. "What if I gave you a chance to make a change? Would you consider serving on the prom planning committee so the event would be more inclusive?"

"Are you serious?"

"It was suggested by the board. You don't have to—"

"I'll do it."

He fidgets with a paper clip on his desk. "Your biggest problem is time. You're going to have to organize this thing fast. It's already January, and the prom's in April. Mrs. Flacco, who usually sponsors the committee, has... dropped out. But I did manage to persuade another teacher to be the sponsor."

He makes it sound like he had to beg, bribe, or torture a teacher to volunteer. "Who?" I ask.

"Mr. Rosen."

My eyes light up. Mr. Rosen is cool. He's young and has a ponytail, and from what I've heard all the girls are gaga for him. But not only the girls—Luke signed up for Mr. Rosen's Life Skills class, even though Luke's basically been living on his own for the past eight months.

"Can I ask people to be on the committee with me?"

"That's up to Mr. Rosen. I'm not sure who's already signed on." Mr. Gerardi stands, brushes by me, and holds open the door.

"Thanks, Mr. Gerardi." I head out. "Really. It's going to be great. You won't regret this."

His smile is kind of jagged. Behind me, I hear him mutter, "I think I already do."

Slipping into the unisex restroom, I text Radhika and Luke:

Guess what? They want us to be on the prom planning committee. Can you believe it? We're going to PIMP THE PROM.

* * *

I catch the bus home, and by the time I get there, I haven't heard back from either Radhika or Luke. Radhika, I can understand. She leaves right after sixth period and has to turn her cell off at home to study. But Luke? I call him as I'm traipsing up the drive to my house. "Didn't you get my text?"

"Yeah, I did," he says. "I just don't know if I can handle another commitment. I have my play, you know."

"Luke, this is what we've always wanted! Our prom. An alternative prom. The way we envisioned it, with everyone having a reason to come."

He sighs. "I know. I'm just really busy. I haven't even written all the music."

"Did I mention Mr. Rosen is the committee sponsor?"

I picture Luke's jaw dropping and drool sliding down his chin. "When do we meet?" he asks.

"I have to talk to Mr. Rosen first, but I'll let you know."

Dad's getting ready to leave as I open the door and slip out of my leather jacket. "Do you need a ride to work?" he asks. "I'm going your way."

"Going where?" I ask him.

He shoulders his holster, which means he's going to the shooting range. He blasts human targets to work off stress. I hate that he's a cop. Couldn't he find a safer job, like Ponzi schemer?

"I don't need to be there for another couple of hours," I tell him. "I'll catch the light-rail." It stops three blocks from the thrift store near Exempla Hospital in Denver.

"Oh, and I downloaded the police scanner, so I'll know if there's an officer down."

He tousles my hair before shutting the door behind him. I wonder if there is a police-scanner app. I'm always afraid that one night I'll get the call, or the doorbell will ring, and the officer on the porch will inform me: "I'm sorry. He died doing what he loved."

What does it matter if you die doing what you love or hate? Especially if the daughter you leave behind has to go live with her psycho mother?

I crank up my nano as loud as possible without my eardrums exploding. For English, we're supposed to choose our favorite opening line from a list we got in class of the one hundred best first lines in literature. So far I have it whittled down to "Call me Ishmael." Brilliant.

"I was born twice: first, as a baby girl, on a remarkably smogless Detroit day in January of 1960; and then again, as a teenage boy, in an emergency room near Petoskey, Michigan, in August of 1974." That's from *Middlesex*, which I actually read and loved. Or, "Lolita, light of my life, fire of my loins." My mind drifts and I think about prom. About what could make it the most magical night of my life. One word: *Radhika*.

How do you tell your best friend you're in love with her without ruining the friendship? Or making it awkward, or scaring her to death because you know, you're absolutely sure, she couldn't possibly feel the same way about you? At the thought of her my palms sweat and all my pores swell. I can't remember the last time I felt this way. It's been a while. Whenever Radhika's near, I want to take her in my arms, kiss her until we're both gasping for breath, then know—*know*—she feels the crush of passion I do. Even though she doesn't, and she can't, and she never will, because Radhika Dal isn't gay or bi or even curious. She loves me as a friend, and it'll never be anything more than that.

I see my cell light up and Radhika's ID appear. My stomach vaults and I toss my homework aside. I have a voice mail, too. How did I miss that?

"Tell me about pimping the prom," Radhika says.

I glance at my clock. Yikes. Time flies when you're fanning the fire in your loins. I fill her in on Mr. Gerardi asking if we'll plan an alternative prom as I sling my pack over my shoulder and rush out the door for work. "You'll help, won't you?"

She says, "What does it involve?'

"I don't know yet. I've never planned a prom, not to mention an alt one."

Radhika hesitates.

"Please. You have to. I can't do this alone."

"Can we talk about it tomorrow?" she asks.

"Sure." I don't want her to hang up, so as I'm sprinting down the drive, I say, "What are you doing?"

"Nothing. I finished my homework a while ago and now I'm just waiting for Mom and Dad to go to bed so I can Netflix a movie."

"Wish I could be there to watch it with you."

The silence stretches, which is unusual between us. "What's going on, Radhika?"

She expels an audible breath. "Mom and I had a fight."

"Over what?" Radhika and her mom never fight. Unlike other mothers and daughters who can't be together five minutes before they start screaming at each other.

"I want to cut my hair short like yours, and she won't let me."

"No!" I blurt out. Radhika can't cut her hair. It's gorgeous. Long and black and sleek as silk. "I'm still trying to grow mine out from the last time I butchered it," I say.

"You didn't. It looks..."

Hideous. I hear the train in the distance and start trotting. "I think you should think about it." Long and hard.

"It's my hair," Radhika says. "I should be able to do anything I want."

She's right. But still.

Radhika says, "My mother's so controlling. I thought I'd have more freedom now that I'm eighteen. You know?"

I send her a mental plea: *Please, please don't cut your hair.*

"I left you a message," Radhika says. "You can just delete it. I'll see you tomorrow."

"Wait!" But the line's already gone dead. The light-rail screeches to a stop and passengers surge out. I hop on board, grab a seat in back, and listen to Radhika's message. "You didn't tell me what your self-affirmation was for today."

My self-affirmation. I forgot. I pull out the calendar

page and reread it: "Undertaking endeavors that seem beyond reach will grow you as a person from the inside out."

Radhika gave me this daily self-affirmations calendar for Christmas. I love it. I'd love it even if I didn't love it just because she picked it out for me.

Undertaking endeavors beyond my reach... That could be anything. That could be prom. That could be Radhika.

When did she leave this message on my cell? I listen again for the time. Right about when she would've gotten home from school. Which means she was thinking about me at the same time I was texting her. Karma? I save her message, the way I do all her messages, to play at night so hers is the last voice I hear before falling asleep.

Provocative, heart-wrenching, hopeful . . .

Read all of Julie Anne Peters's inspiring novels

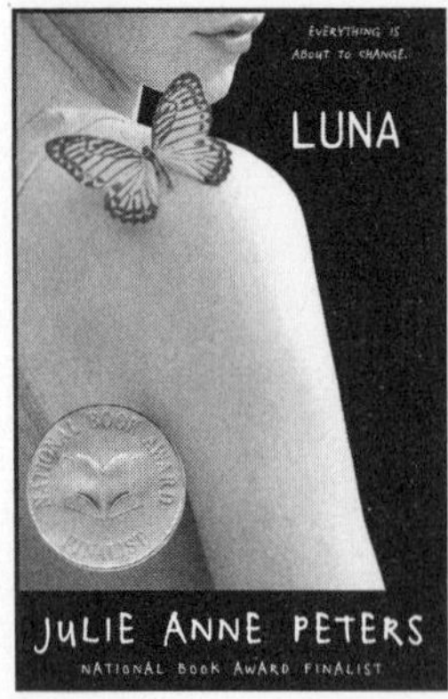

Available wherever books are sold.

www.lb-teens.com

WITHDRAWN

3 1901 05370 9053